Praise for

THE MAKING OF A WITCH

"Based on historical records and events, *The Making of a Witch* by Judy Molland is a profound and poignant story. Set in England in the mid-seventeenth-century, the book accurately describes the risks and challenges women healers had to endure during that era. . . . This well-written story with its compelling plot and authentic storyworld thoroughly captivated me from the first to the last page."

—*Readers' Favorite,* 5-star review

"Those with an interest in this era of history will appreciate how Judy Molland, a descendant of the real-life Alice Molland, uses the sparse details known about her ancestor to spin a tale of resilience in the face of constant misfortune."

—BookLife Reviews

"Alice's impressive drive to help others and to be true to herself, no matter the consequences, will have readers rooting for her when her circumstances look the most dire. An engrossing story of one of the last accused witches in England's history."

—*Kirkus Reviews*

THE MAKING OF A WITCH

A Novel

Judy Molland

SHE WRITES PRESS

Published in 2026 by
She Writes Press, an imprint of The Stable Book Group

1569 Solano Ave #546
Berkeley, CA 94707
https://shewritespress.com

Library of Congress Control Number: 2026904369
ISBN: 979-8-89636-324-8
eISBN: 979-8-89636-325-5

Interior Designer: Katherine Lloyd, The DESK

Printed in the United States

For Joe Baker, without whose support this novel
would not have been created.
Thank you for your love, generosity, intelligence,
and creative ideas.

BOOK 1

CHAPTER ONE

Exeter, Devon. July 1656.

"People of Exeter! Come to the gallows!" The town crier's voice echoed from the end of the lane. The clanging of his bell and the sound of his horse sloshing through the puddles grew louder as he came closer. "Praise ye the Lord! Let us pluck out the devil from our midst!"

Inside a nearby home, ten-year-old Alice Molland had just taken a sip of her warm milk, but her throat constricted, and she could barely breathe. She coughed and spat the milk back into her wooden bowl.

"Is it Goody Luscombe?" She looked straight into her father's dark brown eyes, set deep beneath straggly black eyebrows. "Is she the one they dragged out of her home in the dark of night?"

He nodded from his chair at the head of the table. Her heart lurched and beat so loudly it was all she could hear.

When Alice was younger, her mother, Catherine, had often left her in the care of Goody Luscombe. Now that she was ten, Alice chose to spend many hours at the woman's cottage. Her mother sent her there to fetch sage leaves or pennyroyal or slippery elm, plants she had need of in her work as a healer, and Alice lingered, drawn by Goodwife Luscombe's smile and her fresh corn cakes.

"Did she know she was going to be arrested?" Alice understood why the old woman had shared so much this past summer and insisted Alice pay attention to all the details. Alice had learned from her how to distinguish numerous plants, such as comfrey, mugwort, and chamomile, and how much warm water to add to make the infusions that could relieve suffering.

"I cannot go. You cannot make me go."

"Do not contradict me!" Thomas Molland stood and leaned over his youngest child.

Alice focused on the bloody mark above his right eyebrow, the result of a drunken brawl a few weeks earlier.

"I am your father, and I'm telling you we are ordered to attend this hanging today." He sat, took a long swallow of ale, and plunked his mug onto the table.

"Let us celebrate the death of evil," the town crier's voice bellowed, close to the Mollands' front door.

"Goodwife Luscombe is my friend." Tears pricked Alice's eyes, but she resolved not to cry. She prayed this was a bad dream and she would soon wake up.

The clomping of the horse's hooves grew fainter. Alice's sister Faith, two years older than Alice, sprang from the bench on the other side of the table, her brown eyes like dark moons in her freckled face as she stared at the door.

"Alice, you will do as your father tells you." Catherine stood at the hearth and stirred the potage cooking over the open fire. The earthy smell of potatoes filled the small kitchen.

Alice focused her attention on her mother, a tall woman whose pale brown hair was streaked with gray. "But Mother, you've put me in the care of Goody Luscombe many times. You said she was your friend, a healer of people and animals, like you."

"And she was, but she has used her powers in bad ways and must be punished."

Catherine turned to face her family. "They say a witch has caused the harvest to wither and die two years in a row. Diana Luscombe is charged with being that witch. And she stands accused of causing the death of several pigs and using a toad as a familiar spirit."

"These are lies! Goody Luscombe is a gentle person who would never harm anyone." Alice's words hung in the air, but she got no response. She stared into her bowl. Globules of yellowish cream had formed on the surface of her milk. She had seen men on the streets of Exeter, victims of the Great Wars, clad in dirty rags and missing an arm or a leg. She had even helped her mother prepare a body for burial once. The woman had died in childbirth, and it had been Alice's job to close the eyes so the corpse could not threaten anyone with its look.

But she had never witnessed a hanging and couldn't imagine seeing her dear friend strung up at the gallows. Her eyes moistened. She pinched her left arm, and the pain told her she was fully awake.

Alice grabbed the hunk of oat bread, tore off a chunk, and stuffed it into her mouth. A hard crumb dropped to the dirt floor, and she watched as two skinny brown cockroaches approached, antennae waving as they circled the morsel.

Her father stood, and his bucket-top boots thumped on the dirt floor as he marched from one end of the kitchen to the other. "Look at the streets of our city, littered with all those poor critters, remnants of the Wars. They're starving to death, but slowly, forced to beg like animals. Perhaps hanging may be a more merciful fate for Goodwife Luscombe?"

He came to stand next to Alice. At his feet, both cockroaches grasped the crumb in their pincers at the same time and fought over it. Alice's father crushed one beneath his boot, and it released a loud popping sound. The other cockroach scurried away with the prize.

Catherine lifted the iron pot and crouched down to place it at the edge of the blackened hearth. "We need to prepare ourselves. We are summoned to attend a witch hanging, and we shall obey."

Alice heard the finality in her mother's tone and understood she did not have a choice. Even though her father raised his voice, it was her mother's word that counted.

"Come, Alice. I must speak with you." Catherine stood up and reached an arm toward her child.

Alice took the outstretched hand and followed her mother into the bedroom. They sat side by side on the low box bed.

"Listen to me." Catherine stroked her child's long black hair. "You must attend this execution, or it will be said you were a friend of the witch. Indeed, the suspicion of witchcraft is likely to fall on anyone who does not make their way to Heavitree today, but especially on you and me since we may have been spotted in the company of Diana Luscombe."

Alice nodded as she pictured her friend's round form bent over her oven to pull out risen corn cakes where before there had been only flat lumps of dough. A woman had arrived at Diana Luscombe's thatched cottage one day, and in her arms lay a little girl who cried out in pain. The child had a broken arm, and Alice had learned how to pound on the roots of the comfrey plant to turn them into a paste that Goody Luscombe had packed around the broken limb. The old woman had explained the paste would harden and hold the bone in place to help it mend.

The healer had produced a tiny bottle and given the girl a drop of a brownish liquid. The child made a face, but to Alice's amazement, she soon closed her eyes and fell asleep.

Goody Luscombe had turned to Alice and pointed to the bottle. "Do not speak of this to anyone. It is a secret between you and me and this poor woman."

Alice stared at the reddish-brown birthmark on the back of her left hand with its faint resemblance to an oak leaf and made up her mind. "Do not worry about me." She grabbed her mother's arm. "I shall be right beside you. No harm shall come to us."

"And you promise not to let anyone know that Goodwife Luscombe is your friend? It is up to you, Alice. If you were to let them know anything, it could be bad for all of us. Do you promise?" Catherine clasped her daughter's hands so tightly, Alice thought her bones would crack.

"I promise."

"Come along, you two!" Alice's father yelled from the kitchen.

Alice felt a strong arm around her waist and leaned against her mother's cotton shift, which smelled faintly of ashes and smoke. Together, they would be able to face this dreadful day.

The family stepped out of the cottage and onto the damp ground. People packed the lane, shouting and laughing as they made their way to the gallows.

Thomas shoved his way into the crowd, and the rest of the family wedged themselves in behind him.

The rain had washed away most of the human excrement and rotten carrots and potatoes that generally littered the narrow lane, and a fresh, almost sweet fragrance filled the air. A light wind and the sun made the white clouds scurry away.

It might have been just another beautiful summer's day.

The girls wore their brown woolen skirts, each decorated with two bands of black braid around the hem. Catherine's small face was framed by a lace cap trimmed in white filigree, which lightened the shadows under her limpid blue eyes. In a dark jacket and breeches, his chin smooth, Thomas walked in front of his wife, his large frame head and shoulders above her.

In her left hand, Alice clutched her best conker, the fruit of the horse chestnut tree, which had won every game of Smash the Conker for over two weeks. She gained strength when she gripped its smooth, hard texture between her fingers.

Her right hand was enclosed in her mother's firm grip. Alice smiled as she had promised her mother she would, but within herself, she heard, *Did they arrest Goody Luscombe because she is a healer? Are Mother and I going to be next?* Her throat tightened, and the sour taste of rank bile came into her mouth.

Alice and Faith walked on either side of their mother and jostled each other as they stepped around puddles and occasional piles of dung that remained after the rain.

"Today they permit us to enjoy ourselves!" John Plympton, the tanner, shouted as he strode forward. He usually looked like a tall, ungainly scarecrow, but today he had dressed for the occasion in a hat stuck with brilliant peacock feathers.

Lily Cornock, who lived on the other side of the lane, chimed in: "And about time too! Cor blimey, what do they expect us to do with no alehouses!" Her five children strutted behind her like nervous ducklings.

"The Lord shall prevail!" hollered a loud voice.

Alice looked up to see the two soldiers who guarded their lane. The presence of soldiers did not surprise her. They were a common sight, and her father had told her Exeter had been under military occupation, with soldiers quartered at the castle, since the end of the Civil War in 1646.

But she had never seen the men dressed like this. They wore helmets that resembled pots with metal crowns, long buff coats with back and breastplates over them, secured by bright red sashes. She thought they must be really hot inside all that metal. In their bulky, gloved hands they carried pikes that rose high above them. *What do they use those for?*

John Colbert, the shorter of the two soldiers, yelled, "Death to the witch! Go and celebrate!" His face bore a scar that trailed all the way from his nose to his left ear.

Ambrose Rogers, the other soldier, grinned at Alice in his usual friendly way, and she returned his smile.

Someone tapped her between the shoulder blades. She turned and looked into Mary Ward's pretty blue eyes.

"Oh, it's you!" Alice laughed. The two had been friends for more than a year, but Mary had recently gone to work as a servant at the Greenway house, so they rarely saw each other nowadays.

"Look! Marigold!" Mary produced a grayish-brown toad from underneath her apron.

"She's huge!" Alice remembered the first time Mary had led her to a scummy pond and shown her the tadpoles, blackish on top and dark gray below and surrounded by strings of jelly.

"Watch!" Mary slipped out of the crowd, which moved forward at a steady pace past the two soldiers.

"Mary! No!"

Alice's friend stood on tiptoe behind John Colbert. She held the toad high and poked the creature's belly so that it let out a loud, ugly croak next to the soldier's ear, causing him to jerk his head from side to side.

"Mary should know it's foolish to make fun of our soldiers," Catherine muttered. "They never forget any slights."

Her mother pulled Alice a little closer to her side as they turned the corner into Northgate Street. In front of Alice swarmed more people than she had ever seen there.

She came here often to fetch water or accompany her mother to the wool market and usually loved to get this far, for the street was much wider and cleaner than their own narrow lane. But today it was packed tight with so many people that it seemed to have shrunk.

Around them, people let out roars of laughter, along with shouts of "It be a grand day, to be sure!" and "Good day! You'll be lookin' fine today!" There was music, too—the whine and honk of bagpipes and horns, and in the distance, drums led the crowd toward the South Gate and up to Gallows Cross.

Mary had tucked Marigold back into her apron and once more walked a few feet behind Alice, next to her father, Nathaniel, a tall, bearded man whose bald pate gleamed in the bright sunshine.

"Good morrow, Thomas," he greeted Alice's father, who stepped around his wife and children to walk beside his friend. "We're in fer a vine sight tiday!" Nathaniel had grown up in a village near Cullompton and still spoke with a strong Devonshire accent his neighbors sometimes found hard to understand. "An' the Laurd is favorin' us wi' sunshine! Iddn that right, Charis?"

His wife forced a smile as she looked up and pushed her wiry brown curls back under her cotton bonnet.

Alice wondered if Nathaniel knew about the secret Mary had told her. Her friend had come home earlier than usual one Sunday, her day off work, and discovered her mother taking her pleasure with a man who was not Mary's father. Mary didn't recognize the man, but he had her mother pushed up against the bedroom wall, his breeches down and her skirt yanked up, as he plowed his way into her.

Mary had turned and run straight to the Molland home. Tears ran down her face, and it had taken Alice a while to find out why. Alice had held her friend close and whispered that she must never tell anyone about this. Mary had not responded.

"Well, Nathaniel," Thomas said. "It's true we have had not a single hanging for over a year, not since they got rid of poor old Jeremiah Flattop for stealing from the Hoskins."

"An' a witch, Thomas!" Nathaniel slapped his neighbor on

the back. "Now that be summat else! The first time I seen a witch swing!"

Stay strong for me. Alice was startled to hear Goody Luscombe's soft, singsong voice in her head. She could picture the old woman's face framed by a halo of thick white hair. She had last seen the healer on the eve of the full moon, perhaps a fortnight earlier. Goody Luscombe had sent Alice out to find garlic, useful for fighting infections and killing parasites, and to pick blackberries, whose properties could treat diarrhea and vomiting.

Alice had known where blackberries grew, but it had taken her most of the morning to locate the garlic. Goody Luscombe greeted her when she returned to the tiny thatched cottage close to the noon hour. "What took you so long? Couldn't you smell your way to the garlic?"

As the crowd closed in around the family, the talk grew louder: "Henry Herneman said she put the curse on 'im, 'is wife fell ill and 'is son broke 'is leg," and "Old Ann Southcott and Goodwife Eggins, they brought their children to 'er for help and the littl'uns died."

A drop of sweat from Alice's forehead stung the corner of her eye, and she blinked hard. It came to her that since Goody Luscombe had passed on so much knowledge, Alice had to work to remember everything. She decided to arrange in her mind all she had learned about herbs and ignore all the horrible people around her. And one day she would become the best healer ever in the county of Devon.

"Mother! Where are you?" Faith cried from somewhere in front of them.

Catherine dragged Alice with her as she barged through the throng to catch up with her elder daughter. Alice would have been just as happy to never see her sister again after what Faith had done to Alice's cat, but she said nothing.

Around them, the entire population of Exeter seemed to be out on the streets for this celebration. Cookrow, which extended beyond Northgate Street, was lined with several more soldiers, all dressed in full armor for this festive occasion.

Alice's father had told her that even though the Parliamentarians defeated the Royalists in the Civil War, Exeter had been a Royalist stronghold and was considered far too important to leave unguarded.

She looked up. Above her, a few gray clouds had moved in from the west and brought the suggestion of showers later in the day.

But she mustn't allow herself to become distracted; she had to start recalling Goodwife Luscombe's herbs and their uses. She would start with pennyroyal, a plant her mother often needed for the women who came to her. It was easy to recognize with its light purple flowers rising one above the other and its small, hairy leaves. Goody Luscombe had told her it should be boiled in water and vinegar and would help women to have their courses.

They passed the turn to the wool market, and Alice entered a part of Exeter she did not know.

All around her rose timber-framed buildings much higher than any she had seen before, some as tall as four stories and surmounted by steep vaulted roofs. Over the enormous oak door of the closest house was a shield decorated with a creature painted bright gold that looked to her like a large dog.

"What's that?" She pointed to the shield.

"A lion," her mother shouted above the raucous crowd.

"What is a lion?"

"A beast we don't have in England, and certainly not one I have ever been asked to heal. They say he is very dangerous."

The animal had sharp claws coming out of all four feet.

The crowd moved faster, and the press of people behind them forced Alice to let go of her mother's hand.

More clouds rolled in, but still the sun burned down on the top of her head through her cotton bonnet. Her woolen skirt stuck uncomfortably to her legs, and every cobblestone imprinted itself on her feet through her thin soles.

She turned her thoughts back to the task at hand: The dandelion was Goody Luscombe's favorite plant since it was useful in so many ways. She had shown Alice how to use a small trowel to dig out the roots, which yielded a kind of bitter milk, the most powerful part of the plant. A broth made from the leaves and roots would loosen the bowels and make people pass urine more easily, she had informed her young charge, which made Alice burst into giggles.

She needed to hold this recipe in her head. *Use the roots and leaves to make a decoction in white wine*, she said to herself. Or chop up just the leaves, add a few spicy black berries from the alisander plant, and boil in a broth.

A beggar with a peg leg thrust a wooden bowl under her nose. "Give us a farthing." His face was gray, the same color as the bristles on his chin, and his vacant eyes stared through her. She repeated the dandelion recipe once more in her head to make sure she had it memorized.

She looked away only to see behind her a fat man with a wispy beard who reminded her of a pig. "Kill the witch!" he yelled into her face.

Alice gripped her conker more tightly. She urgently needed to pass water.

The family drew closer to the cathedral, which was visible from almost every spot within the city walls and many without as well.

"Look over here!" Thomas pointed down Southgate Street to the South Gate. "There lies the prison."

Squashed in close to her father, Alice looked up at the huge towers. Long strands of dark hair had escaped from under her bonnet again and stuck to her face. She pushed them back. From a thin slit in the wall hung a shoe suspended on a greasy rope.

"Prisoners let a shoe down like this to get sustenance or money," Thomas informed his children.

Faith paid no attention to her father, but Alice stared up at the old brown leather and wondered if Goodwife Luscombe was in one of those towers.

The crowd was forced to slow down, for only five or six people could squeeze through the archway at one time. The Molland family was shoved against the great pile of bricks and mud that supported the city wall rising high above them.

Then they were outside the wall, where the throng picked up momentum and broke into a run. Alice pulled up her skirt to free her legs and at once felt a kick to her shins, then somebody's elbow knocking into her.

She was desperate to piss but could see no way to break free from the crowd, so she let the hot urine run down her legs.

Nobody cared. The noisy crowd advanced down one steep slope, up the other side, then down again.

The pace slowed as they ascended the final hill. At its summit, outlined against a pale blue sky, stood two ladders propped up on a wooden frame from which hung one solitary piece of rope. Alice stared at the gallows. The crowd had thinned out across the hillside, so she was able to stand still.

I want to go home. Now. But of course she couldn't go home. This was not just a day out. She had to watch her friend be strung up like an animal. The acrid taste of vomit rose in her throat, and she swallowed hard as teardrops rolled down her face.

Keeping her promise to remember all of Goody Luscombe's herbal cures was so painful. Even when her mother came to stand next to her and wiped away her tears, Alice was alone.

Faith had joined up with a group of girls who munched on toffee apples. She flung her head back to laugh uproariously, a movement that caused her blonde curls to dance in the air behind her. Alice had to turn away. *How dare Faith behave in such a foolish, disrespectful way?*

The music grew louder and mixed with the cries of vendors, for there were dozens of little stalls set up around the gallows. Hawkers sold wax images of the witch and pins for pricking.

Alice wanted to scream. Cromwell's soldiers had no use for children's frivolous pursuits. If they were caught playing rounders or football on a Sunday, they could be whipped as a punishment. So why was it that today they were being encouraged to step away from their chores and celebrate the execution of Goodwife Luscombe, a woman who had never harmed anyone?

She turned to ask her mother but saw a rickety cart approaching, pulled by two enormous brown horses. A woman in a tattered brown shift knelt in the cart, her hands bound together behind her back, her head shorn. A priest in a cassock and flat hat stood next to her and held the horses' reins while a sergeant-at-arms rode alongside.

As the cart neared the gallows, the crowd surged forward.

"Witch! You killed our people! Die! Die!" They hissed and stamped their feet.

The chanting hammered at Alice's head. She stared at the woman in the cart, her body slouched over, her head almost touching the cart's floor. Surely this must be a different person. This poor creature looked nothing like the healer who had shared so much with her.

"That Diana Luscombe put a curse on my child, and he died!"

"My wife lay pining for five days because of 'er! Kill the witch! Kill! Kill!"

The taunts wrapped around Alice. She tried to force her thoughts onto the topic of healing plants and what else Goody Luscombe had once taught her, but her mind went dark.

At the crest of the hill, the priest stepped out of the cart and pulled the prisoner up by the arms to drag her out. He walked beside her bent figure toward the gallows and held out his hands to her in supplication. She ignored him.

Alice recalled one spring day when she had gone with Goody Luscombe to pick snowdrops. Alice squeezed her eyes shut so she could picture the tiny white flowers hidden in the long grass. She had found the first one, but then Goodwife Luscombe had shushed her and pointed to where a deer had appeared a few feet away.

"Kill her! Kill her!" came the chant from all around. A soldier moved the two ladders into place.

Alice opened her eyes to see the woman at the top of the hill reach the first ladder. She closed them again to take her thoughts back to that spring day. The fawn still had its spots and tore at a beech sapling as if it had not eaten for days. A light rain moistened the leaves, but she and Goody Luscombe had stayed perfectly still.

Catherine patted her child's back and told Alice to look up.

The prisoner had climbed to the top of her ladder. Alice's heart raced so fast she thought she might die.

From his ladder, the black-hooded executioner leaned over to place the noose around Diana Luscombe's neck and tighten it. Then he climbed down the ladder to the ground.

With one swipe, the executioner yanked the ladder from beneath his prisoner's feet. Goodwife Luscombe's body jerked, and her arms and legs flew out at odd, disjointed angles. Then came a crack as her head fell forward.

The inside of Alice's head wanted to explode. The crowd let

out a tremendous roar. She squeezed her eyes shut, but the deer was gone. Alice could not even see the woods anymore, only blackness. At least Goody Luscombe had died quickly.

Alice opened her eyes to see Diana Luscombe's head bent over the noose while her body swung eerily from side to side.

Alice looked from the outline of the gallows over to the cathedral. She flung her head back to stare at the sky, where dark clouds threatened rain. If God were really up there, why had he allowed Goody Luscombe to die like this?

Her stomach heaved. She struggled to keep the bitter vomit down, but it didn't work. She sank onto the ground and spluttered as a thin stream of whitish liquid poured from her mouth and tears ran down her face.

When she finally stopped retching, the burning sensation that consumed her made her beat her fists into the earth and cry out, "No! No! No!"

CHAPTER TWO

Near Exeter, Devon. August 1656.

"So there 'e be," Jedediah Fletcher pronounced as he pushed open the wooden gate with his wide bottom and pointed to an almost pure white horse tethered to an oak tree on the other side of the field. Catherine had been summoned to tend to this animal.

Alice and her mother squeezed past the farmer, and his two sons—young men in their early twenties—came right behind. The gate swung shut with a bang.

Alice had begged to accompany her mother on this mission to help Farmer Fletcher. Almost a month had gone by since Goody Luscombe's execution, and during that time, Alice had longed to honor her friend and use one of her healing cures.

She got her first opportunity one day when the widow Bradshaw had come by and begged for help with her diarrhea.

Since Catherine had been on her way out to the wool market, she'd turned to Alice. "Can you make the decoction of blackberries and mulberries?"

Alice had nodded and spoken to the widow with what she hoped was an air of authority. "Do not worry. I shall prepare this and bring it to you shortly." The old woman shuffled off without so much as a "thank you," and Catherine disappeared with her basket of wool.

"I know I can do this." Alice's hands had shaken as she pulled out the wooden bowl of blackberries and mulberries she and her mother had picked just a few days earlier. "Goody Luscombe, if you are watching, please guide me."

She'd laid the berries in a pot and added enough water to cover them. "Not too much," she remembered the healer saying. She stirred the berries, and a lovely aroma rose from the pot. Alice smiled. When the liquid had turned a rich purple and the fruit had mostly dissolved, she removed the pot from the fire and strained the liquid through a linen cloth into a jug. *Yes! Alice the healer!*

Despite her new-found confidence, Alice still had so many questions she needed to ask her mother: *How dare those soldiers take an innocent woman and string her up? Does God really live up there, in the sky? And if he is up there, why did he not intervene to save Goody Luscombe?*

She had tried asking questions of Faith, but her sister had laughed and told Alice not to bother herself with such weighty matters. So she only had her mother to turn to, but in their cramped house, there was never a moment when the two were alone. Today's escape from the city would be her chance.

Alice's mother had to earn some money today. For the past few moons, Catherine had earned only fourteen pence a week for spinning and accepted what work came her way so that her children would not starve. Her husband secured laboring jobs when he could, but this morning the family had been reduced to sharing half a loaf of oat bread and a jug of beer for breakfast.

The sun beamed down on them, and Alice breathed in the dizzyingly sweet smell of summer. She was content to be out here even if her empty stomach growled in discomfort. Clumps of dandelions with fine, wide leaves dotted a vibrant green pasture, and as she stepped over them, Alice thought to suggest they return the following day to pick some. She had watched Goody Luscombe prepare the dandelion decoction but yearned to make her own.

At the thought of her dear friend, tears came to Alice's eyes. What if she couldn't remember the dandelion recipe? Never again would she be able to consult Goody Luscombe or see the smile that lit up the woman's face as Alice approached her door, nor would she feel the woman's strong embrace enfold her. She loved this woman who hadn't treated her like a child but more like a younger relative under her care.

Alice used her apron to wipe away her tears. The group approached the center of the field, but the horse did not move. The only sound came from the swish of its tail as it sought to rid itself of the flies buzzing in the summer heat. Farmer Fletcher led the way with Catherine close behind.

Alice paused for a moment and let the farmer's sons, Trewen and Clether, go in front of her. Master Fletcher had told her all his children were named after villages in Cornwall, his father's home.

On closer examination, the animal wasn't exactly white, more the grayish color of snow after it has been on the ground for a day. And even though it stood at least one hand above her, it was still a colt. It was probably two or three years old, close to Alice's age in horse years.

Catherine had just set her basket on the other side of the animal when, with a deep whinny, it reared as far as it could above Alice, a gray silhouette against the bright sun. Two metal horseshoes rose high above her, and she was sure the colt's powerful body would crash onto her. She ran back, collapsed on the grass, and squeezed her eyes shut.

Nothing happened.

She dared herself to open her eyes. The horse had brought its front hooves to the ground. It strove to tear away but instead hopped in an awkward movement.

Jedediah grabbed the rope and held it tight. The animal had to keep still or it would strangle itself. "'Ere, wat bout it then? Wat do yu reckon?" The farmer turned to Catherine, and his intense brown eyes appealed from under his tattered felt hat. The animal let out low, plaintive sounds.

Catherine smiled. "Just give me some time, Jedediah, and your horse will be right as rain." She placed her wicker basket on a bare patch of red earth.

Alice hoped her mother spoke the truth. Most of Catherine's work as a healer of animals had been with pigs and sheep, not with horses.

Her mother crouched next to the horse and lifted its right foreleg by the hoof to examine it. As she did so, the animal flung its head in the air once more and whinnied. Catherine had to let go. The horse's shiny black nostrils flared, and saliva dribbled from the corners of its mouth. Trewen ran over to help his father hold the rope, and the two men struggled to restrain the animal as great shudders shook its body.

The tendons bulged in Trewen's neck, and his ears, which stuck straight out from his head, had turned a deep shade of pink.

"Don't hurt him!" Alice called out.

Alice's mother frowned at her, but the three men laughed. She stared down at her feet and blushed as she saw the little rip at the end of her left shoe where her toenail poked through.

"Alice! I need you over here."

Alice jumped up and ran to stand next to her mother.

With the animal held steady by Farmer Fletcher and his son, Catherine was able to tuck the hoof between her knees.

In response, the animal groaned and leaned its whole weight against her. She teetered and almost fell over. At once, Clether stepped over to help. An enormous man with hair that bristled like a hedgehog, he leaned in and propped up the animal.

When Catherine nodded to her, Alice reached into the basket, pulled out a leather sheath, and handed it to her mother. Catherine withdrew a narrow blade that curled at the tip. Alice stared at the knife but turned her head as the metal glinted in the sunlight. When she looked back, her mother brought the knife down to the horse's foreleg and made a quick incision.

Alice studied the colt's face. Its black eyes were watery, and its jaw trembled and glistened with foam. Its body quivered, too, and it had a strange smell about it, like rotten apples left too long before the cider making. Perhaps Alice could calm the animal.

She tiptoed around her mother and raised her left hand to stroke the horse's clammy nostrils and chin. It snorted at her and seemed to twitch less. When Alice removed her hand, it neighed and once again pulled at the rope.

The oak leaf on the back of Alice's hand moved back and forth on the rough and stringy hide as she whispered to the colt, "Think about all the beautiful things: the first primroses in spring, the smell of fresh grass after a good rain, a patch of blackberries no one has touched." Ants crawled over her feet and inside her shoes, and she bent over to whack them. The horse neighed to call her back.

Catherine did not look up. She had made two separate incisions and kneaded the flesh in both places, but with no success.

Alice inched even closer to the animal's face and remembered what Goodwife Luscombe had told her once: You could calm a restless horse if you breathed into its nostrils. She brought the creature's sweaty nose next to her mouth and exhaled. Her hair stuck to the back of her neck in matted clumps, but she would not be distracted. The creature gradually relaxed beside her.

When Catherine made the third incision, a little spurt of whitish liquid ran out of the leg, followed by a steady trickle. The horse pulled itself away from Clether and stood firm. The man stepped back and shook his arms. "By my faith, I'll be needin' my ale!"

"Careful of yer language!" came his father's response, for everyone knew the punishment for even the mildest swearing was at least three hours in the stocks that stood in the cathedral close.

Catherine reached into her basket, took out a small flask of yellow liquid, and applied it to the incision. She struggled to stand up, so Alice stepped around the horse and put one arm around her mother's waist to ease her up.

"Here. Use this to clean out the wound, and keep the animal still for the rest of the day." Catherine handed the farmer the flask.

"Thank 'ee, m'dear, yu've done wonders." Jedediah Fletcher slipped three coins into her hand.

"An' you too." He addressed Alice. "You'll have to come up 'ere agin to charm the animals like you did today." The words came out from between the gaps in the farmer's teeth with hisses and splutters.

He turned to Catherine. "Be yer littl'un the seventh child of a seventh child?"

"Oh, Master Fletcher! You know I only have the two. Alice is my youngest, just ten years old."

"Well, I jist think yer littl'un has the Gift, you know, the way she had with our critter, calmin' him down." Farmer Fletcher placed his hand on Alice's head.

She stepped away. "Can we go home now?"

"Yes, come." Catherine shook the farmer's hand in farewell, and she and Alice set off across the field. After a few moments Catherine pulled the copper pennies out of her apron. "Look! These will procure us a fine cut of meat at the market tomorrow. We shall go together!" She patted her child's shoulder, and Alice smiled back up at her.

"Well, you be careful with 'er," Jedediah Fletcher called across the field as they squeezed back out through the gate.

The cathedral bell was tolling for evensong as Alice followed her mother down the path that led through the shady woodland. Catherine walked briskly but Alice skipped, so excited was she that Goody Luscombe's beliefs about how to calm a horse had worked. A few days after her friend's death, Alice had gone to Goody Luscombe's cottage to retrieve some of her herbs, but they were gone. Someone had been there before her, and the shelves where the herbs had been laid out were smashed to the ground and the plants swept away.

She'd stopped and looked around to see if anyone had seen her. Then she had backed out and run away as fast as she could.

She and her mother approached the bottom of the slope, but she slowed her pace when she heard the burble of the Longbrook, which called to her as it wound its way toward the River Exe.

The two had not spoken since they left Fletcher's farm, but now Alice implored her mother: "Look, we can stop here for a moment." The path had opened up into a clearing. Alice grabbed her mother's hand and led her over to a tall willow tree on the banks of the stream.

They sat down in the shade of the tree's graceful branches, and Alice craned her neck to stare up the steep slope to the massive city wall that crowned it. "What did Farmer Fletcher mean when he spoke of charms? Did I do a bad thing?"

"No, no. But you did scare him, and me a little, too, by how you were able to put a spell on the colt and calm him. You drew the farmer's suspicion." Catherine set her basket down on the ground and turned to face Alice. "How did you know to address yourself to the animal like that?"

"Goody Luscombe told me that horses are very sensitive, but you could soothe a restless horse if you breathed into its nostrils. So I tried it, and it worked!"

Her mother shook her head and opened her mouth to speak but changed her mind.

"I want to ask you something," Alice said.

"What is it, Alice?" Her mother pulled a small crust from her basket and passed it to her child. "We shall share this today, and tomorrow we shall eat well."

Alice took the oat bread, broke off a small piece, and handed it back.

"I still don't understand why they killed Goodwife Luscombe." Alice had held her thoughts inside for so long that now they all tumbled out like a stream after a heavy storm. "I don't believe she did anything wrong, so why did they have to murder her? And then, if there is a God, why did he let this happen to a poor, innocent woman? Why didn't he do something to stop it? So, Mother, what if there is no God? What if there is nothing?"

There. She had said it all.

Catherine set the crust back in her basket and turned to face Alice. She raised her right hand toward her child's face as if to slap her but instead held her hand there for a moment and lowered it.

"Do not ever ask me these questions again." Her voice sounded like a bow being pulled too roughly over a fiddle string. "You must know they call this blasphemy."

Over the ripple of the Longbrook, Alice made out the pretty sound of a song thrush close by, but all that mattered was that her mother glared at her. The furrow between Catherine's eyebrows deepened. Her mother had never dismissed her in this way before.

"What do you mean, blasphemy?" She stared into her mother's clear blue eyes, which seemed to have darkened.

"Blasphemy means you can be executed if you question the Christian faith."

"Is that why Goody Luscombe . . . ?"

"I don't know, Alice, but you have a lot of questions that make me fear for you." Her mother's voice had lost its taut quality but still had a cold edge. "You need to hold them in, keep them secret. As for why God would let such a thing happen, we must accept that God is good, but his ways are not always known to us mortals."

"Oh." Alice pictured yet again the dark image of Goodwife Luscombe's body silhouetted against the sky, her head bent forward over the noose.

Catherine patted her daughter on the back. She fished out the crust and ate the remainder.

Alice understood that this conversation was over even though her mother had given her no good answers. She had planned to tell her mother about the visit to Goodwife Luscombe's cottage, but now that was impossible. She grabbed a smooth pebble and slammed it into the water.

She stared at the hole in her shoe; her big toe stuck all the way out. It was hard to have so many secrets, so many things she'd been told never to talk about.

"Alice, you should know I am truly proud of you." Her mother reached over to embrace her, but Alice pulled back. Wasn't her mother also troubled by doubts?

Still, Catherine persisted: "I want to teach you everything I know about the care of sick animals and people, as your grandmother taught me."

"And as Goody Luscombe taught me! I want to become the best healer in Devon and share all my knowledge with other healers."

"You are strong and have mighty ambitions. But you need to take care not to draw attention to yourself. The men in charge here do not like girls who are too sure of themselves."

Is Mother telling me I'm too full of myself? Perchance she's right, but this is who I am.

A crash distracted them at that moment, and two full-grown deer bounded through the trees. Their black tails bobbed in the pale sunlight as they leapt over the Longbrook and disappeared from sight.

"Oh, Alice!" Catherine reached to hug her child, and this time, Alice allowed herself to be embraced. Catherine slowly let go.

"So, Mother."

"That's enough, Alice."

Alice did not dare to speak. Perhaps she should just accept that her questions about the existence of God were evil and that something bad might happen to her unless she forced such thoughts out of her head.

Would she go to hell?

She peeled off her buckskin shoes and wiggled her toes around. They were white and squished together. She dipped first one foot and then the other into the chilly water and watched them. For a few seconds, they were some other person's feet, too cold for her to feel. "It's just that I miss Goody Luscombe so much. She was so sweet and kind. And I'll never be able to go to her cottage again, listen to her call Master Colbert an old toad and then wink at me. She was different from anyone I've ever met."

"It may well have been John Colbert who was behind her arrest. I understand you miss our friend, but you still have your family." Her mother did not hug her, and Alice knew she had to bear this burden alone. She bit hard on her lower lip.

The two sat together for several minutes, enveloped by the delicate willow leaves and the pungent smell of wild garlic.

The cathedral bell no longer tolled, and the air was still. It was time to go.

Alice pulled on her shoes and grabbed her mother's hand. She stood up. The city wall loomed above them, a black glow against an evening sky laced with strips of pinkish clouds. It gave Exeter the appearance of a prison.

They strode side by side up the steep hill toward the North Gate, where two soldiers stood on guard. The men said nothing as mother and daughter passed by hand in hand but stood aside to allow for easier passage.

Had Goody Luscombe died because she questioned whether God existed? Perhaps Catherine was right, and Alice needed to put these dangerous ideas out of her head.

Or perhaps she would first seek out her friend Mary, who would surely help her resolve the muddle in her head.

She didn't have to wait long.

CHAPTER THREE

Exeter, Devon. September 1656.

"Alice, wake up!"

Faith grabbed her sister's arm and shook her. Alice opened her eyes to a darkened room.

The two lay on a straw-filled pallet on the ground in front of the hearth.

"Can you hear them?" Faith giggled.

Alice propped herself up on her elbows and stared in the direction of her parents' bedroom. The darkness made the sounds even louder: her father's grunts followed by a low squeal from her mother and a higher noise from her father, which sounded to Alice like a wounded animal. After he let out a loud "Ah!" her mother shushed him and told him they mustn't wake the children.

"There they go again," Faith whispered.

It wasn't the first time Alice had heard her parents' night-time cries, but she had always stuck her fingers in her ears and squeezed her eyes shut. But her foolish sister had forced Alice to listen to those sounds.

"Let's go back to sleep," Alice said. She pulled the blanket over her head. Her mother had explained what a woman and a man do together to make a baby. Catherine had said it was pleasurable, so they sometimes did this because they loved each other, not because they wanted another child.

Alice was in no hurry to hear any more details.

⁂

"I can do this no longer!" Alice flung the two wooden cards into the tall raffia basket, which was full almost to the brim with mounds of wool. "My hands hurt, my arms hurt, everything hurts. My fingers are greasy and smell like sheep piss."

"You behave like a baby!" Faith yelled over the rattle of the door and the lashing of the rain against the thin walls. She sat at the spinning wheel, her blonde head bent over as she threaded the wool in with one hand and turned the wheel with the other.

And you behave like a brute.

Beside Faith stood Catherine, who straightened out the yarn and wound it as it came off the spindle.

Alice sneaked glances at her mother and wondered how she felt after those noises in the night.

Catherine looked from one daughter to the other but said nothing.

It had been over a year since Alice's cat Jaspar, hers since he was a kitten, had disappeared. He'd loved to lick his white paws and use them to clean behind his black ears and over his black head. Every night, he purred and snuggled up with Alice on the pallet, keeping her warm.

One day she came back from the market with some slivers of mutton she'd picked up from the ground to feed her special friend, and her home was empty. Jaspar was gone. Alice asked her friend Jeffrey to help her search for him, and the two raced up and down the nearby streets calling Jaspar's name but discovered no trace of the cat.

They had returned to the Molland home and found Faith. When Alice questioned her sister about Jaspar, Faith wouldn't own up to anything at first but eventually confessed that she had taunted Jaspar, pulled his tail, and thrown water on him. The cat ran away, and she chased him all the way to Northgate Street, where he disappeared.

"Come on, Jeffrey, let's go." Alice pulled on her friend's sleeve, and the two took off toward the busy Northgate Street. Once again, they called "Jaspar, Jaspar," but the calls of people and the clatter of horses and carriages drowned out their voices.

Alice was ready to give up when Jeffrey yelled, "There, over there, curled up behind that carriage wheel!"

As they drew closer to Jaspar, Alice heard a whimper. She bent over to pick up her cat; the fur on one of his back legs was sticky with blood. She turned her head for a moment to avoid the stench of excrement. He growled and hissed at her as she tried to lift him, something he had never done before. "He's hurt," she said to Jeffrey, who crouched down beside her. "His back leg is broken, and he's badly shaken up." She recalled Goody Luscombe's instructions on how to mend a broken bone. "I need to make a compress with comfrey paste to help knit the bone back together, but Faith may try to harm him again if I take him home."

They had decided Jaspar would live at Jeffrey's home, at least for a while, as long as Alice came by every day to take care of the cat. After a fortnight, with the healing almost complete, Jeffrey had suggested he could keep Jaspar, but Alice could come visit whenever she wanted. She had agreed.

Alice had thought she and Faith were friends. She had been wrong, and since then, Alice had wondered if she could ever trust anyone.

Faith's bare arm moved in a steady rhythm as she guided the wool onto the distaff. Alice stared at the cards that lay on top of all that matted fleece and imagined how she might grab one of them and drag its sharp points along Faith's left arm. She inched one hand onto a card and gripped its cold metal spikes.

"Goodwife Molland, Goodwife Molland." The voice was all but swept away by the force of the wind as the cottage door was flung open by a young man who stepped in and slammed the door shut behind him. The thump of the treadle ceased.

"It's my mother. She is abed. I fear she will die."

Alice released the card's metal points. She stared at their visitor and guessed him to be thirteen, three years older than she was. He wore a velvet jacket, breeches, and cloak of the deepest blue, with a pure white linen collar. Rain dripped off his sodden hat and formed small puddles at his feet.

Alice's heart raced. Perhaps she wouldn't have to do any more carding today.

"And Father is away, so Aunt Abigail sent me here. She said you might help us."

"Tell me what ails your mother." Catherine dropped the woolen thread and stepped forward.

"The physician gave her some medicine that did nothing for her. She has the most dreadful stomach pains, and she makes such noises, as if her body were fit to burst."

He took off his hat, and Alice gasped. His hair was a vibrant reddish-orange, almost the same color as the soil that surrounded the city walls.

He reached into the pocket of his breeches, removed a linen handkerchief with a blue *G* embroidered in the corner, and wiped his face. "Please come at once."

Alice wondered why her mother did not reply immediately. Perhaps because it might go badly for her if she succeeded where the physician had failed? Or worse if her mother was unable to help the woman?

"I am Richard Greenway, of the Greenway family," he declared. "I have a carriage waiting outside, and you will be suitably compensated."

Greenway! The family where Mary works.

Catherine nodded. "I shall prepare myself presently."

Richard stuffed his handkerchief into his pocket and replaced his hat.

The rain crept in under the door and filled the small room with a musty smell. Catherine grabbed a rag and wiped around her visitor's feet, which were clad in black leather shoes surmounted by a large buckle.

"Mother! May I come with you?" Alice jumped out of her chair and pressed her palms together.

Catherine looked to Richard, who gave no response, and back to her daughter. "Yes, but only if you can prepare yourself with all speed."

Alice smiled, delighted to accompany the boy with the flame-colored hair, even if it was in the rain. Ever since that day at Jedediah Fletcher's farm, Alice had tried to do as her mother told her by putting her questions about Goody Luscombe and God's existence out of her head. It hadn't worked. She prayed that Mary would be able to help.

She grinned at Richard, whose eyes were a brilliant green, the color of holly leaves.

Catherine waved one arm toward Faith. "Keep the spinning wheel going while I am away, dear." She pointed to the basket beside the table. "And be sure that the yarn is smooth. It must have not a single bump or knot in it. Master Courteney will be at the market on Wednesday, and he will expect it to be perfect."

Within a few minutes, mother and daughter prepared to follow Richard Greenway's rich blue cloak into the street. Catherine clutched her wicker basket, which contained four small jars, each stoppered with a piece of cork. Alice held within the folds of her cloak a small earthenware jar of pennyroyal.

She stepped outside behind her mother. The rain stung her face and sent rivulets streaming down inside her bodice. She clawed her way into the Greenway carriage and flung herself into a corner next to her mother. She spied the widow Bradshaw across the lane, apparently oblivious to the storm, staring in astonishment.

Alice waved at their neighbor. The tips of Alice's fingers and toes tingled with cold, but excitement raced through her body like a wild horse galloping through the fields on a spring day.

With a jolt that threw Alice against the hard wood, they started down the muddy lane in the opposite direction from the church, the market, the well—all the places she knew. The carriage creaked and bumped so that Alice had to grip the bench to avoid falling off. Catherine clutched her basket and stared straight ahead.

Richard sat silently in the opposite corner. Alice wanted to speak to him, but the incessant beat of the rain against the sides of the carriage would have drowned out her voice.

From outside, Alice heard, "Whoa!" She was thrown forward as the carriage jerked to a stop.

Richard flung open the door and leapt out. "It's nothing but our old nag, Daisy. This will take just a moment."

"Where are we?" Alice asked.

"High Street," Catherine replied. "The Greenway house is but a short distance from here."

The carriage had stopped beside a tall house. Alice looked up and counted four stories. The walls of the house glowed white with the window frames a stark black—so different from the pale brown color of the Molland cottage.

Just then, someone opened the house's heavy wooden door.

A portly gentleman in a cape stepped out and spoke with Richard. Then the gentleman raised his pudgy left hand, which had a brilliant ruby ring on the little finger, and signaled a groom to lead a black horse from the side of the house. The man removed a beaver hat from within his cape, pulled it on over his shoulder-length ringlets, and strode over to the servant, who handed him the reins. Without further ado, he mounted the horse and galloped away.

Richard climbed back into the carriage, which jumped into motion again. Alice caught glimpses of shops: a tailor, a haberdasher, and a tobacconist with a display of pipes. Her father had told her that tobacco had been introduced to the west of England only about twenty years earlier and still cost a pretty penny.

One of her father's friends had once brought his pipe to the Molland house and shown the children how it worked. They laughed at him. It seemed silly to burn plants and breathe in their smoke. He told them it was fashionable, that all the rich people had their own pipes and tobacco fresh from Virginia, in America.

"Here we are!" Richard jumped out first and offered Alice his right hand, which she found to be cold and damp. In front of her stood a three-story house, and above the front door, she spotted a shield with a yellow lion painted on either side. From each yellow paw emerged five red claws, and from each mouth came a sinuous strip of red. She shuddered as she remembered the first time she had seen this creature: the day Goodwife Luscombe was hanged.

Richard disappeared around the corner of the house with the horse and carriage. Catherine reached for the brass knocker just as a young woman opened the heavy wooden door. She wore a bonnet embroidered with delicate lace that resembled a feathery spiderweb.

"I am Abigail Greenway," she announced. "I am the head of the house while my brother William is away on business. Enter."

She gestured with a sweep of her long arm. Alice was fascinated that the sleeves of her pale blue gown opened into small folds, and the bodice was embroidered with tiny stitches of gold. *How long did that take to sew?*

They stepped into a wide entrance hall with a polished oak floor and a ceiling that appeared to rise to the roof. Alice wondered if Mary was responsible for the upkeep of the floor. It must be really hard work.

On one side of the hall, a wide staircase led up to the first floor.

"Allow me to take your outer garments." Alice still clutched the jar of pennyroyal but now placed it into her apron and handed over her cloak.

She swallowed hard. The woman smelled of sour milk and lavender, and it made her feel sick. Her mother had told her that rich people did not wash very much and preferred to cover their stink with other smells.

Abigail Greenway held the rain-soaked cloaks in front of her at arm's length and disappeared down a narrow corridor.

The door to an antechamber stood ajar. Alice tiptoed over and peeked inside. She shrieked and stepped back. The head and shoulders of an eight-point deer stared at her from the opposite wall. The creature might have been magnificent once, but one eye had fallen out, and where the left side of its face drooped, a jawbone lay exposed.

Why murder an innocent animal and then watch its head rot?

Catherine grabbed her daughter and was about to speak when Richard appeared behind her.

"This way, Goodwife Molland." He beckoned to Catherine, who released her child.

To Alice, he said, "Wait down here."

"No," Catherine replied. "My daughter is my assistant. If I bring her with me, it is because she must be by my side."

Alice beamed.

Richard said nothing but led the two of them up the staircase and into a room where two maidservants stood, one on either side of an oaken four-poster bed that sat on four squat lion's paws. The gold damask curtains were drawn back to reveal a woman whose curly red hair was streaked with gray. Her tiny head was propped up by two enormous pillows.

The woman coughed and vomited a thin trickle of saliva into a china bowl, which a servant held in front of her. She retched one more time and closed her eyes.

"This is my mother, Florence Greenway. She has been this way for hours. Can you heal her?" Richard asked Catherine.

The servant stepped back, allowing Catherine to move in and place her basket on a small oak cabinet beside the bed. She leaned forward and rested the back of her right hand on Florence Greenway's forehead for a few moments. Next, she touched her patient's neck with her fingertips and peered into her open mouth. Finally, Catherine lifted the golden bedcover and pushed lightly against the woman's belly.

Florence moaned but did not open her eyes.

Alice watched from her place by the door. She tried to remember what Goody Luscombe had told her about the best treatment for nausea. Was it the pennyroyal, whose purple flowers grew close to the ground? Or the root of the gladwin iris with its deep green leaves and stalks that rose as high as her knees? Or something else, perhaps the fern?

"She has taken something bad for her system," Catherine announced. "First we must empty her out, then give her something to ease the pain and calm her stomach."

Catherine turned to Alice. "You must help me." Alice stepped forward but halted when she felt something soft under her feet. Part of the wooden floor was covered with a bright red rug. Around the edge were woven depictions of vines that swirled around yellow lions.

"Come, child."

Alice stamped on the lions with one foot and moved on.

"I think we shall need the fern," her mother said.

Yes, I was right! Thank you, Goody Luscombe.

The fern grew in several hedgerows near Goody Luscombe's cottage. One summer's eve, Alice had accompanied her friend in search of the distinctive plant with its long, straw-colored stem and numerous bright green fronds that alternated on either side.

On that beautiful, clear evening, they had decided to stroll down to the river and pick the fern on the way back. They walked slowly as Goodwife Luscombe's knees bothered her, but at the river, they had spied two glorious swans and their four fluffy gray cygnets. Alice had felt blessed to share this special moment with her friend.

Catherine addressed the servant at the foot of the bed. "She is not with child, is she?"

The young woman smiled. "No, no. She is surely past her time!"

Catherine took the jar with the dried fern leaves from her basket and tapped a small amount of the dark green powder into a glass. "Now pass me the water."

Alice paused. Goody Luscombe had used two plants to relieve pains of the belly. "Should you not add the gladwin iris to the fern?"

"The fern alone can work well. Now bring me the water."

Alice picked up the china ewer from the bedside cabinet and hoped she had not angered her mother. She poured water into the glass until Catherine signaled her to stop. It took a few moments for the powder to dissolve.

Catherine poured the liquid into the open mouth of her patient, who gargled and coughed but eventually swallowed her medicine.

Within a few minutes, Florence Greenway sat up and retched again. This time, it went on much longer. The woman's head bounced up and down as she spewed a greenish bile. Catherine held Florence's hand and murmured, "There, there, my dear. Good, very good."

The smell of vomit made Alice want to retch, and she stepped into the open doorway and glanced next door, where someone was polishing a silver teapot.

"Mary?" she whispered.

Her friend looked up and beckoned to Alice. Mary's brown hair was pulled back under a stiff white cap, and as Alice entered the room, she saw a table laden with an entire silver tea service and several serving bowls.

"Now you see how glamorous is my work! And all for only a few pennies, which I must hand over to my mother. But I am so happy to see you!" Mary set the teapot down and the two embraced until Alice pulled away.

"Mary, I need your help." Alice peered into her friend's deep-set blue eyes and took a deep breath. "You were there when they hanged poor Goody Luscombe. How could God let them kill an innocent woman?"

"What ails you, Alice? You are my dear friend, but you care only to ply me with your questions after we have not seen each other for so long?"

"I'm sorry, Mary. But what do you think? Is there truly a God?"

"Shush! You mustn't say such things." Mary raised one finger to her lips. "And especially in this house. Be careful, and please don't ask me these questions again. I'm sorry." She squeezed Alice's arm.

Alice turned away. Mary had been her last hope. Now she had no one to confide in.

"Alice, come here!"

At the sound of her mother's voice, Alice moved away from Mary and returned to the bedroom. Florence Greenway lay back on her pillow, her lined face gray but more relaxed. She appeared to be asleep.

"I shall have need of the pennyroyal to help to heal her stomach."

As her mother addressed her, Alice strove to push the disappointment from her head and focus on the healing task at hand. She removed the little jar from her apron and handed it over.

"Beware of her hand!" Richard called out. "Keep her away from my mother! She bears an unnatural sign!"

Alice froze at the sound of this upper-class boy yelling at her with his posh accent. Her hands trembled and she could scarcely see anything, her eyes were so bleary. "It's just a birthmark," she muttered.

Richard strode over to Alice and examined the hand she proffered for his inspection. "The mark of the leaf. It may mean redemption, or it may mean the devil. Whichever it may be, I would prefer that you not touch my mother."

Alice pulled her hand away.

"We shall do as you ask since you asked only for my services, and not those of my daughter. Be patient, Alice, the cure is well nigh complete." Catherine turned back to face Florence Greenway, and Richard came to stand beside her.

Alice was left alone in the corner beside the oak cabinet. She ran her fingers over the back of her left hand and traced the outline of the birthmark. Her mother had told her she had big hands, good for healing. *What could be so frightening about a birthmark?*

That night, Alice found it hard to sleep, her heart beat so fast. Richard's voice echoed continuously in her head: "It may mean the devil." What could he do to her? How could she protect herself?

A steady *drip, drip* from the day's rain fell off the roof and onto the ground outside the window. A dog barked in the distance, and then another. Low murmurs came from her parents' bedroom.

Faith lay on one side of the pallet, and Alice pulled herself as far away from her sister as she could. A shiver raced through her. She was alone.

Except that she wasn't. She felt Goody Luscombe's presence next to her, and before them lay the roots and leaves of several dandelions. Goody Luscombe's firm voice told Alice that it was up to her to prepare the dandelion decoction since her own fingers were stiff with rheumatism. With her friend watching, Alice found it easy to pour a little water into a pot set upon a flame and add the flower's parts, although she wrinkled her nose at the potion's acrid stink when she stirred it. After several minutes, it had the perfect consistency.

Goody Luscombe grasped her hand, and Alice could feel the woman's strength flow through her.

When Alicc wokc, it was dark. She stared up at the black ceiling and could still hear Goody Luscombe's voice in her head. She took a deep breath and smiled. Diana Luscombe had always been with her, and Alice would continue to hold her friend within her.

And yet perchance she should take care to cover her birthmark after Richard Greenway's alarm at the sight of it. She had learned that his father was one of the leading merchants of Exeter, so there was no doubt Richard could harm her if he chose to.

She worried, too, for her mother—and, indeed, for herself and her entire family after what had happened to Goody Luscombe. Would she ever again be safe?

CHAPTER FOUR

Exeter, Devon. November 1657.

On a cold Sunday morning, Alice helped her mother set out dumplings for the noon meal, but her numb fingers moved slowly. She brought her fingertips to her mouth and breathed warm air onto them, but the effect lasted only a few moments.

Alice had put the dumplings together the day before. When Oliver Cromwell became the sole ruler of England in 1653, he had issued a decree that there was to be no work of any kind on the Lord's Day. Penalties ranged from a week in the stocks to a hefty ten-shilling fine or a stay in the city gaol for people unable to pay.

It became a habit to prepare Sunday's food on Saturday. The previous evening, Catherine had chopped carrots and onions to make a soup where the dumplings would boil. Alice had stood alongside her mother and first mixed flour with a little salt and some water. Then, her favorite part: rolling the dough into small balls about the size of an egg and dipping them into a bowl of flour to coat the dumplings.

As Alice worked, she thought about her visit to Richard Greenway's house a fortnight earlier. Florence Greenway had fallen ill with the same complaint as last year, and once again,

Alice had accompanied her mother to the Greenway residence to heal her. Alice's heart had beaten quickly at the thought that she might see Richard, but a lone coachman had come to fetch Alice and her mother.

Once the two stood beside Florence Greenway's bed, they had worked together as a team. Alice breathed through her mouth to avoid the sour smell of Florence's vomit, but she stayed next to the patient's bed. As it came time to leave, a servant led the healers down the wide staircase. Richard stood by the open front door. Alice's heart raced, and her palms grew damp. He gave her a brief smile but said nothing as he closed the door behind them. *Is he still suspicious of me?*

As Alice finished setting out the dumplings, her sister squealed, "Ugh! Get him away!" Faith pointed toward the hole at the bottom of the door. A rat's blunt snout squeezed through as it tried to force itself through the hole.

"Maybe it's coming for you!" Alice teased her sister, who had jumped up to stand on the wooden bench. Alice wanted to add that there would be no rat if Jaspar still lived here.

Faith stuck her tongue out at Alice, but Thomas stood up and grabbed the poker from the fireplace. Rats were a common enough sight, but to judge by its snout and whiskers, this one was larger than most. When the fat creature popped out like a cork from a bottle, Thomas went for him, but the rat raced across the kitchen and disappeared behind the stove, its long, skinny tail writhing on the ground.

Thomas replaced the poker and sank back into his chair by the fire. The whole family wore heavy cloaks against the cold. Alice had put on her long skirt under her cloak, but still her body continued to tremble.

"Open up, in the name of the Lord!" came a loud voice on the other side of the door.

Alice stopped breathing. Her mother had begged her not to question anyone about their religious faith and to stay out of trouble with Cromwell's men. Alice had obeyed. *Why is someone coming to our home to threaten us?*

Catherine set down a dumpling and stared at the door, one hand across her chest.

"Open up!" came the order once more, this time accompanied by a loud knock on the door.

Faith sat frozen on the bench, and neither Catherine nor Thomas moved.

I am not afraid. "We have done nothing wrong," Alice declared and unlatched the door.

Before her stood John Colbert. He was accompanied by two soldiers she did not recognize. Tightness gripped her. At the sight of their helmets and drawn swords, Alice stepped back and sat next to Faith. The cramped kitchen seemed to have grown even smaller.

The three men marched in, slammed the door shut, and stopped an arm's length from the table. Outside, the wind whistled around the cottage.

"Our Lord Protector has decreed: no meat eating, no games, no work of any kind on the Lord's Day." Colbert tapped his sword on the wooden table. "What do we find here?" He used the sword to slash one of the dumplings in half. "No meat, I trust?"

"No meat," Catherine muttered.

"Well, we shall see." The soldier grabbed the wooden board with a black leather glove. He took one stride in his bucket-top boots, reached the hearth, and tossed all twelve dumplings into the fire. A line of gray smoke streamed into the kitchen, followed by a burst of brilliant flames. The soldier coughed against the smoke as he strode back and tossed the empty platter onto the table.

Alice's body shook. She could see her own breath, a small

misty cloud in front of her. She stared into the fire and prayed the armored men would leave, satisfied with their work. Her mother had spoken of her fear that something bad could happen on account of the Sunday law, but why had these soldiers chosen to pick on her family?

"What do you want with us?" asked Thomas. "We went to Matins at St. Paul's this morning; we are God-fearin' people." He raised himself so that he stood eye to eye with the soldiers from his place at the other end of the table.

No, Father. Just sit down. Don't make things worse.

The man to the right of Colbert stepped forward, and his shadow engulfed Alice. She gripped the edge of the table and rested her right hand over her left to cover her oak leaf.

The other two soldiers strutted forward so that all three stood in a row at the very edge of the dinner table.

Alice risked a glance at her mother.

In one swift movement, Catherine gathered up her skirt and came to stand next to her husband. Her lower lip quivered.

What is wrong with my parents? These soldiers are evil. We can do nothing to stop them.

"If you think we have any money for meat on the Lord's Day, or any other day, you are most mistaken." Catherine stepped around the table to the opposite side from where Alice and Faith sat and stood before the soldiers. Her hands came to rest above the gray fabric of her bodice.

Thomas's dark eyes fixed on Alice's mother, and his face flushed deep red. Sergeant Colbert stared at Catherine's small fingers. With his sword in one hand, he strode forward and laid his other gloved hand on hers, then slid it down over Catherine's fingers until it came to rest across her bosom.

Alice caught her breath. Her feet seemed frozen, and yet her toes were on fire.

Thomas shoved Colbert away from Catherine and against the soldier who stood beside him. "By my faith, you shall not touch my wife! You heard what she said. Where do you think we might secure money to purchase meat in these hard times? I tell you, we are law-abiding citizens."

John Colbert handed his sword to the soldier beside him and came at Thomas with leather fists.

Alice bit hard on her lower lip.

Her father's black hair was stuck to his forehead, and sweat glistened between the bristles on his chin. He raised his hands against his chest, but Colbert punched him in the belly. Bent double, Thomas's large frame flew against the wall. He landed with a thump and dropped to the ground.

Alice closed her eyes for a moment.

Catherine let out a gasp. "Leave my husband be. He means no harm."

Alice opened her eyes to see how Colbert glared at her father, ready to knock him flat with that iron fist the moment Thomas made to stand up. She silently begged her father to stay put.

"Father!" Faith sprang up from the table, away from Alice and toward Thomas.

No! Don't be foolish, Faith. We could all be dead because of you.

Faith stopped short as John Colbert turned around to level his gloved hands at her. "You should mind your manners, girl."

Faith sank onto the bench and wrapped her cloak around her.

Don't let them see you are afraid, Alice wanted to tell Faith. *Keep yourself to yourself.*

Thomas tried to raise himself by sliding his body up against the wall. Just as he was almost upright, Colbert brought his glove up against Thomas's face.

Alice knew the soldier was out to kill her father. Her throat constricted so hard she could scarcely breathe.

Colbert's mouth was contorted into a strange grimace that raised one side of his face up higher than the other as he jabbed Thomas squarely on the nose. With a thud, Alice's father landed back down on the dirt floor and held his nose as drops of blood oozed between his fingers.

Colbert turned away and grabbed his sword back from his fellow soldier.

Catherine started toward her husband, but Colbert's companions pushed her aside. The three men used their swords to sweep the oaken table clean; a hard, gray loaf of bread rolled under the table, and the day's ale spilled across the dirt floor.

In unison, the soldiers re-sheathed their swords in their red sashes and marched toward the door. "Our general will be glad to know you are keeping observance of the Lord's Day," John Colbert said. The wind rushed in when he opened the door. Two large pots hanging above the hearth rattled and fell to the ground.

The soldiers exited and slammed the door shut behind them.

Catherine threw herself down beside her husband. She cupped his face in her hands and kissed his bloody mouth over and over between sobs, so that her face was smeared in red.

Alice's stomach grew hot as she stared at the sad spectacle of her parents' anguish. Yet she knew it didn't have to be this way. If only her father could control his anger. Colbert had goaded Thomas into a fight, and it had worked.

"This is what they mean by enforcing Cromwell's decree," Catherine cried. "But why us?"

"It's not only us," Thomas said. "They've been going out every Sunday for the past month, knocking on people's doors and hoping to catch them out."

"Ah, Thomas." Catherine's hands still caressed her husband's face. "What is to become of us?"

Alice stared at her father, propped up against the wall, drops of dark blood spattered on the front of his brown doublet.

* * *

The following morning, Thomas sat in the big chair at the chimney corner. He stared into the fire and refused to say anything. His nose was swollen as big as a potato, and black bruises covered the area beneath his bloodshot eyes. The force of Colbert's punch to his face had knocked out his front teeth.

Catherine was out in search of food.

Alice had to get out. As she walked, potato skins, crusts of bread, and even whole cabbages skittered across her path, driven by the wind that whipped around her, but she passed very few people. All the while, she couldn't rid her mind of the image of John Colbert's grimace as he punched her father in the face and the sight of her father sprawled on the ground.

Damn those soldiers. Why are they so cruel? What makes them want to destroy our lives? Don't they have families of their own? Will I ever feel safe?

She decided to visit Jeffrey's house and tell her friend what had happened, thus pushing the ugly memories of yesterday out of her head. Then she would be able to be strong for her family.

Jeffrey was not home, but Jaspar lay snuggled up against the side of the hearth. Alice sat down and gathered his warm body into her arms. When she stroked his soft black fur, he purred and licked her fingers. That's when Alice told Jaspar all about Sunday's events.

* * *

When Alice returned home, Thomas remained fixed in his spot by the chimney.

"Father." She whispered his name as she inched her way toward his chair. He looked red-eyed, and his nose had developed a purplish-blue color.

"Father." Alice spoke again, although her heart was beating so fast that she was surprised she had any voice at all. "I am truly sorry for what they did to you."

Thomas growled. "'Twas not your error. But you must stay away from them." He turned from her to face the fire.

Just before Christmas, over a month later, his nose and eyes had healed, and he had stepped out of the house to procure laboring work.

⁂

Alice stood in a beautiful forest of green poplar trees, their silver-white trunks twinkling under an almost-full yellow moon. The great silence, the immensity of the sky, and the clean smell of the forest surrounded her. Above, amid wispy strands of clouds, the moon slipped in and out of sight like some plump, mysterious fruit.

"Wake up, Alice." Alice sat up at the touch of her mother's hand on her shoulder. "Wake up! You must rise and hasten to church to celebrate the birth of Our Lord."

"Mother." Alice sighed. She lay on her pallet for a few moments to hold on to the sense of peace that filled her. She had learned that by doing so, she could journey in her head to the secret place of her dream at any time during the day.

"Come, child! We are all assembled, and since it is forbidden to celebrate Christmas, we must go under cover of dark. You may think this could be dangerous, but the soldiers are most unlikely to be awake at this hour. We must needs hold on to our faith in these times and pray for Mary's mother, that they may see their error and release her."

Alice shivered. Charis Ward had been dragged from her home eight days earlier and taken away, accused of adultery. In 1650, the Commonwealth Act had imposed the death penalty for incest and adultery, although it was rarely enforced.

Nathaniel had run after the soldiers but had stopped short at the corner of Paul Street when they turned and fired their muskets at him. They missed the top of his head by a beard's length. Now Goody Ward was locked up in the South Gate prison, where no visitors were permitted.

Alice wanted to ask Mary if it was her fault her mother lay in prison. Was it possible her friend had betrayed her own mother? Alice would never know because Catherine had forbidden Alice to visit her friend.

Within a few minutes, the Molland family slipped their way down the icy lane. They clutched each other as they moved forward and joined other soundless shapes, all headed to St. Paul's, their local parish church.

"Our Father, who art in Heaven, hallowed be thy name." Alice chanted with the other members of the small congregation. They knelt in the three front rows of the small church.

She knew these words by heart, and yet more and more as she recited them, she believed she spoke into empty space.

Her eyes grew accustomed to the dim light. She stared at the dark oak wood in front of her, shiny as a result of numerous human hands being placed there over the years and riddled with tiny holes, the telltale marks of woodworm. She wished, as she had a hundred times before, that she might grow another few inches. At the age of eleven, she was only just able to see over the top of the pew. The church smelled especially musty this morning.

"Thy kingdom come." Father Bridgeman stood in front of them in his plain black cassock. With no candles lit, he made an eerie shape. Alice wondered why some people got so upset about how you worshipped God. Surely, he didn't mind if he did really exist; the important thing was that you went to church. Yet her father had told her that during the Great Wars, soldiers fought over this and even killed each other.

Alice's father knelt beside her, his big hands clasped together in prayer, and tufts of dark hair sprouted from his stocky fingers.

"Thy will be done." As they whispered the familiar words, several members of the small congregation shifted their legs. Even though rushes covered the hard, rough ground, the worshippers could not stay motionless for very long.

Alice, too, slid her knees into a new position, conscious of the pattern of indentations that had imprinted itself in the skin over her kneecaps in spite of the long skirt she wore. The crackle of twigs in the freezing air outside the church made her heart stop. Were there soldiers outside, ready to attack?

Around her, the soft chant of the Lord's Prayer continued, and Alice wondered if anyone else had heard the sounds from the graveyard. When no one burst into the church, she allowed herself to breathe again and rested her eyes once more on her father. The flesh under his chin was loose and hung in a fold while the bald spot at the top of his head seemed to glow.

As she stared at his scalp, it became almost incandescent. She blinked, and in her mind, she saw the top of his head gashed open. She gripped the edge of the pew and shook her head from side to side, but the vision remained. Her father lay dead on the ground, head to one side, holding something in his lifeless hands. Blood trickled down his leather jerkin.

Tears rose in her eyes, and she squeezed them shut.

From outside the church came the crunch of footsteps on the frosty ground.

Alice gripped the cold wood of the pew. *Please, God, if you are really there, protect me from whoever is marching toward us.*

"On Earth as it is in Heaven" faded into the gray half-light, and then nobody spoke. Father Bridgeman froze in place, his arms stretched out toward the people who knelt before him. In silence, they all awaited their fate. Alice held her breath. A long, slow creak filled the church as the heavy door was pushed open and the congregation awaited the soldiers' shouts. Instead, Goodwife Babcock closed the door and began her slow shuffle down the aisle as she muttered to herself.

Alice let out her breath.

Around her, the congregants crossed themselves and whispered their thanks to God. "Give us this day our daily bread." The congregants' voices burst out in singsong relief. "And forgive us our trespasses."

Alice allowed herself to let go of the pew and look over at her father once more. Her dreadful vision was gone, and he was the same as always. Alice took herself back to her dream, to the forest and the warm glow of the moon.

She turned her head slightly. Nathaniel Ward sat just behind her father, next to his daughter Mary. Alice tried to catch a glimpse of her friend's lively blue eyes, but Mary refused to look up. Alice wondered if Mary still worked at the Greenway house.

She shifted her gaze to Nathaniel. His gray face, with its sprouty beard, stared up at the priest before them.

On the other side of Alice, the early morning light filtered through a small pane of glass in the chantry chapel and outlined the row of stone statues on its wall. The Puritans had knocked off their heads in the early days of the Civil Wars, declaring that such lifelike creations encouraged idolatry, worshipping someone other than God as though he were God.

Whenever she was bored in church, Alice indulged in her favorite game of imagining the faces of these long-robed figures. She wondered who had carved them and whether the carver had used a chisel. Her father owned a chisel, which he mostly used to smooth out the kitchen table. He had once shown Alice how to use the chisel with a hammer. "Here, just a light touch, and then a little more firm," he had instructed.

"As we forgive those that trespass against us," Alice joined in. "And lead us not into temptation, but deliver us from evil."

Almost imperceptibly, the pace of the prayer had picked up.

"For thine is the kingdom, the power, and the glory," Alice chanted, reflecting on how miserable everyone always looked in church. She decided it must be because their knees hurt, and because it was cold and the service was so boring.

She looked up at the stained glass in the east window, more colorful now that the light had grown stronger. Behind the dark wooden carvings of the rood screen rose the red stained glass figure of Our Lord holding two white loaves and five green fishes. Around him stood people in blue, red, and orange.

When she stared at the beautiful stained glass, Alice forgot that here in the church, the congregation wore black or brown cloaks and barely had enough to eat. The days were short at this time of year, but soon they would get longer, and colorful spring flowers would push through the ground. The world would be beautiful, just like it was in her dream. For the first time that morning, Alice's hands tingled with a faint warmth.

CHAPTER FIVE

Exeter, Devon. April 1658.

"People of Exeter! So perish the adulteress!" The sergeant-at-arms banged his pike on the red dirt as the black-hooded executioner twisted the ladder out from under the convicted woman's feet. The solitary rope hanging in the center of the scaffold snapped taut with the weight of its burden. Goody Ward's shorn head fell forward. Her body twitched one more time and then went still, though her eyes remained wide open and stared into the distance.

Alice shuddered. The cold, damp air intensified the shaking that was already cascading up and down her body. Cromwell's soldiers had arrested Mary's mother less than four months ago, and now she was dead. At the age of twelve, Alice had already witnessed the execution of two women. Who would be next?

But what about the man? Adultery involves a man and a woman. What about the man?

And what was it like to see your own mother die like this? Alice looked around for Mary but saw only a blur of dark cloaks and faces raised toward the scaffold. One of these cloaks belonged to Richard Greenway, who fixed his emerald eyes on Alice. He wore a long black cape, and his red hair fell in curls onto his shoulders. What was going through his head? And whose side was he on?

And what about the man?

"Do not stare!" Catherine poked her child's shoulder.

Alice looked away and pulled her shawl closer around her shoulders, but she couldn't prevent the cold that came from deep within her. And as she looked, it was not Charis Ward she saw but Goody Luscombe. "Kill the witch! Kill the witch!" the crowd had yelled then, almost two years ago. Surrounded by their chants, Alice had stood alone.

"Hallelujah!" cried the priest. "We have conquered evil!" He took a wooden crucifix from the leather belt around his waist, held it up high, and kissed it. Then he knelt and placed his forehead on the ground, which was damp with recent snowmelt. All around Alice, old and young alike dug into their pockets and aprons and pulled out brown wax images of Charis Ward. They stuck her with pins of burnished steel, threw her down, and stamped her into the ground beneath laced-up leather shoes and fancy square-toed boots.

Alice looked to the sky for some sign that God might be watching but saw only massive gray clouds. Her cheeks were stinging, and she caught the fresh smell of approaching rain.

She knew she was better than these citizens of Exeter who took pleasure in watching others suffer, but she also knew she must keep her own counsel.

Alice closed her eyes and brought to mind the small waterfalls she had discovered a few days earlier when she had gone out beyond the East Gate in search of early bluebells. On either side of a stream lay large rocks covered by a thin layer of snow, and it seemed a miracle the icy water kept flowing between them, making its way down shelves of rock six inches high, falling about three feet before continuing across a snowy meadow.

"Come, Alice. We must go." Her mother interrupted Alice's daydream and grabbed her freezing hand. "Your father has already started for home with Faith. We must follow them."

Catherine's words were unnecessary, for the crowd had surrounded the two of them and pulled them into its flow down the hillside. Instead of the snow they had lived with since Christmas, raindrops fell on Alice's cheeks.

The slippery path made her hold tight to her mother's cold hand. Shouts of "'Tis right cold this morning" and "They say it's the coldest winter in living memory!" erupted around her. She hated these people.

When they reached the bottom of the hill and turned onto Magdalen Street, the crowd thinned out to accommodate passing carriages.

The rain turned into a light drizzle. Alice let go of her mother's hand and pulled the hood off her head. "What will become of Goody Ward's body?"

"Hush, Alice." Catherine motioned with her forefinger against her bluish lips. "She will be left for a week and then thrown into a pit on the other side of the hill. A person executed for a crime may not be buried within the city walls."

"That's horrible. But how did they know to arrest Charis Ward?"

"It is well known that Mary's mother enjoyed the company of men besides her husband. And this offense is punishable by death."

"Which men? Why are they not being punished too?"

Catherine placed one hand over Alice's mouth and gave no answer.

But the question kept nagging at Alice: If Charis Ward and these men took equal pleasure in their doings, why was it that Mary's mother had been gruesomely murdered while the men lived on, free as birds?

⁂

The rain persisted on and off for almost two weeks after Charis Ward's execution. Finally, Alice awoke one morning to bright sunshine and almost-clear skies and knew she had to get outside. Her mother and Faith worked together to card and spin the wool, and Alice offered to go in search of dill. She knew exactly where it grew beside the River Exe, and she also knew Catherine had need of it to make a decoction of the leaves, well known as a remedy for digestive problems.

Alice hadn't seen her dear friend Jeffrey since before Goody Ward's hanging, so she set off for his house. He was fourteen, two years older than she was, and she liked that. Alice found boys her own age to be annoying and immature. He was apprenticed to a farrier, but this morning she found him at home. After petting her cat, Jaspar, who purred contentedly beside the fire, she and Jeffrey headed out of the North Gate and down Exe Lane, toward the river. Alice led the way, and soon they arrived at the spot where dill grew.

She bent down and used her fingernails to snip the stems of several dill plants, with their fine, feathery leaves. She breathed in their pungent, slightly minty smell before she placed them in her apron. Dill stems could be almost a foot tall, but Alice knew to leave about a third of each plant in the ground so it would keep growing.

With her work done, Alice came over to sit next to Jeffrey and breathed in the rich, earthy smell of the meadow after the rain. She glanced over at her friend, fascinated as always by his long-lashed blue eyes and the way his brown hair swept back, giving him a permanently surprised look.

"Look, Jeffrey! The ducks! They mean to tell us something!" Six mallard ducks, four males with distinctive green heads and yellow bills and two brownish females, came toward Alice and Jeffrey where they sat beside the river.

"I reckon the ducks are happy for the sunshine at last." Jeffrey lay back on the grass. He closed his eyes, and Alice knew he might fall asleep in no time, as she had seen him do before.

She continued watching the ducks. She loved to study their funny bodies in the water when they plunged down to find food, leaving their squat behinds to stick up foolishly. "Something is amiss with these ducks. There are only six of them, where last time I saw them, there were seven." Alice jumped up and at once the ducks paddled upstream, against the flow of the water.

"Get up, lazybones! Get up!" She yanked on Jeffrey's right arm. He stood up, and the two followed the solemn procession for about a hundred feet until they came around a bend and stopped. At the spot where an ash tree had fallen into the water, Alice spotted a female mallard stuck between two of the tree's branches. She was jammed in by the joint of her shoulder and quacked loudly as she rose and fell with the stream's flow.

"It's the water. Higher than usual, it must have pushed her under, and she cannot move. We have to rescue her!" Alice's heart raced.

Jeffrey stared at her, his pale blue eyes even more translucent than usual. "The mallard is lodged fully six feet out, in the middle of the stream." He put one hand on her shoulder. "To reach the bird, one of us would have to crawl on hands and knees along the slippery trunk of the ash tree and hope not to fall in and be carried away by the icy waters." A tremendous rasping and quacking broke out behind them. "It's but a bird. We cannot risk our lives for such a tiny creature."

In answer, Alice pushed Jeffrey's arm away. She removed the dill stems from her apron and handed them to him. Next, she rolled up her long skirt and tucked it into the apron strings. She didn't care if her shift got wet. She knelt on the damp ground and eased first one knee, then the other, onto the trunk. Behind her, Jeffrey warned her to be careful, but as she moved along, other voices sang out of the clear water and encouraged her to keep going.

Her hands shook, but she gripped the rough bark and inched her way forward. Once she came close to the trapped duck, she realized she would have to let go with one hand in order to free the bird.

"Watch out for me!" she cried to Jeffrey over the babble of the water. The ducks had ceased all noise.

"Stay calm," she muttered to herself while she eased her left hand to a place where she could grip one branch above the water. She plunged the other hand into the stream and discovered where the bird's shoulder was caught, but the water froze her hand, and she pulled back. It took three attempts before she could keep her hand in the stream long enough to push the other branch away from her and set the duck free.

At once, its family members honked and cooed as they gathered around her.

The ordeal over, Alice slithered her way back to the bank and onto dry ground.

"Congratulations!" Jeffrey patted her on the back.

She shook his hand hard and collapsed on the ground, grateful for the warm sunshine. As she looked up, a rush of starlings whirled across the sky and disappeared among the treetops.

The warm weather did not last. It was on a cold morning in the month of May, about a week after Alice rescued the duck, that the parishioners of St. Paul's were directed by the town crier to hasten along to their place of worship, where important news awaited them.

At the sound of the town crier's bell, Alice tensed. "Do we have to go?" She set her card down next to a pile of greasy wool. Faith did the same, and the two waited for their father's response. Catherine was out collecting plants for her herbal remedies.

Thomas pulled himself out of his fireside chair. "What in the name of the devil do they want with us? I fear something bad." He patted Alice's shoulder. "Yes, Alice, we do. It won't help to stay away."

Several of their neighbors stood huddled together outside the church's south door when the three of them entered the enclosed churchyard of St. Paul's. Alice recognized Jane and Susannah Slater, sisters who lived nearby on Corry Street, and gestured to them. Jane responded with a dour look, and Susannah gave a wan smile.

The Molland family made their way to the front of the group and stood next to Ted Wingate. "By God's blood, 'tis cold this morning," he pronounced, his voice echoing in the chill morning air. "They say the River Exe is afloat with islands of ice where fish, fowl, and even people in their boats are frozen solid."

Faith emitted a muffled laugh, and Alice glared at her sister. It was true that the two had been amused by Stick Man, as they called Ted. The man's arms and legs—and even his head, ears, and nose—were thin and pointed, like twigs in danger of snapping if the wind grew too strong. But now was not the time for laughter.

The parishioners grew silent when Father Bridgeman stepped through the archway and read from a parchment scroll. "By order of our Lord Protector of the Commonwealth, General Oliver Cromwell, this church is to be sold, along with twelve others within the city of Exeter."

He lowered the paper and stared down at the earth. "It seems that the military occupation of our city is costly, even though most of the soldiers are quartered on our citizens."

A chill gripped Alice, and her breath created frosty vapor clouds. "What does this mean? How can they do that?"

"Quiet, Alice," Thomas answered. "You must allow the reverend to finish."

"The towers of the churches are to be taken down clean to the roof by the purchasers, and the churches are to be converted into schools or burying places."

Alice's head sank into her neck, and her neck ached. Even if she didn't believe there really was a God, she loved the beautiful stained glass and knew it was important to her mother that they attend church regularly.

She looked up at Father Bridgeman's pudgy, round face and wondered if he could read her thoughts. Four whole cycles of the moon had passed since her mind had shown her the image of her father dead on the ground, and there had been nothing since, but she feared the return of such a vivid picture. Just like when she searched for boll weevils in flour, she knew they were there even if she could not see them.

"First it be the alehouses, an' now they close the churches," grumbled Ted. "Wat d'yu reckon it'll be next?"

Father Bridgeman fished a handkerchief from his cassock and blew his nose.

Thomas turned to walk away, but Father Bridgeman stepped forward. "You'll want to look at what they've already done to our church. Go inside. See for yourself."

For a few moments, everyone stood stock-still. At length, Alice walked up and pushed against the heavy oak door. The rest of the group shuffled in behind her. No one had lit the candles, and yet it seemed less dim than usual. Alice started down the nave but froze in place. The beautiful oak lectern with its intricate patterns of leaves and flowers lay on the ground, chopped into two pieces. Tears rose in Alice's eyes.

Created almost a century ago, the lectern held a special place for the parishioners of St. Paul's since it had been carved by George Tucker, one of their own.

Someone had taken an axe to the rood screen, which separated the nave from the chancel, and jagged wooden spikes stuck up like giant thorns.

Alice gasped and reached up one hand to clasp her throat. These men had smashed up St. Paul's, which she had believed was sacrosanct. And these same soldiers had come into her home and beaten her father for no good reason.

When she looked up, she understood why there was more light than usual for this hour. In the east window, she saw that the bodiless head of Our Lord floated over a gaping hole. Beneath it, shards of red, blue, and green glass peppered the altar.

The cold morning air filled the chancel and wiped out the familiar aroma of lit candles. She could barely breathe.

"Move on out of here. You have had sufficient time." John Colbert's voice boomed from the other end of the nave. He marched down the aisle on his short, stout legs, followed by the same two soldiers who had accompanied him to the Molland home. All three had their long muskets at the ready. "This is no longer your church." The "no" and "longer" came back in a faint echo.

The scar across the left side of his face glowed in the strange light. Colbert turned to face the group gathered halfway down the nave. "Now leave this place. Out of here, all of you."

"But this is the house of God. You cannot take it from us." Faith spoke in a soft tone.

"I said go! This is no longer your church. Leave!" Colbert kicked at the side of the rood screen and signaled with his musket to his two companions.

At once, the three soldiers directed their weapons at the assembled group, which made its way toward the church door.

Alice was left alone. She stared at the east window and tried to bring all the pieces of shattered glass together so that a resplendent Christ figure stood before his disciples and glowed in magnificent reds, greens, and blues. She failed.

At that moment, Catherine hurried into the church, then stopped. "What has happened? What have they done to our sacred place?"

Alice turned away from the east window and walked toward her mother. "They have destroyed it. We don't have a church anymore."

Catherine stared at her child as if she did not understand her daughter's words.

Alice stepped back. Her mother's face bore a faint resemblance to Goody Luscombe's in the way her mouth drooped at the corners.

Would Catherine be the next to go, dragged out of her house and eventually hanged by the neck?

CHAPTER SIX

Exeter, Devon. May 1658.

Even though there was no church to attend, the rules governing Sundays remained the same. Still, a rumor circulated that Oliver Cromwell suffered from malaria and might die at any moment, which gave the parishioners of St. Paul's the hope that they might get their church back.

On this late Sunday afternoon, the sweet smell of rosemary—which Alice was burning to purify the air—filled the kitchen.

Catherine stood before the shelf where numerous herbs were laid out to dry. "I must go out beyond the North Gate."

Alice stared at her mother. "No, you must not. That would be dangerous."

"Rebecca Thorpe has missed her courses by almost two moons and may well be with child. She needs my help, but I have almost none of the fern and gladwin root necessary for my decoction."

Thomas looked up at his wife from where he sat by the chimney. "This is plain foolishness. No woman should think to venture out beyond the city walls as dusk approaches."

Alice understood what her father meant. Two days earlier, a haycart containing six women huddled together had made its way down High Street. They had been arrested for witchcraft, and two sergeants-at-arms had led them to the Castle Gaol. Here, they would await trial at the Summer Assizes.

The prison was known to be a dank, filthy dungeon where, in 1585, gaol fever had wiped out all forty-two inmates as well as the judge appointed to their trial.

But why is it always women who are arrested and hanged? Alice's heart beat alarmingly fast as her mind called up, yet again, images of Goody Luscombe's head bent over the noose and the way Charis Ward's legs had twitched under her prison shift.

"Are you leaving, Mother?" Faith called out from the bedroom. A pain had gripped Faith's innards, and Catherine had instructed her oldest daughter to lie down for a while.

"Yes, but your father will take care of you."

Alice wanted to tell Faith to grow up and not feel sorry for herself.

"I must procure both the fern and the gladwin root. And Rebecca is by no means the first. Ah, these soldiers! Why can they not leave our girls be?"

"Then you would kill the baby?"

"Alice, please. You ask too many questions. I must help Rebecca. I shall explain it to you later."

"I can take your place! I know well what the fern and gladwin iris look like. I even know where to find them." *I am not a young child anymore. I know a lot about herbs.*

Thomas stood up and marched across the kitchen. "I shall go with Alice. It will be safer for two of us to go together." He reached for his leather jerkin, which hung by the front door.

Alice stared at the man whom she had seen sit silently in front of the fireplace for so many hours over the past six months.

"Are you sure?" Catherine rushed over to rest one hand on his arm. "It could be unsafe for you, too, to go out at this time."

"Mother, if you want us to get these herbs, we must leave

immediately. If we return too late to the North Gate, they will shut us out." Alice grabbed her apron from the rack by the door and tied it around her waist. In its wide pocket lay a small trowel.

"She's right." Thomas slipped into his jerkin. "And this is all for you, so be done with your complaints."

"Well." Catherine pulled on the iron latch to open the front door. "'Tis a pretty time of year, now that the evenings are longer and the air warmer. I suppose, as long as you make haste. Go down to the woodlands by the brook. You have no need to go further, and you can return before dark."

"Mother, I told you—I know where to go." Alice hoped this outing with her father would help to heal them both from the wounds inflicted by Cromwell's men.

"Watch yourselves well. I shall remain here to take care of Faith. And hurry! You must return before the eight o'clock curfew, when they will close the gate."

Thomas pulled the front door shut, and he and Alice headed along Paul Street.

As they rounded the corner toward the North Gate, Alice heard a voice calling to her: "Wait! Alice!" She turned to see Jeffrey, who bounded along the side of the street to avoid the mucky kennel in the center. He grinned when he caught up with her and brushed his long hair off his forehead.

"Alice! Where have you been? Are you headed out to search for some herbs? May I accompany you?"

Alice reached out to embrace her friend, but Thomas interrupted them. "We must hurry. We don't need a third person."

Alice turned to look at her father. "Why speak to Jeffrey like that? He can walk fast."

Thomas shook his head. "I'm sorry, Jeffrey, but Alice and I must go alone." His tone was firm. He stepped away and walked toward the North Gate.

Don't order me around like that in front of Jeffrey. Alice looked back to her friend and then ran to catch up with Thomas. She didn't want to see the disappointment in Jeffrey's eyes.

⁂

Alice and her father had covered almost half a mile, moving down the hill outside the city walls.

They spoke little as they slipped and slid on the damp earth, but Alice's thoughts consumed her. *He shouldn't have talked like that to Jeffrey. I can speak for myself.* She wanted to chide her father for his words but decided against it. The most important thing was leading him to the fern and the gladwin.

"Primroses!" Alice stepped off the muddy path and reached between the roots of an oak tree where the tiny flowers were tucked away. "Look how pretty they are!"

The sight of these pale yellow flowers with their darker yellow centers brought tears to her eyes, for they celebrated the end of a cruel winter with their gentle beauty. Perhaps they also meant that her nightly torture would come to an end.

Ever since being ordered to leave St. Paul's, Alice had been tormented by strange dreams. She was in a city that looked like Exeter, but a familiar street led to a castle she had never seen before. Another night brought her to a grand house where her family and others were gathered for a celebration, but as she stepped in, she realized she was naked.

She had come to dread the nights.

"We have a task at hand, Alice. Primroses are not our concern. We must climb back up the hill before the gate closes."

"Yes, but look!" Alice pointed a few feet ahead of them, to the spot where she'd caught sight of a patch of bluebells with six violet-blue bells hanging from each stem. She ran down and picked one.

"Well, thank the Lord if this dreadful winter is over."

Alice smiled and breathed in the sweet smell of the bluebell. She remembered being told that if you turned a bluebell flower inside out without tearing it, you would win the one you love. That didn't concern her today, but the appearance of these beautiful flowers made her hopeful. The god of churches didn't exist. Here, she became alive.

"Well, perchance it will do no harm to pause for just a moment. I sometimes wonder where you came from," Alice's father said, "with those deep brown eyes and black hair."

"But you have dark hair."

"Used to, more like!" He laughed and rubbed the bald spot on the top of his head. "Not black as a starless night, like yours, with that pale skin. If I did not know better, I might say the fairy folk had something to do with you."

He took hold of Alice's hand. "And you have a strength of spirit that your sister lacks. Hold fast to that strength, Alice." He looked up at the sky. "But we must hurry."

Alice strode off between the oak trees, her heart full. Thomas followed her over the muddy ground.

"In spite of what your mother says, I can distinguish the fern, so this will be my task." He stood beside a clump of ferns and bent to pick one from the bottom of the stem.

Alice stared at her father's fingertips, covered in red mud. She had deliberately led him to this spot where grew the brake fern, which was small and had broad green leaflets with a pale center, unlike the royal fern, which was much taller, with brighter green leaves.

She took a deep breath, and the energy rose up from the earth and rushed into her body.

Thomas nudged Alice's arm. "We dare not delay any longer. The evening will close in on us. But before we can return, you must take us to the gladwin iris. I know your mother said it was close by."

She took him down a narrow path to the irises, which lay in a shadier part of the wood. One patch had leaves with sharp edges that were thicker in the middle; the other had tall reed-like stems that had yet to produce leaves. *Why can't I remember which is which? I'm sure Mother has shown me how to tell them apart.*

She turned to her father. "We need to take the root of the gladwin iris for Mother's decoction, but it lies right next to the yellow iris, which Mother has no use for. With neither of them in bloom, I can't tell the difference."

"It matters not. Let us collect both of them. We must get back before nightfall, when they will lock us out. Hurry!"

Alice took the trowel from her apron and slid it into the dirt to remove the two sets of roots. The ground was saturated, which made it easy to reach under the roots and ease them out of the earth.

She placed them in her apron, and the two stepped out from the woods to begin the climb to the North Gate. The sky had clouded over while they gathered the herbs, and a thick blanket of gray hung suspended above them, giving blurry, amorphous shapes to the trees that lined the path. The two of them hurried forward, and Alice had to trot to keep up with her father.

In the half-light, she could just make out the square shape of the tower surmounting the North Gate and the small hovels that bordered the roadway. The hill seemed much steeper than when they had descended.

"They are preparing to shut the gate!" her father declared. "I shall go ahead and let them know you are close behind me."

Thomas marched forward with the advantage of his leather boots and longer legs.

Alice struggled to walk fast. Her buckskin shoes squelched, and she had to stop periodically to pull off the clumps of wet earth that stuck to her soles and untangle her skirt, which wrapped itself between her knees. "Wait for me!"

Her father, ten strides ahead of her, turned. "Do not worry. You will be safe."

"But Father! I should walk beside you!" She drew closer to the North Gate and tried to run faster but tripped over her skirt and fell face-first into the slippery mud. Panic swept through her as she pulled herself up and wiped her face with the sleeve of her bodice.

A musket shot pierced the murky silence of the evening. The sound of it crashed into her head like a cannonball. "Father! What have they done to you?" She gripped her head between her hands.

She stumbled up the last part of the slope and reached the gateway.

"Och eye! He was not lying, by gad! Here comes the wee lass!" Alice heard the voice from the other side of the wall.

"Come here, girl." A soldier she had not seen before walked under the great stone arch and came toward her. He aimed the point of his musket at her. "But hurry. 'Tis past curfew time, you know."

Alice had to force herself to breathe. Her mind conjured up an image from her dreams: She started out on a familiar path, but it turned into a thin, icy trail at the edge of a cliff. If she slipped, she would fall hundreds of feet. In front of her, Goody Luscombe's body hung from a rope, but the face in the noose wasn't Luscombe's—it was her own.

"Get in there!" The butt of the soldier's weapon prodded the small of her back.

She stepped through the gateway and shuddered.

She already knew what she would see, only this time she would never be able to squeeze her eyelids and rock her head from side to side to make the ugly picture go away.

Thomas Molland lay on his side on the ground, the fern leaves still in his hand. Where his left ear should have been, a white bone stuck out. All around it, the flesh protruded, discolored and pulpy like a turnip left to rot in the sun. A continuous stream of blood dribbled from his open mouth.

"Hurry home to yer mother," the soldier commanded. "Tell her if she does not collect the body within the hour, we shall dispose of it. And let this be a warning. It is a mistake to disobey the curfew."

Alice stared down at the face she had seen so clearly in her vision a few moons earlier. "Hold fast to that strength," he had said. She gasped as her mind swirled with images of her father: slumped on the floor, his face smeared with blood, and sitting in his big chair telling her stories of the Great Wars.

With a wail that came up from her stomach, she flung herself across his body and cried out over and over, "Oh, Father, Father."

"Your life could be in danger if you remain in Exeter, Alice, so I shall send you away." Catherine stirred the pottage over an open flame while Alice and Faith chopped the beans and barley bread she would add to the mixture.

"But you need me here!"

"Yes, but more than that, I need you alive, and you'll be better off with your Aunt Sarah and her family in Ivycombe for a few weeks."

Alice hesitated. It had been over a fortnight since her father's death. In her mind, the same thoughts repeated themselves: Her father would still be alive if only she had not put her own wishes first by stopping to admire the primroses and pick a bluebell.

Alice tried to explain all this to her mother, who sought to comfort her child and assure her that his death was not Alice's fault. Alice knew differently. She had killed her father. She remembered his strong hands with tufts of black hair on the knuckles, the scar above his right eyebrow. She especially remembered his words to her: "Hold fast to that strength."

And yet she couldn't believe this had really happened. How could her father be dead? Where was he now? Even when the image of the blood flowing from his mouth came back, her mind refused to accept that she would never see her father alive again.

"I need to visit the place where Father is buried."

Catherine had paid Ted Wingate and John Plympton to carry her husband's body to Bartholomew Yard. The two men had dug a grave, and Father Bridgeman had conducted a brief burial service.

"We cannot abandon him."

"We have not abandoned him. Your father is at peace now, and he would want us to protect ourselves from any further harm. You will only gather suspicion if you visit his gravesite."

Alice watched her mother wipe away a single tear from her cheek. "In that case, Mother, I shall leave this very day."

"No, the three of us will leave tomorrow. It will do me good to see my sister, and besides, a mother cannot send her youngest daughter to make this journey alone."

"But Mother," Faith piped up. "Let me stay here and guard our home while you two travel to Ivycombe. It is Alice who is in danger, not me."

"No. We are a family and must stay together. Even though you do not like to go far, you will come with us."

Are you not afraid to be here by yourself, Faith? Look at how those soldiers broke into our home, destroyed our food, and attacked our father. Imagine what they might do if they discovered you here alone.

The next morning, the three remaining members of the Molland family set out on the two-day journey to Ivycombe. In addition to a few clothes, Alice took with her the small sword that her father had kept from the days when he fought for the Parliamentarians. She marched at a fast pace. Catherine and Faith complained, but Alice couldn't help it. With each foot she stomped into the ground, her thoughts unfurled further. *It wasn't all my fault. That Scottish soldier didn't have to pull the trigger. I felt so blessed to be out in those woods, but he tried to take it all away from me. He won't succeed. I will do something to avenge Father's death.*

CHAPTER SEVEN

Ivycombe, Devon. June 1658.

Alice had been in the village of Ivycombe for almost two weeks. Her mother and sister had stayed for only one day. They couldn't afford to miss the wool market, the family's main livelihood, for too long, and Catherine didn't want to leave her home empty.

Since Alice might well be in danger because she was a witness to her father's death, Catherine had insisted that her daughter stay in Ivycombe for at least another two or three weeks, until it was safe for her to return.

Alice did not object. She loved the absence of Cromwell's soldiers, although she did miss her mother and how they worked together to produce decoctions of pennyroyal and mugwort.

On this bright, sunny afternoon, Alice's Aunt Sarah had instructed her son Matthew to pick dandelions along with Alice. Sarah was renowned for her healing skills, and as Alice knew well, the plant's roots and leaves could be used for many purposes, such as helping with the passage of urine and procuring rest for those unable to sleep.

The two worked close to a tall hedgerow, shaded by a hawthorn tree whose delicate white flowers, tinged with pink, were poised to open. They had an unusual spicy smell, almost like almonds. Alice stood up to breathe in their scent, but it was the sweet aroma of the bluebell that came to her, the one she had picked on the last day of her father's life. Tears welled up in her eyes, and she blinked to make them go away. She recalled the feel of her father's strong hand on hers when he told her to hold on to her strength, and it was so painful not to cry out loud.

"I have a question for you, young Alice." Matthew walked over to her. His gray eyes sparkled and his lean, taut body revealed not an inch of fat.

Alice swallowed hard. She didn't like it when Matthew called her young. She was twelve, and he was only three years older.

Still, she smiled at her cousin, who had become her close friend since her arrival in Ivycombe. She rarely saw his father, Uncle Henry, since he was so busy around the farm. And Matthew's older brother, Caleb, worked at a tin mine up on Dartmoor and came home only at the weekend.

"Tonight is the full moon. Our group will gather to celebrate at our special place. I would have you join us."

"Does Aunt Sarah know about this? Will she come too?"

"Yes and no. Mother knows of my doings but is not part of the group. We gather in a circle at our sacred site, an oak grove not far from here, and perform some simple rituals to honor the power of the moon."

Alice hesitated.

Night after night, she lay on her pallet, her stomach twisted in pain as she listened to the thudding of her heart. Engulfed in darkness, she swam in a dark tunnel with only a peephole of light in the far distance. At times, a shudder took over her body, and she wanted to yell at her father that he should have waited for her and not gone through the North Gate alone. If only she had not stopped to admire flowers but instead had insisted that they head back up the hill when it was still light, before the curfew.

This morning she had woken up sobbing, her heart knotted so tightly she could barely breathe.

Her father's death had confirmed for her that there was no God—if there were, why would he have let her father die for no good reason? Why hadn't God spoken to her and warned her not to go into the woods for her mother's healing herbs?

Yet even as she acknowledged what she had known for so long, that God did not exist, it left an emptiness within her that she was desperate to fill.

Perhaps Matthew was right and the full moon celebrations would help her.

She looked up. "Thank you, Matthew. I would love to go with you tonight."

Alice stood in a circle along with ten others as the full moon held the hushed group in its soft embrace. Matthew had instructed her to watch and listen, and excitement had bubbled up inside of her as her cousin led her the mile or so beyond Ivycombe to this oak grove.

She stared at the makeshift altar he had created. Beside a goblet containing water stood another chalice. Next to it lay a platter of salt, a small knife, and a flickering tallow candle fixed on a wooden block.

After a few moments, Matthew stepped out of the circle and picked up the knife with his strong, sunburned hands. He held it high in the air and chanted, "I cleanse thee, O creature of water, and charge thee in the name of the Lady and the Lord." With one swift move, he plunged the knife into the goblet of water.

"Blessings be upon this creature of salt in the name of the Lady and the Lord." With his left hand, he tipped several grains of salt into the water, stirred the mixture with the knife, and placed the knife on the ground. Next, he picked up the goblet and stepped over to the edge of the circle he had swept earlier with a broom. Alice watched him turn to the right, step around the circle, sprinkle water, and repeat, "I purify with water and salt."

Alice had no idea who the Lord and the Lady were, nor why Matthew sprinkled the circle with water and salt. She would ask him later. She did know that she had come alive in this moment and was no longer filled with emptiness. She stared at a majestic oak tree at the far end of the grove. Tiny pale green acorns peeked out between its deeper green leaves. She breathed in the sweet evening air. It was late on this long summer day, and the sun had almost set. When she looked up, the moon smiled down on her and her heart danced with joy.

Once Matthew had replaced the goblet and moved back to stand beside Alice, a young woman in a brown cloak stepped up and lifted the candle from the altar. Alice recognized her as Philippa, the blacksmith's daughter. A few days ago, Aunt Sarah had proposed that the two girls spend an afternoon together.

When Alice had walked into the blacksmith's shop, the distinct tang of molten metal hung thick in the air. She'd stopped for a moment to watch as Philippa, with her long blonde hair and mouse-like eyes, gathered the remains of a horse's hooves and cast them upon the fire.

"It's considered unlucky to leave the shavings about or to simply throw them away," she explained. Her tone was sharp, almost rude. Yet along with the severity, Alice had detected a sadness surrounding Philippa.

Under the full moon, Philippa stepped around the edge of the circle, just as Matthew had done, and recited, "I warm this circle with fire and air." The candle's acrid odor filled the air for a moment and then evaporated.

In this oak grove, at least, she seems calm and happy.

Philippa set the candle back on the altar and once more took her place in the circle. Silence fell. And yet to Alice, it was not silence; it was a rush, like a flock of birds who burst forth from the ground to soar upwards. Her heart danced and excitement roared through her body.

She wondered, *How can these simple incantations touch me so deeply?* She was caught up in the power of the universe and glowed with a light that burned within her.

The group kept its gaze fixed on the altar. Even Matthew, although he stood beside her, appeared far away. An owl hooted from a nearby tree, and in the distance came the occasional splash of the river against rocks.

Perhaps I am experiencing magic. Matthew had explained to her earlier, as they'd crossed the stone bridge, that it was very simple. "We all have the power to change the way we see things, the way we think. But you must concentrate hard to allow this power to come into you."

"I understand!" Alice had exclaimed. For surely it was magic that allowed her to talk to Goody Luscombe even though the woman was dead?

After a few more minutes, a woman with graying hair, clad in black, stepped forward, took the knife, and held it aloft. Alice joined the rest of the group members as they fell in line behind her, and like Matthew, she turned to the right and led them around the circle. At each of the four quarters, she stopped and chanted,

Ho! East, South, West, North!
Here I come to call ye forth,
Attend ye here with joy and mirth,
Air and Fire, Water and Earth.

Alice, along with the other moon worshippers, returned to her place in the circle. The older woman did not move but still held the knife up toward the sky as she called out:

Wondrous Lady of the Moon
Mistress of the night and of all magics
All-wise Lunar Mother
We greet you
At the waxing of your powers
With a rite in your honor.
We pray by the Moon
We pray by the Moon.

Alice was mesmerized by the chants but had so many questions for her cousin. *Who is the woman in black? Why did she address the four directions? Why did she hold the knife up in the air? Why did you put salt in the water?*

The woman replaced the knife on the altar and joined the group sitting on the ground beneath the oak trees' sturdy branches. The air had grown cool and misty, and it would have been completely dark if not for the full moon.

No one spoke. Each member of the group stared ahead. Alice did not dare break this precious silence.

After several moments, Philippa rose and reached for the second cup on the altar. She held it high and declared, "Bless this drink we share with thee." She took a small sip and returned to her place in the circle. Then the wooden cup was passed around. When it came to her turn, Alice drank. It felt like the small ale rushed through her body as if the nearby river had become part of her and carried her away to a magical realm beyond this circle.

To her amazement, she wanted to cry, and her throat hurt from the tears she held bottled up inside.

The light from the moon faded as clouds filled the sky and the mist turned into a heavy drizzle. The drops that rested on Alice's hair began to soak through and made her shiver. She feared she might faint and breathed deeply to bring herself back to the circle.

The group finished the ritual drink and rose in unison. Alice followed Matthew as they moved around the circle, walking opposite from the direction they'd walked before, and chanted:

East, North, West, South
Now begone and take thy rest.
From the Lady be thou blest,
East, North, West, South.

Once the magic tools were taken up, the moon worshippers vanished into the night. She and Matthew hurried back to the farmhouse under the bright moon. Even though she still shivered as the water dripped from her hair, Alice wanted to skip and run back to dance under the oak trees and thank them for the magical gift she had received this evening. For it seemed to her that she had come home to where she belonged.

***

Alice took some time falling asleep that night. Matthew had cautioned her not to speak of the evening's ritual to anyone outside of their small circle. So now she had another secret to keep, just like when Goody Luscombe had told her never to speak of the magic potion she had used to calm a sick child, and when her mother had warned Alice, as they set out for Goody Luscombe's hanging, that she must not reveal herself to be a friend of the healer.

She lay on her pallet and listened to the rain thrumming on the thatched roof.

Her body was on fire. *Did Goody Luscombe take part in such rituals? If so, why did she not take me? Did she think I was too young for them?*

Yet while Alice pondered this, the image of her father appeared to her: His thick hand grasped the fern leaves, and blood dribbled from his mouth.

When sleep finally came to her, it brought the familiar nightmare where she relived her father's death, but tonight it was different. That soldier once again emptied his musket into her father's head, but this time, Alice grabbed the weapon and aimed it straight back at him. With one shot, the Scottish enemy was dead.

CHAPTER EIGHT

Ivycombe, Devon. June 1658.

The day after the full moon gathering, a Wednesday, Alice sat on the sheep-bitten grass and watched Matthew work with Thunder and Whipster, the two sheepdogs, to round up the last of the ewes and bring them into the sheep pen. On this blustery day, the sky looked washed out, with the sun barely visible behind feathery clouds. All around was the bleating of the lambs and the low *baaing* of the ewes, along with the intermittent jangle of sheep bells.

Matthew had explained that for the last fortnight, the lambs had eaten alongside their mothers while continuing to nurse. "Gradually, the lambs need less milk as they consume hay and other solid foods, and the mothers produce less milk. When the lambs no longer need their mothers' milk, they will be led to pasture, out of sight and earshot of the ewes." Alice had promised to help move the little ones, but she hated the idea that some of them would end up being sent for slaughter.

She breathed in the rich scent of honeysuckle and looked out over the Devon farmland she loved: fields of irregular shapes and sizes, all bounded by tall green hedges to ensure the livestock could not escape. A single five-bar gate in each hedge marked a farm entrance. And everywhere, there were sheep; Matthew had told her there were twice as many sheep as people in Devon.

Alice relived the previous evening and realized how natural and joyful the ceremony had been. It was nothing like worshipping at St. Paul's before it had been shut down, where her knees hurt as they rested on the stone floor while she prayed to God to forgive her for all her sins. But what sins was she supposed to have committed?

⁂

Matthew came over to her, his eyes clouded with weariness.

She reached out to take the sunburned hand he offered her but then noticed some large leaves growing out of a nearby ditch. She scrambled up and went over to the ditch. "Comfrey! Your mother and I searched to no avail all morning, and it's right here."

Matthew bent to pick the leaves, but Alice pulled him back.

"No, you must grab only by the stalk, for the leaves will make you itch terribly." She plucked one hollow stalk close to the ground and placed the plant in her apron.

"How do you know these things?" Matthew smiled, and the tiny dimple on each side of his mouth deepened.

"I had a wise teacher, a cunning woman, for a long time, and my mother instructs me too. I aim to become the best healer Devon has ever seen."

She was surprised to hear herself say these words and marveled at the idea that she wanted to share this with Matthew. Yet at the mention of her mother, Alice missed Catherine and longed to reach out and touch her.

"Look, yonder," she said, "behind the primroses." She pointed to a spot close to the hedge as the two sat down on the grass. "Those hairy brown stems and pairs of pale green leaves—that's loosestrife. Soon it will have spikes of bright yellow flowers. Taken internally, it's good for all manner of bleeding." She remembered how her mother had introduced her to loosestrife one afternoon as they walked near the Longbrook.

She turned to face Matthew. "But you have your magic rituals. There was something in that circle that I had not known before. Who are the Lady and the Lord? And how did that woman know those chants?"

"Shush! Keep your voice low." Matthew placed a forefinger against his lips. "That woman, as you call her, is Sybil Privet, and she learned those chants, and many more, from her grandmother. They've been in her family a long time."

"But the Lady and the Lord? Is that like Mary and Jesus?" Alice had so much to learn and hoped she could take it all in.

Matthew shook his head. "No. Mother insists the whole family attend church on Sundays, and so we do. But our gatherings are quite different."

"What do you mean? How are they different?"

Matthew opened his mouth to answer her but then looked toward the sheep pen. "Damn! Four of those silly sheep have escaped their pen." He stood. "Where are my dogs? I'll have to chase the sheep myself."

"I shall come with you." Alice jumped up, and the two marched toward the pen at the other end of the long field. Alice had to almost run to keep up with her cousin. They passed numerous lambs who joyfully leapt, hopped, and head-butted, and she wished she might frolic with them.

"Tell me more about your moon worship." Alice knew Matthew was worried about his sheep, but she still had so much to ask him.

"Alice, stop with your questions. I must get these sheep back into their pen. And you can help if you grab the bucket near the entrance to the pen and shake it once the sheep go through the gate. The bucket is full of oats, which they love."

Alice tried not to feel disappointed as she and Matthew ran down the slope to the pen. Once there, Matthew walked toward the runaway sheep, and Alice reached over the side of the pen to grab the bucket. The grassy stink of so many sheep hit her at once. She took a step back and breathed through her mouth. The animals mostly had white faces, although she spotted the occasional black one. Some of them let out *baas* like growls and grunts while others produced shorter, higher *baas* that resembled songs. Alice had not paid much attention to the sheep that grazed around Ivycombe, but now she found herself fascinated by their antics.

Matthew's sheepdogs had reappeared, and in a trice, they rounded up the escapees and forced them back into the enclosure.

Alice continued to breathe through her mouth. She turned back to the pen's entrance, leaned over, and shook the bucket. When the sheep ambled over to her, Matthew shut the gate and came to stand next to her.

It was late afternoon by now, and the air had grown warmer as the clouds thinned, allowing beams of light to shine through.

Alice was still pent-up with the need to ask Matthew more questions. "Can we talk a little longer? I am still so excited by last night's ritual."

"We can, but we must soon return home for supper."

Once they were both seated beside a farm gate, Alice spoke first. "You said your gatherings are different from attending St. Michael's. What do you mean?"

"Philippa could explain better, perhaps. She brought me into this group. We find more truth and peace in our oak grove than in any church. Instead of one male god who judges us from his place in Heaven, we hold to the idea of a female force and a male force, the Lady and the Lord, present equally. These forces are everywhere, even within us. Does that make sense?"

"I think so." Part of Alice wanted to shout out for joy that of course she understood, but another part held her back. How could she tell her mother about Matthew's beliefs? "But what about air, fire, water, and earth?"

"We and the land around us are all made of these elements. We are part of the land, just like the plants you speak of and the oak trees where we meet. But we humans have a fifth element: our spirit. Is this all too much for you?"

"No. Well, maybe." Matthew spoke with such passion it scared her a little. "Do you gather together often?"

Two curious lambs ran toward them. The little creatures bleated and leapt up to turn in the air, their white ears flopping up and down. Alice looked at Matthew, and they both laughed out loud.

"Then these funny lambs also have this life force within them?"

"Alice, you are speaking our language!"

Alice beamed at Matthew's praise.

"As for how often we meet—when the moon reaches its waxing phase, that is the richest time since it's when we feel the most power and energy from the moon's brightness. But we may also meet at other hours for some special purpose: to raise the energy to ward off sickness or to bring good luck for the harvest."

"And are you able to do these things?"

"Well, we have produced a fine harvest of corn these past two years. That's how long I've been a member of our group. We can initiate change when we come together as a group, but we each need to reach down inside ourselves, control our thoughts and our spirit."

Alice thought that sounded really hard, and she wondered if she would be able to do what Matthew described. "Does Philippa have that power?"

"Philippa is a very special friend to me."

"I can see that, but she spoke harshly to me the other day, for no reason I could tell." Alice spoke in a calm tone. She didn't want her cousin to think she disliked Philippa.

"Philippa's life has not been easy. Her mother died a long time ago, and—"

They were interrupted as a cry rang out. "Come here, you!"

Margary Badcombe, the innkeeper's wife, approached on the other side of the gate with a woman whom Alice had not seen before. A badger bolted under the gate and crossed the field to disappear under the hedgerow.

The women stopped when they spied the two cousins.

"And what are you doing over here?" Margary examined them with an intense gaze.

"Helping your father too good for you, is it?" The other woman addressed Matthew.

"Not at all! Father gave me dispensation to leave after a long day. And now we must return for supper." Matthew and Alice stood in unison. "Fare thee well!"

At this, the women walked away, and Alice and Matthew made their way home.

To Alice's concerns that Margary and her friend seemed unfriendly, Matthew laughed out loud, but Alice could not be entirely at peace for the remainder of the day. She also came to understand that accepting all Matthew had spoken of was more complicated than she had thought. It wasn't enough just to enjoy her feelings of excitement. And she still hadn't asked him about the significance of the water and the salt.

Philippa's tiny bedroom was crammed full with five people, and the pungent smell of sweat, blood, and vinegar made Alice feel nauseous. Philippa had taken ill the day before, just four days after the full moon ritual.

It was close to noon. Philippa's body was enclosed in a sack-like cloth, but her arms and legs were covered in thin leeches whose mouths sucked at her skin while their tails twitched frantically, thrilled with their blood feast. Philippa looked so far gone in her delirium that she appeared to be unaware of her surroundings as she tossed from side to side and sweated profusely.

Alice winced. Even though she had misgivings about Philippa, Alice hated to see a human being in such a wretched state.

"Please, sir, stop. You're hurting her," Matthew implored.

Alice and Matthew, along with Philippa's father, stood in front of the pallet where Philippa lay. A heavyset man knelt beside the pallet, and Alice understood him to be the barber-surgeon who had been summoned from Exeter.

Alice had been seated at Aunt Sarah's kitchen table earlier that morning, repeating her cousin's words about the Lady and the Lord, when the front door burst open and Matthew strode in, his face flushed and his breath coming in short gasps.

"It's Philippa," he said. "I decided to stop at the blacksmith's for a moment on my way out just to say hello to her, and I found her in a terrible state. She took ill yesterday, and she looks dreadful. She moans, says she hears strange voices in her head she can't control. Then she complains that she has pains from something bad she ate, but she has taken only water for the past twenty-four hours. Do you know where my mother is? I'm sure she could help."

Alice shook her head. "Aunt Sarah left to pick comfrey in the place where we saw it, by the sheep pen. But she probably wandered further to see what other herbs she could find."

Matthew shook his head. "Damn! She will be too late. Philippa's father has summoned a barber-surgeon, but I don't want the man anywhere near her."

Alice had heard of barber-surgeons but never met one. She knew only that Goody Luscombe had despised them for their lack of knowledge about herbal medicines and their use of bloodletting for almost every ailment.

She stood up and embraced Matthew, whose eyes looked ready to spill tears. "I'm sorry your mother is not here. Perhaps I can help." As she spoke, Alice thought of her own mother, who would surely know how to heal Philippa. Sorrow gripped her. She had been so caught up with the mysteries of the moon ritual since the night at the oak grove that thoughts of her mother and father had not entered her head.

Now Matthew approached Philippa, but the surgeon stood up and pushed him away. While the man stared at Matthew with his right eye, his left eye seemed to wander around on its own, unable to settle.

One by one he yanked the leeches off, immersed them in a jar of vinegar, and replaced them on Philippa's limbs, where they sucked and twitched even harder than before.

Finally, he pulled off all the leeches, applied a dirty rag to stanch the flow of blood, rinsed the leeches in a jar of water, and threw them into a leather pouch.

"That will be two shillings. Leave her be for now, but keep an eye on her." Philippa's father handed over the money, and the barber-surgeon picked up his bag and marched down the stairs.

Alice followed him outside, where he prepared to mount a piebald horse tied in front of the smithy. "Please sir, how can you be sure the use of leeches will restore my friend to good health?"

"Simple child. How can you know anything of these matters?" He did not turn to look at her but placed one foot in the stirrup and pulled himself up into the saddle.

"I just seek to understand." Alice knew she risked his wrath.

"The girl has a wretched fever, probably because some witch has put a spell on her." He spat out the words. "The bloodletting will help her heal. I have to ride back to Exeter." He grasped the reins to turn his horse around and trotted down the lane.

Alice stared after him and a tremor went through her. This barber-surgeon with his thin lips and one wandering eye had spoken of a witch. Did he believe that? Or was it an excuse in case his gruesome methods turned out to be no cure at all?

The following day, Alice was determined to ask Aunt Sarah for advice. Even though she was frustrated that she didn't know how to cure Philippa's illness, Alice hoped Aunt Sarah would be able to help. Alice knew that Philippa had turned to Matthew's mother earlier in the year when she'd felt the constant need to pass urine but couldn't.

An infusion of parsley, made with the whole plant, had helped clear her urinary passage then, and that's what Aunt Sarah made Philippa swallow now.

Two days later, Philippa's fever finally broke, and she was able to take water and a little bread. By week's end, she was on her feet again, albeit moving slowly.

A few days after Philippa's fever broke, Alice woke to the sound of sobbing, and it took a moment for her to understand that the tears were hers. She knew she must return to the magical oak grove. She had dreamed that her father was alive and had shown her how to build a wall, one of the skills he had learned while serving as a soldier in the Parliamentarian army. But then he vanished, and she ran through the streets of Exeter searching for him. Except it wasn't Exeter, it was a town she didn't recognize, and she had no idea where she was. And she was alone.

Still in tears, Alice took a few minutes to pull on her shift, dress, and apron, fix a cap on her head, and set out for the stone bridge. She carried her father's small sword with her. It was a lovely warm morning; the sparrows chirped, and she even spotted a beautiful male goldfinch with its yellow and red markings. The bleating ewes called to her, but she knew she must visit the site of the ritual before attending to the sheep.

She stepped carefully into the ring of trees and sat on the grass, still wet with the morning dew, in the center of the oak grove. "I miss you, Father," she whispered. Her tears slipped from her eyes and fell to the ground. In response, she heard her father speak: "Hold fast to that strength."

Joy swept through Alice when she recognized the rich timbre of her father's voice. She stood and held the sword up high above her. "Thank you, Father. I promise to avenge your death."

Alice spent that day with Matthew.

"We've secured the sheep in their pen, as you know, and we are ready to move the lambs away from their mothers. That's where I need your help."

"But aren't the lambs sad to be away from their mothers?" Alice hesitated. "Matthew, I've been here a long time, and I should return to Exeter. I don't mean today. But perhaps tomorrow?"

"Dearest Alice." Matthew embraced her. "I shall miss you but trust that you will take with you all that you have learned from our moon ritual. And I thank you for your help."

After that, the two worked hard under a bright sun in an almost-cloudless sky.

Alice's task was to carry water from the well beside the farmhouse to a big trough in the pasture where the lambs were to be led.

She dipped one wooden bucket into the well, then the second, and attached them to the rope that hung around her neck. She started out away from the farmhouse, but the rope hurt so much that she stopped, pulled it off, and sat down. "I cannot do this. Why didn't Matthew tell me how hard this would be?"

She could hear Matthew as he encouraged his sheepdogs, and within a few minutes, Alice called out to the Lady and the Lord to help her. A lightness filled her, and she jumped up, emptied about a third of the water from each bucket, and replaced the rope around her neck.

She moved forward and sang "Greensleeves," her favorite song: "Greensleeves was all my joy, / Greensleeves was my delight, / Greensleeves was my heart of gold / And who but my lady Greensleeves?" She had no idea who Greensleeves was, but it was clearly a love song, and as she sang out loud, the sun grew less oppressive, and her burden grew lighter. "Greensleeves was my delight," she intoned, and joy filled her when she remembered she would see her mother within two days.

She continued toward the upper pasture and passed close by Matthew, who supervised the border collies as they rounded up the lambs. "Come-bye!" he called, which encouraged the dogs to move to the left. Next he called "Walk up!" to urge them forward. His red face was covered with sweat, but he waved and gave her a big smile.

Alice broke off her cheerful singing when she gazed at the lambs' sweet, innocent faces and listened to their sad bleating, as if they knew that most of them would be sent for slaughter at Martinmas.

All morning and into the afternoon, Alice carried buckets of water up to the trough. On the eighth trip, she emptied the last bucket with a loud sigh. She pulled off the rope, placed both hands on her shoulders, and rubbed to take away the pain. She had never worked so hard. That evening at supper, she ate a small serving of pottage before she fell into a deep sleep on her pallet.

The next morning, she set out for Exeter, her few possessions in a sack slung over her shoulder. She had given her father's small sword to Aunt Sarah, who had found it to be a perfect tree trimmer. Matthew accompanied Alice. He would make the first day's journey with his cousin and take her to a friend's house in Ashleigh, where she would spend the night. The road to Exeter was well signposted from there, and by the end of the second day, Alice would be home.

She was so excited to share with her mother all she had learned about the Lady and the Lord, the power of the moon, and so many other things. She also knew she must do something that would make her father proud of her. But would Catherine listen to her daughter? Or would she grow angry and forbid Alice to speak of such dangerous ideas ever again?

CHAPTER NINE

Exeter, Devon. May 1660.

Alice heard a loud rap on the front door and hastened to open it so as not to disturb her sister. Her good friends Jane and Susannah stood in front of her, work caps gone and mugs in hand. Even Jane smiled instead of wearing her usual severe look.

"Come out with us and celebrate!" Jane invited Alice. "Charles the Second, eldest surviving son of Charles the First, has been restored to the throne of England. Long live the king! Oliver Cromwell is dead! His soldiers have left, and we have our city back again."

Her sister, Susannah, was equally animated. "And even better, the sheriff of Exeter has decreed that the conduits that bring water to the citizens of Exeter shall flow with red wine for a full twenty-four hours!" Susannah's cheeks were flushed, and she pointed to the passersby who laughed and clutched large tankards as they ran down the lane.

"I cannot join you." Alice mumbled the words.

Her two friends ceased their laughter.

"When Faith came home two days ago, she complained of an ache in her head. She lay down at once upon our mother's bed. Within a few hours, her face was flushed crimson and covered by a red rash, and she was unable to stand. Faith needs me here. Go and be merry. Drink for me."

"I am so sorry." Susannah spoke before she and Jane turned away to join the throng.

Alice stared after them. She knew the return of the monarchy was important after the years they had endured Cromwell's rule, but she could not bring herself to smile. As she closed the door, Faith coughed, and Alice hurried to her sister.

"Look!" Faith sat up in bed and pointed toward the open door. "Stay away from the red bird that hovers over there!"

Alice turned to look but saw no red bird. "You must rest," she assured Faith. With one arm around her sister's shoulder, Alice encouraged her patient to lie down again. She could hardly bear to look at her sister's face where the red rash had turned into blisters that resembled giant soap bubbles filled with fluid.

What kind of healer am I if I turn away from Faith? I must put all else aside and focus solely on her. That is what a healer does. Especially with my mother not well, I am Faith's only hope.

Catherine sat slumped in the big chair by the hearth in the kitchen, where she spent much of her time these days.

Faith shifted in her bed, unable to rest easy. She sweated so that her body gave off a sweetish, pungent smell that made Alice want to vomit.

"Help me! Water!" she pled.

Alice reached for the jug and poured yet more water into the wooden cup. She held it to Faith's mouth, but most of the liquid dribbled out onto the woolen blanket.

"Thank you," Faith muttered, and for a while, she fell into a light sleep.

Alice gazed at her sister and wished she could do more for Faith.

For a moment, she thought of Jeffrey. She wasn't sure he was her best friend any longer. After her return from Ivycombe, almost two years ago, she had tried to explain the moon ritual and the magical oak grove to him, but Jeffrey's face had grown stern, and he'd spoken in a strange, cramped voice. "You should dismiss these ideas, Alice. They are dangerous."

She pushed those thoughts aside and closed her eyes to take advantage of this moment of peace, but she was soon awakened by a shriek from Faith: "Look at those bright yellow daffodils growing in a blue pot beneath the window!"

Alice was about to explain that of course there were no daffodils since they bloom in March. Instead, she jumped up, took Faith into her arms, and rocked her sister. Although she was annoyed with herself for being so affected by Faith's fusty odor, soon Alice had to seize a white linen handkerchief to cover her nose, for Faith's stench was reminiscent of flesh put upon the fire.

Alice had heard that an English doctor pronounced the best treatment for the pox was to leave all the windows open, keep a sheet or blanket no higher than the invalid's waist when lying in bed, and drink plenty of beer. Alice disagreed and kept the front door closed in addition to shutting all the windows. She also covered her sister up to her chin. As for beer, that's not what Faith asked for.

A barber-surgeon had advocated bloodletting, just as Alice had seen Philippa endure in Ivycombe, only instead of leeches, this barber-surgeon proposed bloodletting from the tongue as a cure for the pox.

Alice dismissed all these ideas but had already started the one treatment she believed in. A few months earlier, when smallpox had spread in Exeter and killed almost 10 percent of the population, she and her mother had boiled the root of devil's bit in wine and kept the decoction in a small jar. Catherine had explained to Alice that this was the best remedy for a pestilential fever. Now Alice moved to the kitchen to retrieve the jar, unstopped it, and bent over Faith to force the brownish mixture down her sister's throat for the second time that day.

"Ugh!" Faith made a face as she swallowed the potion.

"I'm sorry." Alice patted her sister's shoulder, but the loud clang of bells drowned out her voice.

"What is it?" Catherine peered into the bedroom, and Faith sat up.

"I believe the cathedral's noonday bells are exceptionally loud today in celebration of our new king. Don't worry, they will soon cease."

Catherine shuffled out of the room, and Alice helped Faith to lie down again.

The bells fell silent within a short time, but soon, the fever rose in Faith even while she slept. All Alice could do was wipe her sister's face and hold Faith's damp hand. She stared at her sister, whose blonde hair stuck to her sweaty cheeks. *Is Faith going to die? But surely, if I am a healer, I should be able to save my sister.*

In the early evening, Faith stirred awake and declared that she was hungry. Alice had kept some thin broth warm, mostly just water with some onions and carrots, and she poured the liquid into two cups, one for Faith and one for their mother. She herself would eat later. Catherine wanted to help, but Alice encouraged her to stay seated.

Once Faith had taken the soup and was able to hold the cup and feed herself, she thanked Alice and snuggled back under her blanket.

Perhaps she isn't going to die. Perhaps I was wrong. Please, Faith, get better. Please.

In the early light of morning, Faith stirred again, and Alice noticed a change in her sister's breathing. Faith gurgled as if she wanted to clear her throat but couldn't. Alice rolled Faith onto her side, but still the gurgles continued.

She was unsure whether Faith could hear her, but Alice lay on the bed next to her sister and talked to her about the new king, about what a beautiful day it was, and about how special Faith was to her sister. After a while, Alice decided to sing "Greensleeves," but she soon drifted into sleep.

It was Catherine who woke Alice to tell her it was over: "Faith has gone to her maker."

Alice was momentarily confused, but mother and child embraced for several minutes. Neither of them cried. Alice's father had died only two years earlier, and her heart contracted, a refusal to weep because it was too painful.

Faith didn't deserve to die like this. No one deserves to die like this. And I couldn't help her. Why does the world have such horrible diseases?

It was almost three weeks after Faith's death, in the middle of June, when Alice brought a basket of spun wool to the Exeter wool market that took place every Wednesday. Even though Catherine's condition had improved and she was well able to do the spinning, Alice had to take on the hard work of doing all the carding. She stepped into the tall building with its high roof and numerous stalls and breathed in the sweet, grassy smell of wool. All around came the noisy shouts of sellers and buyers.

"Good morrow, Alice."

Alice started. Before her stood Richard Greenway. For a moment, she was back in the carriage with her mother, on the way to tend the frail Florence Greenway. But now she was fourteen and had not set eyes on Richard for at least a year. His voice had a distinctive earthy quality she did not remember from before.

"Good morrow," she replied tentatively. She looked up, and Richard's deep green eyes challenged her beneath his fiery red hair. He reached for her, and she found his hand to be warm.

"And what brings you here to seek out a lowly spinner?" She removed her hand.

"You are much more than that, Alice. My mother is fit and well thanks solely to you and your mother. Since you ask, I shall tell you that I seek your assurance that I may call on you again, as necessary. The physicians bring no succor."

She did not answer right away. Had he sought her out specifically to ask this question? "I should be most pleased to attend you and yours. As long as my birthmark no longer disturbs you." For though it was he who had singled her out, she realized that, unlike in the past, she now knew herself to be a match for him. What could he possibly know of what she had suffered with the death of her sister?

"On the contrary, I find it most distinctive." He stroked the back of her left hand with one finger.

A delightful shiver passed through Alice.

"They say you have learned well the healing arts of your mother." He raised his voice to be heard above the cries all around: "Over here!" "A shilling, I said, a shilling!" and "'Tis not right! You are a rotten cheat!"

He continued. "They even say you have a gift for it."

"They say many things," she countered, conscious of a game they were playing together but unsure of the rules. "I trust the other members of your family are well?"

"Yes. You have a smile like an angel, Alice. Perchance you are an angel, with those magical healing arts?"

At this, she laughed and excused herself as she needed to talk to Master Courteney, who approached across the crowded alleyway.

Richard swung his short black cloak around and was gone, much to the interest and suspicion of the small group of spinners who had gathered to watch this unusual encounter, including Alice's neighbors, the widows Bradshaw and Drew. It was generally considered unseemly for a gentleman of rank to seek out a woman of lower birth in public.

After that Wednesday, the figure of Richard Greenway occupied Alice's daydreams. For even though she knew well that Richard's father would be horrified at the notion that his son had shown interest in a lower-class girl, she understood that something important had passed between them, and she wanted to hold onto it.

She was disappointed when he did not seek her out at the next Wednesday market, nor at her home.

Three months after her encounter with Richard, Alice rose early to go to a spot near the North Gate to pick mint leaves for relief of her mother's colic.

It was mid-September, close to the time when day and night were equally long. Soon, the days would get shorter and the long, dark nights would set in. Alice had seen how her mother's hands and feet turned blue with the cold, and she worried that Catherine's ailments would increase over the winter months. Her mother was such a slight person now; she had lost so much weight.

Sometimes Catherine forgot that Faith had died and called out for her oldest daughter. Whenever that happened, Alice had to explain that Faith was no longer with them. Catherine wept, and Alice sought to comfort her. Alice missed her sister's lively smile, but she herself did not cry. She just held her mother.

The air on this Monday morning was cool, and a purplish-orange light lit up the horizon as Alice turned the corner from her lane to see the dark outline of the city wall emerging a hundred strides ahead of her.

She stopped. Just visible in the dim light, ten-year-old Dorcas Killigrew stood at her front door, clad only in a thin nightshift.

The girl stared at her cat, Miranda, on the opposite side of the lane. Miranda snarled, and her ginger fur and mangled tail were raised in fury against the three mongrels that surrounded her.

The mangy black and brown creatures had their mouths wide open to reveal sharp teeth, and their tails stood high in the air behind them.

Alice recognized the mad dogs that terrorized the streets of Exeter, and she knew the cat's plight was hopeless. Her mother had instructed her that these creatures had no interest in humans, but Alice should leave well alone were she to encounter them.

She hurried over to Dorcas and put her arms around the girl. When she sensed the tremors that shook Dorcas's thin body, Alice squeezed her more tightly to protect her against the horrific scene before them.

It struck Alice that without her beloved cat, the girl had no friends. Dorcas's mother had died when the child was just three years old, and Alice had last seen Dorcas's father seated outside the market with a filthy bowl in his hands and flies crawling over his face. His legs had been blown off during the Great Wars, and every day he squatted on his bottom and begged for food.

Alice used one hand to stroke Dorcas's cheek, and the girl's body folded itself into her. Together they watched as the short-haired animals taunted the cat from either side and moved in to attack in stages. At first, the cat hissed and spat, but when a crack rent the air, a dull croak came out of her mouth. Alice sensed Dorcas's sharp intake of breath, a jab against Alice's own stomach. She placed one hand over Dorcas's eyes, but the girl pushed it away.

With a growl and a snap of jaws from the largest mongrel, Miranda's back legs were broken, and finally, the cat lay on her belly in a pile of excrement. The dogs shuffled away in search of their next prey.

Alice let go of her charge and grabbed a stick that lay beside the open doorway. She stepped over to the dying animal and struck hard against its neck. With a dull *thock*, which Alice knew she would remember always, the creature's head fell forward. After all the animals she had helped her mother heal, this was the first she had destroyed.

She looked up. Nicholas Symcox, who reeked of onions and whose shirt was undone and loose outside his breeches, stood before her. "How dare you disturb our peace at this hour?" he grumbled before ambling off.

Alice spat after him. She undid her apron and used it to scoop up Miranda's body. It weighed heavy, and she stared at the blood from the creature's legs as it soaked through the linen cloth, spiraling out into ever-widening circles.

"Run to my home and fetch the spade which lies against the wall!" Alice commanded Dorcas. When the girl disappeared up the lane, an image of Alice's cat, Jaspar, appeared in her mind, his black-and-white fur gleaming. She wished she could reach out and touch him, but she knew Jeffrey took good care of her cat. Or perhaps Jaspar was Jeffrey's cat now?

Within a few minutes, Dorcas returned, and Alice led her along first one narrow lane, then another, to the graveyard behind St. Paul's church.

They stopped outside the northeast corner of the little plot of land, and Alice lay her burden on the damp earth. Dorcas still did not speak, but her hands trembled as she dug furiously. To Alice, it seemed as if the girl possessed the force of a full-grown man when she threw the earth into a pile behind her while tears streamed down her cheeks.

Within a few minutes, the two of them had created an ample hole. Dorcas stood up and chanted, "Miranda is dead! Miranda is dead!"

Alice crouched down, slid her hands under the lifeless body, raised the cat whose ginger fur was matted with clumps of blood, and placed it into its special grave. With their bare hands, the two girls picked up handfuls of earth and flung them over the body while Dorcas chanted, "Miranda is dead! Miranda is dead!"

Alice marveled at Dorcas's instinct in finding these simple words, which seemed to leech out her pain much like a poultice on a wounded arm. Yet she was nervous that the sound of Dorcas's voice might cause them to be noticed, and she wondered if it was against the law to bury a cat in a place intended for humans.

She was glad when Dorcas ceased her lament and slipped away into the churchyard, where the girl intended to gather something. And though it seemed to Alice that they had done all they might, still she thought of Matthew and his special rituals and wondered if something further was necessary for burying a beloved animal.

She wondered, too, if it mattered that this cemetery had lain deserted, no longer hallowed ground, for two years when St. Paul's had been sold off. Only a few months ago, when King Charles had ordered the restoration of the Church of England, did the city of Exeter see fit to buy back the church, although they had yet to repair the east window or replace the rood screen.

Dorcas returned a few moments later and carried two twigs of yew, which she lay precisely in the center of the small mound.

The two stood for a moment, hand in hand. "Thank you," Dorcas murmured.

Alice put one arm around the girl's shoulder, and they slipped away.

A few hours after burying the cat, Alice and Dorcas had cause to visit St. Paul's again. With the return of the monarchy to England had come compulsory church attendance and the requirement that the youth of the land be able to repeat the entire catechism before their mandatory confirmation. To ensure this, young people were required to attend a series of classes.

"Child, speak up!" Alice overheard. All around her in the small vestry, a chorus of voices chanted the many verses of the catechism.

"My duty towards my neighbor is to love him as myself and to do to all men as I would they should do unto me: to love, honor, and succor my father." Alice bowed her head.

Why do I have to sit here and repeat these words if I don't even believe in this God? And my father is dead.

She peered up at the bewhiskered face of Father Hobbes, the Anglican priest who had been assigned to St. Paul's now that it was once more a place of worship.

I am no longer a child but a full fifteen years old. She looked down at her fingernails, still muddy in spite of her efforts to clean them, and folded her arms so that her hands did not show.

Since her return from Ivycombe, she had found no one in Exeter with whom she could share her experiences at the full moon ritual or her conviction that a belief in one male God didn't make sense. Not even Jeffrey.

She looked over to where he sat, his brown hair swept back as usual and curling up where it touched his neck. She and Jeffrey had shared so much: her gratitude when he'd agreed to take care of her cat; his fear of his father, who turned on his mother and beat her when he had one too many pots of ale. And the good times: They both loved to walk in the rain and fantasize about whom they might marry. She had thought they could tell each other everything.

"To submit myself to all my governors, teachers, spiritual pastors," Father Hobbes encouraged Alice.

"To order myself lowly and reverently to all my betters," she continued methodically while imagining herself at her favorite place: an enchanted body of water she had named the Green Pool. Here she had spent many hours charmed by the water and seen the constant small changes in its color, fluctuating between transparent green on a summer's day and a deeper, murky green after a rainstorm. She had watched the willow trees go from bare branches in winter to the yellow catkins of spring; she knew the tiny field mice vanished as night came earlier and earlier but returned when winter faded into spring. As she herself grew taller, it came to her that she was part of those changes, not a distant observer but another tiny creature in a big world.

"To be true and just in all my dealings," Alice mumbled. The words were already very familiar to her, for unlike most of her companions, she had the advantage of being able to read the catechism.

Catherine Molland had sat her child down night after night over the past year to teach Alice how to read. These days, Catherine often awoke with pain in her back and legs, which made the search for healing plants too arduous for her. This duty she had assigned to Alice and had presented her child with her favorite herbal jar, the small earthenware pot etched with thin black lines.

Although Catherine's body grew weaker, her eyes were still strong, and reading was a skill she was determined to pass on to her daughter. She used the Bible and began with a passage from Genesis, "In the beginning, God created the world," and another from the New Testament, "And behold, there were shepherds abiding in the fields." Alice already knew these words by heart, so Catherine pointed at each word, one at a time, and instructed Alice to say them over and over.

Even as Alice relished this newfound skill, she questioned

whether any of these stories were true. She had wanted so much to tell her mother about her experiences within the circle in the oak grove at Ivycombe, but she could not; her mother had told her it was blasphemy to question the Christian faith. She wanted to stay close to her mother.

She had questioned her mother as to what might have caused Philippa's illness.

Catherine had replied that some girls and women were more prone to infections of the bladder than others. "For these females, the place where their urine comes out can attract diseases. And sexual activities may also cause harm."

Alice had not known what to reply. Was it possible that Matthew and Philippa had lain together?

Alice pushed aside her questions. That afternoon, she was stuck in a gloomy vestry. She looked around. Today, twenty candidates for confirmation sat on joint stools in a dank room that let in light only through a tiny slit of a window.

She recited, "To bear no malice nor hatred in my heart."

"To keep my body in temperance, soberness, and chastity." Father Hobbes's voice spoke close by her ear, edged with annoyance this time.

Alice twitched at the feel of the priest's hot breath on her neck and his cassock brushing her arm.

She continued the prayer, "And to do my duty in that state of life unto which it shall please God to call me."

Alice looked up. Father Hobbes now stood over Dorcas, who wept uncontrollably.

"Please, please, do not beat me," Dorcas said between sobs. "I . . . durst say . . . I . . ." She sat back, unable to speak more.

The musty space grew silent as its occupants watched the portly priest pull Dorcas up by the elbows and force her to look at him.

"You shall obey me," the priest implored the child. "It is the law of the land that you should be able to recite the catechism in perfect order before your confirmation." He added in a gentler tone, "But you have time."

Dorcas still sobbed.

"It is fully a month before you must appear before the Lord Bishop of Exeter."

The priest moved away from Dorcas.

As Alice watched her friend weep, a howl made its way up from her gut and filled her body with the need to cry out. She had not shed a single tear at the time of Faith's death. She pulled her linen handkerchief from her bosom to stanch her tears, stood up, mouthed "Farewell" to Father Hobbes, and hurried out through the low archway.

She scarcely noticed the difference between the vestry and the brightness outside. Alice passed by people who strolled along Goldsmith Street and enjoyed the late afternoon sun, but they were distant to her. A numbness gripped her body and froze her thoughts. She walked forward—oblivious to those around her or to where she was headed—until she turned the corner a moment later and saw the great cathedral looming over her, its two towers rising above the rest of the structure as if to survey the citizens of Exeter.

She stopped and threw herself down on the grass that surrounded the cathedral on two sides. The numbness had vanished and her heart beat frantically. How dare this enormous structure hold the people of Exeter in its sway and pretend to protect them? There were said to be over thirty churches in Exeter, as well as this cathedral, but what good did they do? Her sister, her father, and Goody Luscombe were all dead, and how had these houses of God made any difference?

She looked up at the enormous stone building that reached

high above her, impervious to her presence. She had heard that it contained the longest nave in the world, but what did that matter to her? A series of tall, pointed turrets ran the length of the nave on the outside. On the west front of the cathedral were three rows of statues, some with their heads missing. Who were these people? Above them gleamed a giant stained glass window, and even higher yet, another one that was smaller.

A memory arose in her: Faith's wheeze as she called "Help me" when she'd attempted to sit up and reach for the mug of water. And the smell of her toward the end, like rotting cabbage, so that Alice had to hold her breath, though she was ashamed to do so. "No, no, no!" Alice pounded her fists on the cathedral green's perfectly maintained lawn, to the astonishment of a few passersby who quickened their pace.

She beat on the ground for several minutes until, unable to bear the sight of the awful cathedral any longer, she stood up. She needed to go to the Green Pool.

She walked fast to get away from the cathedral, first down the grassy slope to Southern Hay, then across Southernhay Lane, to the place where her enchanted pool lay. Although the early evening air was cool, the sweat crept down Alice's back. The pool lay surrounded by a world of shivering willow trees, their long leaves brilliant with the greenish-yellow hue of autumn. She brushed against the leaves as she made her way between the trees and sat at the water's edge. She took a deep breath and lay back on the damp earth. Above her, the first few stars emerged from the darkening sky.

When she heard a splash, she looked across the pool to see a stately gray heron. The bird had planted its long, thin legs in the pond's shallow waters, and the bird's bright yellow beak was immersed in the water as it sought its next meal of fish. Alice felt honored by the presence of this beautiful creature. She had come home.

CHAPTER TEN

Exeter, Devon. September 1660.

Father Hobbes leaned forward and focused his deep-set eyes on Alice. The two sat in the vestry at St. Paul's, where he had summoned her. "I am disappointed in you. I waited a day to summon you since I expected you to seek me out first and apologize for your behavior. I may find it necessary to report your actions to the Lord Bishop of Exeter." He sat back in his chair, stroked his mustache, and waited for Alice's response.

Two days after her abrupt escape from St. Paul's vestry, Alice had received a message that the priest required her presence immediately. It was the last Tuesday in September, and she was busy carding in preparation for the wool market the next day. She looked over at her mother, who let Alice know that Father Hobbes's command must be obeyed.

The questions raced through her mind as she stared back at him: *Does he know I went to the Green Pool? But how could he know? And what does it matter to him?* She pushed a few strands of her long black hair back under her cap. They were damp thanks to a light autumn drizzle.

At least she knew he had called her to this dank vestry, which smelled faintly of mold, to force her to apologize. But why would this man with his neatly trimmed mustache want to report her to the Bishop of Exeter?

"I can explain. I would never dream of being disrespectful to you or your church." She hoped he believed her. She paused to watch an errant daddy longlegs make its way up the stone wall of the vestry.

"My sister Faith died three months ago. I had been numb, unable to weep for her until I watched Dorcas cry. Her tears released something in me, something I could not contain. I had to leave rather than sob in front of everyone. Surely, as a man of God, you understand and would want to comfort me?"

"You didn't ask for comfort." Reverend Hobbes banged a fist on the low table that separated them. "I feel this is a game for you, Alice. You are an attractive young woman and may be able to use your looks to persuade others of your beliefs. But I care about your soul. Our Lord Bishop has made these confirmation classes mandatory. You disobeyed him when you ran out as you did."

He doesn't listen to me. He knows only that I didn't obey the rules. No wonder I cannot believe in his God. And what did he mean by that reference to my appearance? Her body gave an involuntary shudder.

"I am concerned for you, Alice. Some in this parish already consider you a troublemaker, and you do yourself no favors when you rush out of this vestry like a madwoman. You need to grow up."

Alice bristled. *He presents himself as my advisor who wants only to help me.* She had a sudden image of her mother at home, worried about her child, and decided to let the minister believe she appreciated his advice.

"Thank you, Father. So that you know I am not a troublemaker, I promise to bring my mother to church every Sunday and attend every class before my confirmation. And I am sorry if you feel I have been impolite." She spoke these words as a vision of the gray heron at the Green Pool popped into her mind.

"And if you will excuse me, I must return home since Mother will be worried about me."

The minister nodded his assent. She stood up, strode to the low wooden door, unlatched it, and headed down Paul Street.

Months later, on the second Thursday of April, 1661, Alice leaned over to peer into the depths of the Green Pool. Susannah and Jane stood on either side of her. All three were naked and tried not to tremble as they stood at the grassy edge of the small body of water, bathed in the light of the full moon.

Alice had kept her promise to Father Hobbes in the months after their meeting. She had completed her catechism classes, received confirmation from the Bishop of Exeter, and accompanied her mother to church every Sunday. During this time, Alice had also invited Dorcas to live at the Molland home. The girl accepted the invitation with delight, and it made Alice happy to have help with the carding. She still missed her sister and sometimes imagined that Faith sat beside her, but Dorcas's sweet nature made her easy to work with.

When the rain held off, Alice and Dorcas stepped out together to gather herbs such as mugwort, dandelion flowers and roots, and comfrey leaves and roots, and Alice made the weekly trip to the wool market. Otherwise, she stayed home, determined not to cause any trouble.

But on this night of the full moon, Alice had to go to the Green Pool. This time, she had invited her friends Jane and Susannah to come with her so that they might honor the moon together.

Jane had at first resisted Alice's request. She especially did not want to undress and step into the cold water, convinced that someone would see them and take advantage. After much persuasion from her sister and Alice, Jane had finally agreed to join them, but only this one time.

"Shall we begin?" Alice whispered, and the other two nodded. Their slim bodies were outlined in the glowing light of the moon, with no clouds to obscure them.

"Spirit of the moon, be with us tonight," they chanted in unison. "Guard our pool and keep us safe. Ye mighty powers of air, protect us and give us strength." Already facing east, by design, they turned to face south, west, and north as they chanted the appropriate elements: fire, water, and earth.

Alice stepped first into the green water. Her feet landed on mud, and the water came up to her knees. Her body shook, and yet she took comfort in the chilly waters of this perfectly circular pool surrounded by weeping willows. Susannah and Jane followed her into the water, and Alice moved further in; the water enclosed her and covered her thighs, the small triangle of hair between her legs, her belly, and finally, her breasts. Her feet met small, slippery rocks; she curled her toes around them and grew stronger, charged by a magical energy.

With a splash, Alice plunged headfirst into the water. A chill gripped her center and radiated outward through every part of her body. As she held her breath and stayed under, the cold gradually transmuted into warmth. Some indefinable life source existed here, perhaps from an underground spring. She was vibrant and could defeat anyone even though money was so scarce she had barely eaten for the last two days. She and Susannah had decided they had to do something to alleviate the suffering that the poorer citizens of Exeter endured. They would discuss this the next day.

Still underwater, she wondered what Matthew would think of this ritual. In the past year, she had seen her cousin only once, and briefly. And although they had both affirmed their enduring friendship, Matthew's affections were focused on Philippa, whom he was about to take as his wife. Alice wanted to be happy for him but knew she could never bring herself to trust Philippa.

But now Richard Greenway had come back into her life. He had sought her out a few times at the Wednesday wool market. Always he made sure to brush against her arm or her hand; that touch sent flutters through her and filled her dreams with his image.

Then, just last week, he had sent a servant in a carriage to request her presence for his mother, who had fallen ill again.

After Alice had induced Florence Greenway to expel a greenish-brown liquid and had soothed her pain with the pennyroyal, which allowed her to sleep peacefully, Richard led Alice to the kitchen, where they sat by the hearth. She was amazed at the size of the room, which was at least three times bigger than the Molland kitchen, and two dozen gleaming pots hung on metal racks that ran the length of the room. Richard took her hand, thanked her, and asked how they might meet again.

"I am at the wool market every Wednesday." She withdrew her hand and noticed his chin bore the beginnings of a wispy beard. "I also have a special place I like to visit. I call it the Green Pool."

His emerald eyes focused on her, and she liked the feeling of having power over him.

She explained how she had to cross Southern Hay to make her way to the pool and then stood up to leave.

"Thank you," Richard had said. He had given her a brilliant smile and summoned a carriage to take her home.

Alice surfaced and spluttered from lack of breath.

Jane and Susannah kicked their feet in exhilaration and laughed with shrieks of pure joy.

"Now you may understand why I love this place!" she called out.

"Oh, yes!" Susannah replied. "It is a magically charged place, indeed. A faery place, I dare say. But let us not stay too long, for fear we shall be discovered. Come, we should make haste."

Alice flipped over in the water and glided toward the edge of the pool. With each stroke, she reminded herself of the lesson this pool always taught her: Whenever life grew too hard, as it had after Faith's death, she must explore beyond the city walls to feel alive again.

⁂

The day after the ritual at the Green Pool, a Friday, Susannah came to the Molland home, as the two had planned, to discuss what action they might take to deal with the poverty amongst Exeter's carders and spinners.

"Three pence a day, the price of a barley loaf. How can they expect us to live on that?" demanded Susannah. She slammed her pot of ale down on the kitchen table.

Catherine looked up from where she stirred a vegetable stew over the hearth.

"We should move outside." Alice placed her right hand on her friend's shoulder. "It may well upset my mother to hear our conversation."

The rain had ceased, and behind them, dusty pink clouds straddled the horizon while the sky above glowed the color of pale lilacs.

The two sat on the wooden bench. Alice placed her ale on the ground and fixed her gaze on her friend's clear brown eyes. "I have an idea to share with you. I overheard something wonderful at the wool market last Wednesday. A peddler passing through from Somerset told us what happened a fortnight ago in the town of Street."

Alice leaned forward. "A good number of the local spinners came together and marched toward the meat market. As they approached, their leader yelled, 'Fire!' The market emptied abruptly, and the spinners rushed in and made off with whatever took their fancy."

"Were they arrested?" Susannah sat up straight.

"No! Nothing happened to them. What do you think? Could we do that?"

Susannah yanked off her white bonnet and her chestnut brown hair fell onto her shoulders. "Alice! With you as our leader, yes. We can do this. Let us begin our planning at once."

On Sunday afternoon, two days after Alice and Susannah met, fifteen of the carders and spinners who lived close to Jane and Susannah's home on Corry Street gathered in their kitchen. Alice and Susannah stood in front of them. It had been Alice's idea to hold a meeting to organize a protest, but now she was unsure. She was only fifteen, and some of the women in the room were several years older.

Although the sun beat down on the cottage, the group had decided to keep the front door shut. Alice's cheeks grew warm. The stale smell of cooked vegetables hung in the air.

"Let us begin." Alice scarcely recognized her own voice, which came out with a note of authority. "We must take action in the face of the dire conditions we are forced to live in."

The room gradually quieted.

"We need only decide what action will work for us."

A young woman about Alice's age, who wore a delicate lace cap, spoke in a firm voice and raised one fist in the air. "We can deliver a petition to the Chamber demanding an increase in wages for carders and spinners. Let them know that, at times, the clothiers refuse to pay the spinners even a single penny, forcing them to take goods for their work."

At once the comments flew:

"Do you really think they will listen to us?"

"They don't give a damn about the people of Exeter but care only to maintain themselves."

"And they are all men who fancy themselves so much better than women. They would mock us and send us on our way."

I need to take control. I projected myself as the leader.

Alice clapped her hands. "If you don't like this idea, who has a different plan?"

A woman in front of her raised a wrinkled hand and suggested, "I say we refuse to work until they raise our wages."

This time Susannah responded. "Without a doubt, the clothiers and merchants would instantly find others willing to replace us."

The sweat trickled down Alice's back, and her hands shook. She knew it was time to speak with authority about the idea she and Susannah had discussed. "I have a plan that has been used before, and I am confident it will work."

The group fixed their attention on her.

"Here's how we shall proceed."

On the first of May, a Thursday, Alice knew she must calm herself. The market raid would take place the next day, and she had dreamt that she, along with all the other women, had been arrested and thrown into gaol. Once awake, she grew upset with her mother for no good reason and knew she had to gain control of herself.

That evening, she came alone to the Green Pool. Before she set out, she had anointed her red candle with rose oil and cast a love spell as she visualized herself and Richard together.

On this warm night, Alice sat at the edge of the pool and

dangled her feet in the clear water. Overhead, in the branches of the willow tree, a breeze blew continuously; the leaves shook with a passionate hissing, a rising and falling that resembled breathing.

"Ah!" She jumped at the realization that she was not alone and turned to hear someone say her name. She knew at once that her spell had worked.

"Alice." Richard moved toward her.

"How did you know to find me here on this night?"

She stood before him awkwardly, and the water dripped onto her bare feet. She had decided to abandon her coif for the evening, and her long black hair fell across her shoulders to touch the edge of her bodice. Richard was clad in a linen shirt with a ruff at the collar and matching cuffs on the wrists, covered by a blue velvet doublet. Over this, he wore a short black cape, which reached to his breeches.

Alice smiled at the way his long red hair glowed in the moonlight.

"Are you afraid to be here with me?" he asked.

Alice looked up at the inky black sky dotted with tiny pinpricks of light. The moon was a bright orb. "No." Inwardly, she trembled but forced herself to continue. "I feel blessed to be out here with you on this night."

He took one step toward her, took her right hand in his, and kissed it. "Alice," he whispered again.

This time, she gazed into his clear green eyes. She had dreamed so often of this moment, but now that it was here, she knew not how to respond.

In a trance, she watched as he took her arms, wrapped them around his back and under his cape, and drew her to him. She rested her head against his chest, detecting a scent reminiscent of horse chestnut.

He stroked her hair. "My Alice," he muttered, and Alice knew she might lose herself in his rich voice, as lush as a ripe fruit.

She looked up at him. At once, his warm mouth pressed a gentle kiss on her. She smiled. He pulled her even closer and crushed his lips against hers, as if he wanted to devour her. It scared her a little, and he ceased.

The two stood in each other's arms for several moments and listened to the perfect silence. After all the brief encounters at the market where their hands had touched and shoulders had brushed against each other, and after that time in the Greenway kitchen, Alice could scarcely believe that what she had envisioned for so long was real.

Richard finally spoke. "Come." He took her hand and led her back to the shelter of a pair of hawthorn trees, their new leaves just beginning to emerge, and then laid out his cape for her. Slowly, they eased to the ground. They did not speak, but Richard reached to pull Alice up against him, and she was lost in his musky scent as he kissed her over and over. With her breasts flattened against his chest and her arms around his back, she gave herself over to the delight of his kisses. She wanted nothing more than to hold on to this moment beside this beautiful pool forever.

Eventually, she voiced her concern that she should leave since Dorcas could be worried for her.

Richard pulled away from her and flashed his brilliant smile. "Have I told you that you have beautiful eyes?"

She laughed in response, and all consideration of foolishness vanished as a wave of love for this man swept over her.

Before she left, he made her promise that they would meet at the Green Pool again on Whit Sunday, just three weeks away.

CHAPTER ELEVEN

Exeter, Devon. May 1661.

"No, no! It should simmer slowly, not race at a fast boil." Alice grabbed the earthenware pot from Dorcas and held it above the flame. "You must clasp it thus."

Dorcas stretched out her thin hands and took the pot as she was instructed. Even while she directed Dorcas, a shiver passed through Alice at the thought of kissing Richard the night before. Her body was curiously alive, for Richard's touch had ignited a fire within her.

Alice was teaching Dorcas how to boil the comfrey root. Once Dorcas had prepared it to Alice's satisfaction, the two would take the solution to Agnes Furze, who had complained of blood in her urine for a sevennight.

Alice reached around Dorcas's slight frame to stir the contents of the pot. "You see how it develops exactly the right consistency when I stir it—a liquid, but not too runny?"

The girl nodded, although she held her nose and looked away.

"Yes, I know—it smells like horse dung, but it is the cure that Goody Furze needs. Next time, if I am called away for some reason, can you prepare it yourself? With perchance a little help from my mother?"

Dorcas looked up, and the glimmer of a smile lit her face.

Catherine shifted her weight in the hard chair and leaned forward. She tried to pick up the thread from the spinning wheel between the thumb and forefinger of her left hand but groaned. Her joints had stiffened, and she flexed them back and forth to loosen them.

"There, that's perfect," Alice congratulated Dorcas. Together, they lifted the pot from the flame and laid it in front of the hearth, where the liquid might cool.

"You make a fine team," Catherine declared. "Look at you, Alice, taller than me and with that beautiful hair—black, just like your father's. And now you have a wonderful assistant in Dorcas."

Alice smiled, pleased she had invited the girl to live with them in exchange for her help with carding and the preparation of medicines. And, of course, to be a companion for Catherine.

Alice came to stand beside her mother and rested one hand on her shoulder. For a moment, Alice remembered how cold her toes had been in the waters of the Longbrook on the day when the two of them sat there after they had tended to Farmer Fletcher's sick horse. It was then that her mother had first pledged to teach Alice all she knew about herbs and healing.

Nowadays, it was a fine balance that Alice walked every day with her fiercely independent mother, who resisted help. Nevertheless, Catherine was still a superb spinner, probably the best in Exeter. Alice leaned over to kiss the top of her mother's head and sat at the other end of the table, next to Dorcas.

The two young women settled into their job of carding, but Alice's thoughts were still filled with the magic of the night before and how her body had tingled at Richard's touch.

"What ails you?" Catherine chided her. "At the rate you work, we shall surely starve to death."

"Forgive me," Alice replied and focused her attention on her task: holding the card where she had placed the fleece in her left hand while pulling the metal teeth of another card through the fleece with her right hand. It was a delicate job, for she had to exert enough pressure to smooth out all the tangles without tearing the wool apart.

She had to finish her work promptly so she would have time to meet with Susannah and be sure all the details of their plan for later that day were in place.

***

The noon bell tolled from the belfry of St. Mary Steps Church by the time the crowd of spinners and carders had gathered at the bottom of Stepcote Hill. It was Friday, market day for meat, fowl, fish, and dairy products, so many of the citizens of Exeter, as well as those from nearby villages, had gathered in the center of the city.

Alice had chosen this spot to meet, conveniently close to the meat market, because she knew the authorities paid little attention to the western section of the city, where lived some of the poorest citizens of Exeter.

She looked down to survey the group that had assembled in the shadow of the city wall that rose some twenty feet above them. On the other side of the wall, the land fell off sharply down to the banks of the River Exe. Here lay the fulling mills and the tenter racks where cloth was taken to be finished and hung out to dry.

The spinners were well aware that the fullers, clothiers, and merchants all made a fine living and that the Exeter serge market flourished. Yet they themselves were close to starvation.

Alice looked down and saw perhaps forty women, dressed mostly in plain woolen bodices and skirts, their hair pulled back under linen coifs, waiting in the faint mist of a drizzle. Alice was flanked by Susannah, whose chestnut brown hair flowed freely, and Jane, who had shorn her curly locks and had the startled appearance of a sheep. The lean, hungry faces all around Alice reflected the deep emptiness in her own belly, for she, her mother, and Dorcas had eaten only a thin soup of potatoes and carrots for the last two days.

For a second, the image of Richard flashed into her mind, but she pushed it away.

"Hear me," she commanded at the last stroke of the bell. "For our victory, we depend upon quick action. This hill is steep." She turned and indicated the narrow steps with a sweep of her long arm. "But we should move as one swift army, not a raggedy group of soldiers." She hoped her tone conveyed a confidence that they would be victorious, although she heard a slight tremor in her voice.

As one, the silent crowd moved up the narrow street like a moorland stream anxiously forging its way through the undergrowth to the river. The plan was straightforward. Once Alice reached Smythen Street, she would raise her right hand, and each woman would count to one hundred. They had practiced this several times at their meeting to ensure they all counted at the same rate.

When Alice got to the final number, they would already have entered the market, and each woman would raise her hands and yell "Fire!" as loudly as she could. Ten of the women would actually start small fires with the bundles of straw concealed under their long skirts. This would cause a panic, and stallholders would flee, allowing each woman to rush in, grab as much meat as she could handle, and leave.

Alice grasped the raspy woolen material of her skirt and lifted it high in order not to trip as she strode upward. She mounted the steps and found she was no longer hungry or nervous but consumed instead with a forceful energy that would allow no failure.

On either side of her, Susannah and Jane marched with equal determination.

At the crest of the hill, Alice's stomach hitched at the pungent, bloody odors of the meat market. She remembered that her mother had brought her here once and told her that Exeter had held a weekly market for its citizens since the thirteenth century, and that by 1281, the city was the only one in Southwest England to have three market days a week.

The thought that the blood of pigs, hogs, sheep, and rabbits had been spilled in Butcher Row for over three hundred years made Alice feel queasy.

They had passed few people on their way up the steps, but as they grew closer to the market, Alice heard shouts and laughter. She was glad of the hustle and bustle since it would provide easier passage for the market raiders.

When Susannah, Alice, and Jane reached Smythen Street, with Butcher Row a short distance ahead, Alice raised her right hand—the signal for each marcher to start the count.

She lowered her hand and heard *one, two, three* inside her head. The light rain had ceased, and above them, a pale sun forced its way through the clouds. By the time she reached the number fifty, Alice, Susannah, and Jane had arrived at the entrance to the meat market on Butcher Row.

Alice stared at the stalls that lined the narrow street on either side, about thirty altogether, spaced six feet apart. Miniature Union Jacks, with their red, white, and blue colors, hung from some of the stalls. Long rolls of canvas, held up by poles and draped over the stalls, protected the meat and other products from the elements.

While Alice stood still, Susannah walked off to her right, and half of the women followed her as she led them behind the stalls, where they could not be seen by the crowd in front of the stands. At the same time, Jane moved to her left, and the remainder of the women came after her to place themselves where they might not be seen.

Alice continued the count as the market raiders filed past her. She had to force herself to stay focused amidst the sounds of butchers hawking their wares, dogs barking, horses neighing, and shoppers gathering to exchange gossip, as they did every Friday.

Have I put all these women's lives in danger? What if my plan doesn't work?

She glanced at the stalls immediately in front of her and clenched her fists at the sight of so much meat piled up. All those cuts of beef loin, capons, ducks, and geese mocked the poverty of the women who had to survive on three pence a day.

We have to do something. I must stay strong.

She took long, slow breaths to calm herself. Still, she continued the count and laughed to see a little boy run past her as he chased a pair of pigeons.

When the last of the women had disappeared, Alice reached the number ninety and walked over to stand behind the first stall to her right, on which lay at least twenty meat pies and several strings of sausages. The light, bloody smell almost made Alice vomit, but then she inhaled the earthy aroma of pipe tobacco.

She was startled to see in front of her a tall gentleman who held a clay pipe to his mouth and wore a boater-style hat decorated with blue ribbons. She recognized Sir William Greenway, Richard's father, and prayed he would not turn his head. To her relief, he seemed engrossed in his conversation with a black-coated man, and the two strode away from her.

When the word "hundred" entered her head, Alice raised both hands to her mouth and bellowed, "Fire!" Immediately, the call of "Fire!" echoed in the air, yelled out by the women who stood behind the market stalls. At the same time, the ten designated women pulled out bundles of straw from beneath their skirts, and each struck a knife against a sharp stone to set the straw alight. Sparks flew immediately, ignited the straw, and sent streams of smoke into the air.

For a second, the market held its breath, stunned by the sound of the most frightening event of all—the biggest threat to its livelihood and, indeed, that of the whole city. The smoke that rose into the air convinced the butchers and stallholders this was a real fire, which might spread fast. Several of them raced over to the sources of the fires and stamped on the ground.

It was in this melee, as deftly as if they had spun the finest thread, that each woman ran into the empty stalls, grabbed a leg of lamb, a rump of beef, a couple of rabbits, and vanished into the city's narrow lanes.

Alice herself did not look around but darted forward and seized three pork pies along with four strings of sausages from the stall in front of her. She lowered them into the especially deep apron she had worn for the occasion and made her way to the North Gate and her home.

Although she was proud that the market raid had succeeded, Alice feared the men might seek revenge.

When Alice presented her mother with the meat pies and the sausages, Catherine greeted her with a wan look. "I thank you," she murmured. She took her child's hand in hers and said, "Stay by me a while."

Alice sat on the hard floor next to her mother's chair, Catherine's frail, bony hand within her own. When she looked up, her mother's watery blue eyes pleaded with her. "I am afraid for you," she whispered. "You are so much like your father."

Over the following week, Alice stayed within her own home and assigned all necessary errands to Dorcas. She made an exception only to bring Agnes Furze, who lived just two lanes away on Goldsmith Street, the comfrey liquid.

When she stepped into the stale air of Agnes's one-room cottage, Alice saw at once that the old woman's condition had worsened. She lay on her pallet, her coarse gray hair pulled back from her face and her mouth slightly open. Alice tiptoed over to kneel beside Agnes but drew back slightly at the smell of her foul breath.

She didn't want to alarm her patient, so she reached for the woman's tiny hand, scarred by the white marks of old knife cuts and dotted with liver spots. She caressed it, and after a moment, Agnes stirred and smiled at her visitor.

"Alice," she muttered.

"I have the decoction of comfrey root for you." Alice smiled. "Here. I am sure it will help." She lifted the half-full mug with one hand and attempted to prop up Agnes's head with the other, but it slipped back. In the end, Agnes had swallowed just a small amount before she fell back on her pillow, asleep again.

"Is she all right?" Alice heard a voice behind her and turned to see a boy of about eleven, Dorcas's age, at the front door. Under his mop of curly black hair, he had a scar running down his left cheek, just like John Colbert, the soldier who had come into Alice's home and beaten her father. She shuddered.

"Are you Alice?"

Alice flinched. *How does this child know my name?* She stood up and replied with a brief nod of her head.

"My name is Lewis, and we live next door. Mother comes over to keep an eye on Goody Furze."

"Thank you. She's asleep, but I would be most grateful if you could check on her later today. And my assistant will visit this evening."

With that, she exited, relieved that Agnes had a good neighbor but worried that the old woman looked so fragile, a twig ready to snap in half. Once she returned home, Alice instructed Dorcas that she must attend to Agnes before the end of the day.

From the girl, Alice learned that the Chamber had it under consideration to lay charges against Alice, Susannah, and Jane, who had been identified as the leaders of the market raid.

She worried that the authorities might watch her now or perhaps send people to spy on her. Then, with a week to go before their Whit Sunday meeting, Richard came to her front door.

His green eyes glared at her. "You have brought dishonor upon yourself," he pronounced and marched away.

CHAPTER TWELVE

Exeter, Devon. May 1661.

Early on the Thursday following Richard's visit, Alice and her mother began working on the huge tub of fleece Dorcas had brought back from the wool market.

Alice sat at one end of the kitchen table and prepared the wool for spinning. At the other end of the table, Catherine pulled threads from the carded wool to wind onto the spinning wheel.

The two worked in a silence broken only by the scrape of the cards and the light click of the wheel. The small kitchen grew stuffy as the morning sun beat down on the cottage.

The fleece smelled of sheep piss, and her hands were clammy with the heat, but Alice didn't care. At least the pain in her fingers and arms provided a distraction from the questions that plagued her. *It's been almost three weeks since the success of the market raid. Are my fellow carders and spinners in trouble? I have heard no word. Mother has shown her disapproval of me, as has Dorcas. But what of the authorities? Will they prosecute me? And Richard?*

"It's over!" Dorcas flung open the front door and shouted her news. "They posted a notice at the Guildhall that the Chamber has decided not to pursue any legal action against the market thieves." She stopped to catch her breath and push back the soft curls that had escaped her cap. "They explained that Cromwell's rule had brought about much violence and fear, and they wished to assure the citizens of Exeter that life had returned to normal and it was not worth their time to pursue charges. Signed by the members of the Chamber: the mayor, eight aldermen, and sixteen councillers.

"But they added a warning to the three leaders not to cause any further trouble, or the consequences would be severe." Dorcas finished up her speech and stared at Alice.

I took pity on her, and now she judges me.

Catherine put down her thread. "You can be sure the authorities will keep an eagle eye on you, my child."

"But, Mother, are you not pleased with this news?" Alice set her carders down and walked over to Catherine. For almost three weeks, she had expected a thump on the door, as had happened when Cromwell's men strode into her home and destroyed her father. Only this time, a member of the Chamber would have come to arrest her.

She placed one hand on Catherine's shoulder. "Can you not be happy for me?" Her heart beat so fast she thought it might explode.

"Just be careful not to bring more shame to our family."

"I shall take care, Mother. This is wonderful news, is it not? But, Dorcas, I had no idea you could read so well."

"I found Jeffrey at the Guildhall, and he read the notice to me." The girl's cheeks flushed red, and she giggled.

"Jeffrey! Is he well? I haven't seen him for months. And Jaspar? How is Jaspar?"

"Jeffrey looked well, but he wanted me to tell you Jaspar is failing. The cat sleeps a lot and seems uninterested in his food."

In a flash, Alice remembered the day Jeffrey had helped her find Jaspar after Faith chased the cat away. She could still picture the spot where they had found him, curled up behind a carriage wheel, his back leg broken. He had growled and hissed as they drew near. Jeffrey had taken care of him ever since, for almost six years.

"I must visit him, and soon. But Dorcas, come sit next to me. The carding will go faster if we work together."

By the time Whit Sunday arrived, three days after Alice learned there would be no charges laid against her, she had made up her mind that Richard would meet her at the Green Pool. She reasoned that in spite of his sharp words to her, he must have welcomed the Chamber's decision, and surely, he had not lost his attraction to her after the passionate kisses they had exchanged?

She sat at the grassy edge of the Green Pool, her feet and ankles immersed. The moon was on the wane, but the emerging stars were bright as fireflies and created a translucent haze over the surface of the water. She had taken in only a thin crust of barley bread and a little water, so her body was taut with energy, but her mind was unable to focus on anything but the feel of Richard's body against hers.

Alice breathed in deeply through her nose and exhaled through her mouth. She repeated this pattern five times to calm the rapid beat of her heart.

A rustle sounded in the willow trees behind her. Startled, she looked around to see a large doe appear out of the grayness and amble over to drink from the pool just a few feet away from her. The animal sauntered back into the trees and disappeared. Alice loved that she and the deer were just two parts of the natural world, her life force.

After several more minutes, Alice's feet grew cold. She withdrew them from the water and dried them with her skirt. Where was Richard? They had arranged to meet at sunset. Now, the arrival of twilight meant the shape of the trees around her grew blurry, although warmth still stirred the air. She would wait only a little while longer. How dare he break his promise to her?

"Good evening." Richard spoke from behind Alice in a high-pitched voice.

He came to sit beside her on the grass but placed himself an arm's length away. "I have something I must say to you." He did not look at her.

"I trust you will apologize for your delay." Alice surprised herself with these words.

"I hesitated because I was not sure to find you here. Let me speak briefly, and then I shall be silent." Richard grabbed a strand of red hair and twirled it between his thumb and forefinger. "I hope you can forgive me for my harsh words to you last week. However, you should know my father holds you in poor repute, although he knows well you do not face prosecution."

The strain in his voice resounded within Alice, but now that Richard was here, she could not bear to have this night snatched away from her.

"I imagined that might be so. But you are not your father, I think?"

He slid closer to her, and she trembled as his leg brushed against hers. She placed one hand on his arm, determined to dismiss all doubts from either of their minds.

"No, I am not my father." Richard took a deep breath, and Alice prayed that he, too, had decided the evening was too precious to lose. "For I love nothing more than to jump on my horse, Duke, and ride off into the countryside, while Father is perfectly content to stay within the city and attend to his business."

"Then look up at the heavens. See how brilliantly the stars shine."

Richard leaned back to gaze upward.

Alice smiled at the sight of his high forehead and fine aquiline nose, slightly flared, profiled against the dark sky, and the way his red hair fell back across his shoulders.

"Alice, listen." He turned to face her. "I am deeply fond of you, which is why I am here now. But you need to assure me there will be no more attempts to disrupt the meat market."

Alice hesitated. She wanted to explain to Richard how the carders and spinners had scarcely enough to eat, and her actions were designed to help them. On the other hand, the way his leg touched hers made her desire him even more.

"No more thievery." She made the promise, although it annoyed her that he made himself superior to her.

"Do you enjoy poetry?" Before Alice could answer, he went on, "Are you familiar with John Donne?"

Alice could not restrain her laughter but saw by the way Richard moved his arm away from hers that she had hurt him. "Forgive me." She patted his arm under the velvet cape. "It's only that our worlds seem so far apart. Would that I had the time or the money to purchase books of poetry."

"Then next time we meet, I shall bring my favorite poems and read them to you!" He took her right hand in his and kissed her palm.

A shiver ran up Alice's arm. "I should like that."

"But I do have something for us to share this very night." From within the folds of his cape, Richard withdrew a small silver flask. "My father's finest Bordeaux wine." He pulled off the top and passed the drink to Alice.

She raised the metal to her lips, and the rich liquid flowed down her gullet and into her stomach, infusing her with a warm glow. Alice had never experienced a taste so smooth and pure. She handed the flask back to Richard and watched him place his mouth where hers had been.

Once he had drunk, he replaced the top and turned to her. "Do you remember the first time you came to my house?"

She nodded. "And the first time you addressed me in the market, and my fellow spinsters were fain to die of curiosity."

"I think we both knew this might happen from the time we first saw each other." Richard stood up and reached one hand out for her.

"You were terrified of me and my birthmark!" Alice took his hand and rose to stand next to him. She became aware again of the faint scent of horse chestnut. "I trust that is no longer true?"

In response, he brought his mouth to hers. Alice tasted again the fine wine and surrendered herself to him, drawn by a force she could not stop as Richard's strong arms tightened around her.

They stopped kissing for a moment, and he brushed his lips across her face. He thrust his tongue into her ear and gently licked, which made a warm ache spread throughout her body.

Gradually, he inched away and rested a hand on her bodice. He cupped one breast and lowered his head to kiss the line where her bodice lay across her bosom. "You have beautiful breasts."

She reached up to trace the firm outline of his jaw with one hand and heard his sharp intake of breath as she reached inside his shirt to caress the soft curls on his chest. His skin was hot beneath her fingertips, and his heart beat with the same frantic rhythm as her own.

His hands moved to outline her face, trace the line down the center of her back, feel the softness around the crease in her buttocks. He moaned as he thrust himself ever so slightly forward.

He lifted his head and sought her lips once again, and their mouths locked together, more urgently this time. Alice wanted only to lose herself in this man.

"Let us move back a little, under the trees." He removed his cape and spread it out on the soft grass beneath a willow tree. As one, they lay down together, enclosed by the lushness of the willow leaves.

He kissed her gently at first but grew more insistent. Her body ached for him as she responded to his kisses. The sprouts of stubble on his chin thrilled her, and she licked around them.

He pulled her to him more roughly and loosened the ties of her bodice with one hand, cast it aside, and caressed her breasts through the linen shift. Gently, he eased her away to unfasten his own doublet. Immediately, they clung to each other again, and her hard nipples rubbed against his warm skin.

"Oh, Alice." His velvety words warmed her neck. "Oh, my love. But wait, I want to see you."

He moved off her and she stood up, proud to reveal herself in this magical place. He untied the bow at the back of her skirt, and she stepped out of it. Her linen shift was her only protection. She pulled it over her head, flung it to the ground, and wrapped her arms around her waist. A light breeze caused the nearby willow leaves to swish back and forth.

"Now it is your turn," she whispered.

In a few seconds, he stood next to her, shirt, boots, stockings, and breeches off. His manhood stood out in readiness, which surprised her, but she looked away to gaze up at Richard, who was taller than her by several inches. His eyes devoured her, the black hair that reached almost to her waist, and the lines of her body, more softly rounded than his. She liked the way her full breasts glowed in the moonshine and how her nipples had grown hard.

In one movement, she lifted up her arms for him, and he carried her over to his cape. Softly, he laid her down, and as he placed himself next to her and smiled, her body was swept by an ocean of heated sensations. She reached out one hand to stroke his firm stomach. He looked so blissfully content.

He moved toward her, caressed her arms, and ran his fingers down the outside of her legs. "You smile as I have never seen you smile before."

Alice realized it was true, for she could not stop herself.

They lay side by side, still aglow with pleasure at the discovery of each other. In wonderment, she reached up for him, stroked the fine line of his jaw, and eased her fingers down his body and onto his belly button. Tension pulsated through her; she thought she could never get enough of him.

When he leaned over to brush his lips against her temple, she reached one hand lower to caress the inside of his thigh. He groaned and slid over to place himself on top of her. His hardness pressed between her legs, and she wanted only to feel him inside her. She opened herself up to receive him and heard him mutter, "Oh, my love." When he entered her, she felt a twinge in her groin, but then the pain was gone. After that, she experienced only pleasure as he moved within her.

She gazed up at the brilliant stars in the darkened sky and the wonder of the moment gripped her.

She wished it to last forever, but his dance grew more insistent, and his hands gripped her arms. "Alice, oh my Alice, oh yes." His body heaved with a great shudder. After a few seconds, he brought his lips to her face with gentle kisses and moved to lie beside her.

Their bodies were damp with sweat, and Alice detected a sweetish scent when she lay one arm across her lover's chest.

"Next time, I promise to go more slowly. I could not help myself, Alice. You have been my dream for so long."

Alice lay back. At this moment, she was sure she could die of love for this man. All she wanted to do was spend the rest of her life with Richard Greenway, their souls conjoined as one.

Later that night, as Alice turned the corner into her dark lane, her body still alive with pleasure, she was surprised to see the dull glow of rushlight inside her home. A moment later, Dorcas emerged and ran toward Alice.

"Alice! Where have you been? You should have been here. Agnes Furze. She is dead. Lewis ran over here to tell you."

Dorcas's voice cracked and caught in her throat. She wiped away tears and sniffed loudly. "According to Lewis's mother, Goody Furze was up and about this morning and looked much better but announced she had decided not to go to church even though it's Whit Sunday. She said not to worry about her, but she needed to rest for a while. When Lewis stopped by several hours later, Agnes's face was very pale."

Dorcas paused to blow her nose. "He saw that one hand stuck out from under the coverlet, and he touched it but drew back because it was so cold. She was dead."

Alice struggled to take in what the girl had told her. She knew Goody Furze had been in poor health, but how could she be dead? "We should go over there to wash and lay out the body and wrap her in her shroud. And perchance we can help in other ways."

"Of course." Dorcas turned to close the door, and the two hastened down their lane and toward Goldsmith Street.

They approached Goody Furze's cottage, where someone stood in the open doorway.

"Stay away!"

Alice and Dorcas took one more step forward.

"I mean it. Stay away. We don't want you here." Lewis's voice boomed out and echoed in the dark. The rushlight behind him outlined his silhouette in front of the small cottage.

"Lewis, you know me. It's Alice. We're here to help you. I know how to prepare a body for burial. Please allow me to enter."

Lewis stepped so close to them that Alice could make out the scar on his face. "You are forbidden to go anywhere near Goody Furze's body. We don't want you here to meddle. Leave us alone with our sorrow."

"But Lewis—"

"Leave at once. You are known as a troublemaker in this city, and now you have caused our dear neighbor to die with that potion you made her drink. You should never have touched her. Go!"

He spoke with the force of a full-grown man though he was but a child.

Alice feared his voice might wake the entire neighborhood. "As you wish. I understand you are in sorrow, as am I. I shall return on the morrow."

She took Dorcas's hand, and the two set out on the short walk home. Neither of them spoke. Dorcas cried soft tears and withdrew her hand to wipe her face.

Alice could not control the thoughts that raced around inside her head. *How dare that boy speak to me like that? It must have been his mother who put words into his mouth. He knows I cared for Agnes. I visited her almost every day for the past few weeks. Does he think me evil because he knows of the market raid?*

The two turned the corner into their lane and stopped simultaneously. The sound of squeaks and hisses came toward them. Just visible in the half-light of the moon, several rats raced past, their long tails thumping on the ground as they ran.

"Ugh! Let us hurry." Alice strode forward.

Within a few moments, they stepped into the Molland home. Dorcas mouthed "Good night" to Alice and lay down on the pallet by the hearth.

Alice joined her but knew she had to come to peace with herself before she could sleep. *I did not cause Agnes to die. I did all I could to help her recover. That's who I am: a healer.*

Goody Luscombe had not visited her for some time, but Alice recalled Luscombe's powerful exhortation to her: "Stay strong for me."

My father would surely give me the same encouragement. This eleven-year-old cannot stop me.

And yet, just as it was with Faith, I was unable to save Agnes. How good are my healing skills? And will the citizens of Exeter hold me responsible for the death of Goody Furze?

CHAPTER THIRTEEN

Exeter, Devon. May 1662.

On a brilliant Tuesday evening toward the end of May, Alice passed under the archway of the North Gate and made her way down the steep slope to the Longbrook. There, she would meet Richard. Her body was already on fire with the thought of his caresses and kisses.

Although it had been nigh on a year since their first tryst, they had met but a few times over the past months. Winter days were short and the nights long, and this year had seen freezing temperatures and ice floes on the Longbrook and the River Exe.

When she reached the end of the path leading to the stream, she recognized Richard's silhouette. Her breath caught in her throat, and she stopped. The sight of his long, sensual fingers splayed out on his leg made the familiar tingle race through her. She walked, then ran, toward him.

He grabbed her and brought his mouth to hers for a deep kiss. A flame passed between them and ignited both of their bodies. They pulled apart for a moment and stared into each other's eyes.

Richard placed one arm around her back, the other under her knees, and picked her up. The sun was intense, but he carried her to the shade of a sturdy beech tree with a huge domed crown and laid her down on the dense carpet of fallen leaves.

Richard unbuttoned his breeches, and Alice helped him push them down. She wanted only to feel her lover inside her, but it happened so fast that she almost laughed out loud.

She lay in his arms for several minutes and breathed in his scent of horse chestnut. "Let us linger a while longer by the water."

They stood up as one, and he swiftly pulled up his breeches. Together they walked to the grassy edge of the Longbrook and sat beside the gray striated boulder that had become their accustomed meeting place.

The warm air embraced them, and the scent of fresh grass assured Alice that spring had truly arrived. Bright sunshine filtered through the leaves of the trees around them and cast long shadows while the brownish waters of the stream flowed before them.

Alice stroked Richard's shoulder-length red hair. "My love, it is wonderful to be with you again. And I must thank you for your gifts to my family." Although their encounters were rare, Richard had arranged for food to be delivered to the Molland home at least once a week: a sack of potatoes, a rump of beef, or a barley loaf.

She ran her fingers along his sleeve. Unlike the blue velvet doublet that he usually wore, this one was silky and smooth, and she relished the touch.

He did not respond to her but instead gazed steadfastly into the burbling waters of the Longbrook.

She needed to bring him back to her. "What is it that you do every day in preparation to take over for your father?"

Richard turned his head, and she trembled as his emerald eyes focused on her. "I know you may well think to envy me." He brushed the evening gnats off his face with a sweep of his long fingers. "But my life is very constrained. I have little freedom to do as I wish."

"Do you want me to feel pity for you?" She pulled away from her lover.

"No, no." Richard brought her hand to his lips. "It is only that you understand how important you are to me, but that you and I cannot be together as often as I would wish. Do you believe me?"

His intense eyes begged for acceptance, and Alice leaned over to cradle him.

The loud, clear phrase of a song thrush trilled behind them. "I believe you. But if you would only speak a little of your thoughts as you awake, the tasks which you must perform. It would help me to know you better."

"My father's factor was my teacher."

"Your father's factor?"

"He is a trader who acts as an agent for my father in the buying and selling of wool products."

A lone mallard drake, resplendent with its green head and yellow beak, lazed in the water before them. For a moment, Alice recalled the duck she had rescued with Jeffrey. *Would I save a stranded bird in the same way if I had been here with Richard, instead of Jeffrey?*

Richard picked up a small stone and flung it directly at the bird. His aim missed, but the drake took off, furiously flapping its long, pointed wings in the air.

I rescued a duck, but Richard would seek to kill this drake.

Alice stared at her lover for a moment but said nothing.

"Master Giles is my teacher's name, a funny old man. He resembles nothing so much as a toad. You know, I have never said that out loud before. You see how you influence me! My instruction began at age seven. He came to our house and taught me how to keep the ledgers, in addition to reading, writing, and Latin grammar. And all the while, I wanted to ride my horse, Duke, out into the country. It is truly not very exciting to be the son of a merchant."

Alice looked down at her hands, the nails cut almost to the quick out of necessity so as not to interfere with the carding. She had watched her best friend, her father, and her sister die. No, her life was not exciting. And she had no free time to indulge in expeditions on horseback.

"And your sister, did she take lessons with you?"

"Christina?" Richard laughed and reached for the small metal flask that lay beside him on the grass. He took a long swig, wiped his mouth with the back of his hand, and passed the drink to Alice. "No, I rarely see her. The business of a merchant is considered men's work."

"It would not be so if there were no man in the household."

Alice raised the proffered flask to her lips and drank slowly to sway her thoughts against an argument with Richard. "I told you before how my mother has instructed me in the art of reading." She replaced the flask on the grass.

"What books has she used to instruct you?"

"Chiefly the Bible. And I find reading marvelous." She arranged her woolen skirt over her knees. "But it's true you seem little interested in the business of your father."

"You know me well enough, Alice!" Richard curled a strand of red hair around his forefinger. Alice realized he often did this when he needed to concentrate. She was unsure whether she liked the habit or found it irksome.

He eased over to her and wrapped one arm firmly around her shoulder. "I think I love to hear the bleating of sheep and the jangle of sheep bells much more than the sound of my quill pen as it notes the week's profits from the serge market. Indeed, our love of this place, away from the confines of the city, is what binds you and me so tightly, is it not?"

"And yet you are obliged to follow in your father's footsteps?"

"My father wants me to accompany him in his business dealings, although he is the one to make all the decisions. For my part, I would far rather read poetry and dream of you than worry about the price of serges or negotiate with the Company of Merchant Adventurers."

Alice stared at him. It was as if he spoke another language.

"This is the guild to which all veritable cloth merchants belong. Through them, the wool of Exeter is carried to many parts of the world."

Alice held her breath, aware of an invisible string that drew Richard from her. It pained her, but she had to speak.

She inched away from him so that his hand was no longer on her shoulder. "Do you see how strange our situation is? The wool of Exeter begins its life in the hands of carders like me. Carding and spinning is hard and tedious work, and we get but pennies for our labors while your father grows rich." *Have I said too much? Will Richard turn away from me?*

She saw her words had not surprised him.

"Alice." He took her left hand and held it tight. "We both know our love would seem impossible to others, but it is real. There are vast differences between our two worlds, and yet together we have found a pure joy. But enough of this." Richard pulled away from her to reach into his cape. "Here." He presented her with a white cloth that contained a small object.

Alice took the gift and unwrapped it to discover a delicate silver necklace from which dangled a tiny heart. What she had taken for a cloth was a linen handkerchief, and one corner was embroidered in blue with the Greenway family crest and the initials *RG*. She gazed down at Richard's initials and the silver heart and willed herself to believe their love for each other was all that mattered.

"Thank you," she whispered and kissed him.

Richard gazed at her and lifted her hair to kiss the back of her neck. "As Herrick says, 'Gather ye rosebuds while ye may, Old Time is still a-flying.' Let us enjoy the moment and savor what we have now."

Richard pulled her to him in a rough embrace, and they held each other tight.

After a few moments, Richard suggested that if Alice sought to see more of his life, she should peek in at one of the gatherings of merchants that took place in the square within sight of the cathedral. "But now let me read you some poetry before we part." To her delight, he shared with her a sonnet by Shakespeare:

Like as the waves make towards the pebbled shore,
So do our minutes hasten to their end,
Each changing place with that which goes before,
In sequent toil all forwards do contend.

The mention of the shore made Alice long to travel to a beach, for she had never set eyes on the sea. Richard promised he would take her soon.

⁂

Three days after her meeting with Richard, on Friday afternoon, Alice squatted down to pluck the small pods from the mustard plant that grew behind the Molland cottage. From them, she extracted the awl-shaped seeds and placed them in a small basket. Her mother was lethargic and drowsy through most of the day, so Alice hoped a decoction of the mustard powder, mixed with cinnamon and dissolved in rose water, would help Catherine quicken her spirits and cleanse her body.

Several neighbors had asked for this mixture as Alice's reputation increased for her ability to both heal and to listen with compassion to those who approached her with their troubles. Yet she heard still Lewis's voice: "You are known as a troublemaker in this city."

At the same time, her mind wandered constantly to Richard—the way he caressed her breasts and gently licked inside her ear. But a moment later, she stopped herself, angry that her lover refused to acknowledge the unjustness of a system that kept her in poverty while his family gained more and more wealth.

With her basket close to full, Alice stepped inside and set it on the low wooden table. She stood under the bunches of herbs that hung from the beams above her and pounded the tiny seeds with a wooden pestle to crush them into a fine powder.

Catherine lay asleep on her bed, and Alice had sent Dorcas out to search for pennyroyal and eyebright.

After several minutes, her arms ached so much that she had to set the pestle down. As she stood still, she became aware of the argument going on inside her head: *He loves me. Almost a year has passed, and his very touch continues to thrill me*, was countered by *Once his father finds out about you, that will be the end of it.* Then came the reply: *No, Richard will never abandon me.*

A loud rap interrupted her turmoil. She opened the front door and was surprised to discover Jeffrey.

"Alice, I cannot stay long."

"What is it? You seem sorrowful. Is it Jaspar?"

He nodded. "I thought you would want to know. He lived longer than I expected; I know you've visited him several times this year. Yesterday he disappeared, wandered off to die alone, as cats do. I am so sorry to bring you this news, dear Alice."

They embraced, and Alice was caught up in images of Jaspar and his adorable white paws. She did not cry, but a numbness gripped her.

"Thank you for your attention to him. You are a good friend."

"And now I must take my leave." Jeffrey turned and left her alone in the doorway.

Alice picked up the pestle and attempted to go back to smashing the seeds, but she found she had little energy. *Did Jaspar suffer before he died? Should I go in search of his body?* She hated to abandon the cat, but knew she likely would not find him, for he might have traveled a mile away in any direction. And what of Jeffrey? Did he somehow know about Richard?

⁂

On the second Thursday in June, a warm drizzle that noon didn't deter people who strolled about the railed-in space known as the Exchange for Merchants, the place close to the cathedral that Richard had suggested Alice observe if she wanted to learn more about his life.

Alice and Susannah stood huddled on the other side of the railings and listened to conversations.

"If only they would let our goods through! These endless battles in the Channel will surely be our death knell."

"And for what purpose? No winner, no loser, except us merchants. Ah, to think that we believed this Charles to be any different!"

Alice stared at the tall-crowned hats with wide brims that were decorated with feathers and ribbons. She also saw low hats with shallow crowns, some festooned with large ostrich plumes. Yet she wanted Susannah to understand that in spite of their fancy clothes, these men could also be wonderful human beings.

"Look, over there!" Alice spoke in as natural a voice as she could muster. "Is he not handsome, with all that red hair and such a gainly manner? This is Richard, the man I have told you about, my lover." She paused. She had never said that word aloud before, and the sound of it made her smile.

Alice watched Susannah peer through the row of silver birch trees to rest her eyes on Sir William Greenway, who sported a tall black hat decorated with gay ribbons, and next to him, Richard Greenway wearing a wide-brimmed hat.

Eager to gauge Susannah's response, Alice stared at her friend and the tiny drops of water on the top of her beige linen coif. Susannah's face revealed nothing.

"This is your Richard? I see he may have a certain charm, Alice, but you cannot possibly suppose that a gentleman of his standing can take you seriously?" Susannah placed her hands on her blue woolen bodice and stared at Alice. "We must leave. Come. Let us walk down to the West Gate."

"The West Gate? Can we not talk here?"

"No. I am most ill at ease." Susannah stepped away, and Alice had no choice but to follow her friend as she moved from the cathedral and turned first down Broadgate and then into Fore Street.

Halfway down the street, beneath a brightly painted signboard advertising fine tobacco, Alice lay one hand on Susannah's arm. A constraint gripped Alice and she had to speak. "What irks you, Susannah?"

Susannah shook her head. "Calm yourself, Alice. I see you are troubled, and I want to show you something at the West Gate. I believe it will help you."

"All right, but let us move quickly." *Why does Susannah not tell me what is on her mind? This is most unlike her.*

The drizzle had ceased, and the air was filled with a fresh, earthy scent as the two young women continued further down Fore Street with its uneven rows of houses built of cob, some pale cream, others of a darker buff color.

As the massive city wall came into sight, the road descended and resembled a quagmire, deep with ruts and sticky with mud. Alice was forced to lift up her skirt and tread carefully to avoid a fall.

She yelled that they should not go further, but Susannah ignored her.

At the end of the street, they turned left into the pure mud of Westgate Street. When they reached the West Gate, Susannah led the way under the crenellated tower that surmounted the narrow passage, then stepped out on the other side of the wall.

"Look, Alice." She pointed to where the River Exe flowed beneath them. The sky had cleared, and Alice saw a cluster of new buildings—barns and sheds and cottages—flanking a stretch of mown grass on which stood row upon row of wooden screens hung with lengths of cloth.

"I have seen all these before." For a second, the long racks appeared to Alice like neatly arranged gallows.

"Then you understand, Alice. Exeter grows rich from the woolen industry. It turns the most money in a week of anything in England. The merchants make a fine fortune from this cloth while we carders and spinners starve."

Susannah raised her voice. "Just last year, you led the rebellion into the market. But today you betray your own kind by your affection for Richard Greenway, whose father is one of those despised merchants."

Alice took a deep breath. Had she been wrong to think she could rely on her friend? "Susannah. You are my dearest friend, which is why I wanted to confide in you. Richard is surely part of the merchant class. But we are in love." The knot in Alice's chest grew tighter.

"You led us spinsters triumphantly up Smythen Street, not many feet from this very spot, and into the market." Susannah's dark eyes beseeched Alice. "It was because of you that we succeeded. What has happened to you? Where is that Alice now?"

"She is yet here!" Alice planted her hands on her hips. "I think you cannot know what I feel, how love transforms everything, how Richard and I are only complete together, how we need each other. I chose to speak to you of Richard because I considered you my friend, but that is no longer true. Clearly, I cannot trust you."

Alice turned her back on Susannah, stepped under the arch of the West Gate, and cursed how the mud sucked at her pattens. First Jeffrey and now Susannah. It was clear there was no one she could trust.

She stomped her way up the steep slope and muttered, "I have no need of friends. I can take care of myself."

CHAPTER FOURTEEN

Exeter, Devon. August 1662.

On a sweltering Tuesday afternoon, Alice, Catherine, and Dorcas labored to prepare the wool for the Wednesday market. The sun beat down relentlessly on their cottage and made the air within thick and heavy.

"I cannot go on." From her hunched position, Catherine placed one hand on the arm of her chair and attempted to pull herself upright. Instead, the effort proved too great for her, and she fell forward across the spinning wheel. Left to its own devices, the wool unraveled onto the dirt floor.

Alice and Dorcas threw down their metal cards and rushed to the other end of the table. They stood on either side of the slumped body and gently lifted Catherine from the wheel.

Alice held her mother while Dorcas filled an earthenware mug from the ewer by the door. She brought the mug to Catherine's bluish lips and forced a little water between them. To Alice's relief, her mother opened her eyes and raised her head.

"It is wickedly hot in here." Alice wiped her mother's brow with her own apron. "And no surprise that you should pass out. But you must rest. We shall carry you to your bed."

Alice and Dorcas stood on either side of Catherine, placed her arms around their shoulders, and lifted her up.

The sight of her mother's droopy eyes on the face that had once seemed so strong made Alice long for the times when she and her mother had explored the woodlands outside the city walls together in search of mugwort, chamomile, and comfrey. Those days were gone.

Alice and Dorcas cradled their precious load as they progressed into the bedroom. They laid Catherine upon her box bed, and Alice eased the freshly laundered sheets around her mother.

"Dorcas, fetch the lavender water." Alice was thankful the two of them had prepared a distilled water from the purple flowers just a few days ago.

"Here." Dorcas returned at once. She carried the fragrant liquid in a wooden dish, along with a strip of white cloth.

"Breathe easy while I apply this," Alice said to her mother. She brought the linen soaked in lavender water to Catherine's temple and nostrils, and a pale pink color rose in her mother's cheeks. Catherine reached one hand to rest against Alice's. Just then, someone banged on the front door.

"Tell whoever is there that I may not be disturbed."

Dorcas left the room. Alice turned her attention back to her mother, who loosened the cotton bonnet from her head. Thin strands of gray hair fell across the pillow.

"It's a servant from the Greenways." Dorcas rushed in. "The one who brings us weekly supplies of food. I have brought him inside, for fear he might be observed."

"Tell him I shall be there presently. And Dorcas, perchance we shall have need of more lavender. You recall where we found it, at Southern Hay?"

Dorcas nodded. "I shall leave at once." She slipped out through the doorway.

Alice looked toward the bed and met Catherine's stern look.

"Be careful." Alice could barely make out her mother's words, so weak was Catherine's voice. "Those gifts of food from Richard Greenway come at a price. You have spoken of him as a good friend, and perchance he is. But his father wields tremendous power in our city."

Alice stepped out of the bedroom, and just inside the front door, she found Walter, Richard's personal servant. His broad grin revealed a chipped front tooth. "My master wants you to meet him tonight at the place you have agreed upon." He wiped the sweat from his brow with his woolen sleeve and broke out into a high-pitched laugh.

"And here's what you should wear." He handed Alice a black cloak.

"I cannot go, for my mother has taken ill. Tell your master it must needs be tomorrow."

Alice took the garment Walter offered her and pushed back her annoyance that Richard had chosen this moment to summon her for their planned visit to the seaside. She forced herself to smile at the boy.

"Go! I must return to my mother." She opened the door, and a merciful breeze of fresh air entered the room.

"I shall inform Master Greenway." Walter turned and his bobbed head disappeared into the muggy air. At the same moment, Alice noticed the bulky shape of her next-door neighbor, the widow Bradshaw, who stood close by in the kennel. She pretended to throw away refuse, but with her wide, beady eyes and round form, she reminded Alice of a squirrel who liked to fuss over every little task.

She paused by the open door and watched her neighbor bustle away. Alice moved back into her home and placed the cloak on the kitchen table. When she stepped into the bedroom, she found her mother in tears and realized she must have overheard the entire conversation with Walter.

Alice leaned over to embrace her mother. "It's all right, Mother. I shall take care."

"What you are doing is dangerous." Catherine's words came out in a quaver between sobs. "You know Thomasina Furze holds you responsible for the death of her mother."

"Thomasina is merely distressed at her mother's death. Dorcas and I tended well to Agnes, but there was nothing more we could do for her."

"Whatever you say, Thomasina shares her opinion of you with anyone who will listen. And now you risk being seen with the Greenway lad."

Alice excused herself to go to the kitchen. The sight of Catherine's tears, for which Alice was responsible, made her ache with sadness. *Is it true, what my mother says? I cannot bear to see her cry like that.*

Later that day, Alice stood before the still waters of the Green Pool. Catherine had slept most of the afternoon while Alice and Dorcas struggled for several hours to complete as much carding as they could. Finally, Dorcas had flung down her cards and declared she could do no more, her arms hurt so much. Alice put down her cards too. The effort of holding her right arm straight to avoid straining her wrist as she drew the right card over the left meant that she had been forced to take short breaks. But eventually, she had to stop.

Alice had taken this opportunity to visit the Green Pool and pick the blackberries she knew her mother liked. She also needed to calm herself before her adventure with Richard the following day.

Just as the fiery sun began its journey below the horizon, Alice lowered the basket full of purplish-black fruit to the ground. She turned to face north, away from the sun, and declared:

Ye mighty powers of air,
I summon, stir, and call you up,
To guard my circle and witness my rite.

She paused for a moment and inhaled deeply to experience the presence of air. Then she moved through the other three directions and invoked in turn fire, water, and earth. With the circle cast, she seated herself cross-legged within the sacred space, lit a red candle, and stared into it. She sought to conjure the image of Richard, as she had done so many times before. But this time was different: Although he appeared swiftly in her head, seated at a long table, he focused his gaze on the table before him. She continued to watch him and knew he wanted to invite her to come sit beside him, yet something restrained him, for he would not raise his eyes to look at her.

What does this mean, that he refuses to look at me? I fear something bad. He has promised to take me to the seaside. Will he keep his promise?

Alice's head pounded with muddled questions she could not answer. She decided she must wait until the morrow, when she could address Richard directly. She banished her circle with the familiar words:

Ye mighty powers of air,
I thank you for attending my rite
And ere you depart to your fair and lovely realms
I bid you hail and farewell.

She repeated the chant for each element and made her way home, but she could not force the image of Richard's bowed head from her mind. What did it mean?

⁂

In the early evening of the next day, Alice proceeded across the Exe Bridge clad in the voluminous black cloak Richard had given her. She had seen the bridge's many arches from far away; now that she walked above those arches as she crossed the river, her body trembled in a fever pitch of anxiety. Although it was the hour of vespers, the sun still burned, and she sweated within her heavy garment. Richard had told her the Seven Stars was on the far bank, next to the bridge, and he would wait for her behind the inn, close by the river.

For a moment, Alice pictured her mother and Dorcas the way she had just left them, seated outside with mugs of ale. Catherine had woken early this morning, her face bright, and announced in a strong voice that she was ready for work. The three women had toiled all morning to complete the spinning for delivery at the market.

Alice had waited until she heard the church bell calling worshippers to evensong to announce that she had an important errand and intended to leave at once. She wondered if her mother and Dorcas spoke of her at this very instant as she continued down the center of the narrow bridge and stared at the points of her black shoes. It was only when she almost walked into the house marking the end of the bridge that she looked up and saw the inn no more than sixty feet before her.

And to the right of it, a dark figure on a bay horse. She slowed her pace, for she desired to take in her lover's form, his slender body, elegant as a poplar tree. She took a deep breath and crossed the muddy field to where he waited. Yet while the sight of him thrilled her, she was still troubled by her vision of Richard at the table and his refusal to acknowledge her.

They did not speak. Richard leaned down from his horse and offered Alice a black-gloved hand.

She pulled her cloak to one side and climbed onto Duke's back. Three hefty men emerged from the alehouse and glanced over in interest but soon turned back to their conversation.

Richard and Alice set off at once. She decided to wait before sharing her concerns with him, and he announced that they would follow the course of the river as it made its way to the sea. "We are headed toward Exmouth, where we shall look out over the English Channel. Our secret destination is no longer secret!" At first he rode the horse at a canter, but he soon pushed Duke to move faster, almost into a gallop.

Alice wrapped her arms around his waist and lay against his woolen cape. The warmth from his back entered her body, and she drew herself into him, seeking to match the rhythm of her breaths with his. She paid scant attention to the irregular fields and clusters of cottages as they flew by.

After what seemed to Alice a very long time, Richard slowed Duke to a trot and reined him in to a stop. The two dismounted, and Alice looked up at the clear sky, a different hue than she had seen before. The pellucid blue infused the countryside with a delicate light.

"The sky is wonderful!"

"It's just our fair county of Devon at her finest for you." Richard secured Duke to a tall oak tree. "I have chosen the eastern end of the beach, a secluded cove where we may be entirely alone and hidden from the eyes of the world."

Richard took Alice's hand and led her down a narrow path between tall hedgerows. After about one hundred feet, they came to a wooden gate. It swung open easily, and they stepped into a wide pasture. To judge by the short grass, Alice imagined sheep grazed here.

Close by her feet, a small stream bubbled along, and beside it grew bright yellow sunflowers, now closing up for the night. She picked a couple and arranged them in the front of her bodice. Their stems came to rest between her breasts, and she liked the touch.

The sea lay at the end of the path that cut across the field. It shimmered in the evening light, its dark waters decorated by the whitecaps of sporadic waves.

"The water! Look how the sunlight seems to make the waves sparkle!"

"And here we will walk along a sandy beach, while further east, the shingle beaches begin, going from Budleigh Salterton onward into Dorset."

Alice scarcely heard him. She stared ahead, and the vast expanse of water seemed to free her from the confines of the Exeter city walls.

With the path wide enough for only one person, she followed behind Richard as they wound their way across the meadow and down to the beach. They continued mostly in silence, for she had no desire to speak, only to feel the warm air and soft ocean breeze reach inside her.

The path widened as they arrived at the golden beach. When Richard stopped, she moved forward to stand beside him, and he rested one hand on her shoulder.

Before her, the vastness and the tremendous powers of the waters perpetually in motion called to her. She looked as far as she could see to where the ocean met the sky. A brilliant orange sun hung just above the horizon and distributed its light over the water. Alice cried tears of joy as she surrendered herself to the magic of the moment.

"Come! To the waters!"

Within moments, they were at the shoreline, pulling off their shoes and venturing into the sea.

"It's colder than the Longbrook!" Alice grasped her skirt with both hands and splashed in the water.

"And it seems to please you!"

The cool waves nipped at Alice's feet as she held still and closed her eyes. She listened to the splash of the whitecaps and took in the pungent scent of seaweed. When she licked her lips, she discovered a salty taste. It was as if she had traveled to another land and become a new, different Alice.

"We should walk along the beach. Come!"

They picked up their shoes and turned away from the setting sun. In a trance, Alice followed Richard along the golden shore, and her feet sank delightfully into the warm sand. At the end of the beach, they scrambled over dark rocks, and tiny crabs scuttled away from them. Alice grabbed Richard's hand for fear she might fall on these slippery stones.

As he led her into a small cove, she turned to see the sun had disappeared below the horizon, but the sea and beach were bathed in a soft glow.

Once they were inside the cove, they flung off their cloaks, laid them one on top of the other, and sat down.

From his breeches pocket, Richard withdrew the silver flask, but Alice touched his hand. "First, you must hear me."

Richard pulled away. "What is it?"

"I have had a vision that makes me question your intentions toward me. Am I a game for you, a toy that amuses you?"

"Why do you ask these questions? I have told you I love you and will always protect you. It matters little that our lives seem so separate, for we both know we belong together. Others can perhaps not understand, but we have each other. That is all that matters."

As he spoke, Alice heard a tremble in Richard's voice. She gazed into his wide green eyes.

"I have brought you here this night as a gift to you, to celebrate our love. Let us not argue but instead enjoy this beautiful beach." He again proffered the silver flask. This time, she took it and drank deeply of the Bordeaux wine. She wasn't sure if she believed all he said, but she decided to push her worries aside.

Once they had both partaken, Alice inched closer to Richard. Their bodies brushed against each other with a feather's touch, but her gaze still focused on the shimmering green-gray sea.

When he placed his arm around her shoulder and squeezed it, Alice looked at him, and his warm mouth met hers, a gentle kiss.

They eased down so that they lay together. They said nothing, but Richard pulled Alice into his arms, and she was lost in his musky scent as he kissed her over and over. Overwhelmed with pleasure, she gave herself back to him.

The pale outline of the waxing moon smiled down at her. Determined to seize this moment and make it hers, she unbuttoned her lover's doublet and the shirt beneath. He pulled off both garments and quickly loosened his breeches. Then he reciprocated her gesture, freeing her from her linen bodice and her long skirt.

They lay back and stared at each other in wonder. Richard's hands rubbed all over her body, at first tenderly but gradually more fiercely, igniting her. The flow of energy moved between them and united them.

Whenever they had lain together before, he had shown her the beauty of giving herself freely, in a gentle and passionate way, as they opened their souls to each other. Now she knew the other side of that force, a fierceness that made her tremble.

In the distance, she heard the soft splash of waves as they hit the shore. "Listen to the rhythm of the magical ocean."

He held her face between his hands and kissed her gently.

The dance of their union made her want to cry out loud for joy. She snuggled up to him and stroked the fuzz of his chest hair. When she reached over to kiss his nipples, he moaned, and she kissed him on the lips before dropping kisses on his neck and along his collarbone. With gentle licks, she used the tip of her tongue to trace the inside of his ear, exactly as she had learned from him.

In response, he pulled her even closer to him and kissed her hard.

She knew he sensed the extreme tension and vibrancy in her body and understood that he could not hold out for long.

"Oh, Alice."

She heard him groan, and within seconds, they had united and moved together. She wanted only to keep him there, their bodies in perfect communion as they held each other.

"Rogue whore! Brazen witch!"

Alice heard the accusations as she turned the corner into her narrow lane. Ahead of her stood the widow Bradshaw, round eyes ablaze, waving her short arms in fury, gesturing at Alice. "Rogue whore! Brazen witch!"

She stood beside another woman, whom Alice did not recognize. "Thou art a base scum'd bitch, a base strumpet! Beggarly whore!"

Alice had sensed eyes watching her return on previous nights but had dismissed her fear and convinced herself that her imagination ran wild. Now she knew absolutely that she had been seen. Worse, she knew that soon, the entire neighborhood would know of her liaison with Richard.

Her heart thumped and "Beggarly whore!" rang inside her head. She hurried forward, anxious to be within the safety of her home.

CHAPTER FIFTEEN

Exeter, Devon. October 1662.

Alice stared at the frothy liquid and knew it had happened, as she'd feared.

This Tuesday in mid-October marked about six weeks since her visit to Exmouth with Richard. She had taken the fern or the pennyroyal every time they had lain together, but for the past several days, she had sensed changes in her body. Tiredness overtook her, and she needed to pass urine frequently.

The malty smell of her breakfast beer brought a sour taste of vomit to her mouth and confirmed what she already suspected: that she was with child by Richard. She pushed the beer aside and reached instead for the jug of water.

A fierce autumn wind caused the front door of the small cottage to rattle ceaselessly, and it made Alice feel all the worse. Rain had lashed down for most of the night, a southwesterly storm blowing in from the Channel. From the grayness of the sky, the storm looked set to last all day.

Alice poured herself a mug of water to wash away the acrid taste, but when she sipped it, her stomach heaved, and she took no more. She looked up to see the eyes of Dorcas and Catherine focused on her.

"I have missed my courses these six weeks. I believe I am with child." *There, I have said it aloud.*

Catherine took Alice's hand in hers. "It's that man, is it not?"

Alice nodded.

"Do we not have a ready supply of pennyroyal, or brake fern, or gladwin root? You know well how to prepare a mixture which will promote your courses."

"No!" Alice surprised herself by her vehemence.

She withdrew her hand from her mother's and went to stand by the hearth. "This is a child conceived in great love, Mother. I cannot willfully cast it aside."

"You may find yourself cast aside in its place." Catherine coughed as the wind drove a cloud of smoke from the hearth across the kitchen. "As you know well."

Dorcas grabbed Alice's mug and took a long swig of beer. "What will happen to us?"

"Nothing will happen to us. I shall speak to Richard."

"Ah, the daughter of a poor spinner will speak to the son of a city merchant." Catherine's distinct voice resonated in spite of the howling wind outside. "Well, perhaps he may bring you to your senses if he is truly as kind and devoted as you say. I am your mother, and I have known for a while what ails you. I have already prepared a special potion. It stands beside my bed."

Alice did not move. Whatever might happen to her, she knew absolutely that she already loved the child within her.

"You must know you are already in danger with your reputation as a troublemaker. The uproar at the market, then Agnes Furze's death, and now a bastard child? Think what you are doing."

"Mother, cease your complaints. Once I speak with Richard, we shall find a way forward together. No need for your help."

Catherine stared at Alice in silence for a few moments. "There is yet another possibility."

"Yes?" Alice suspected she knew what her mother was about to suggest.

"Jeffrey would marry you and take care of you. He has been your friend these many years and holds you very dear. Think of what lies ahead and protect yourself. You are fully sixteen years old, of an age when you should consider your own marriage and family. For I shall not live forever."

Alice walked over to her mother and placed one hand on her shoulder. "I cannot do it, Mother. Jeffrey is like a brother to me, but this is Richard's child."

Catherine's brittle bones trembled beneath her shawl. "You are a willful child, Alice. You should learn to take advice from others."

Alice sent Dorcas to the Greenway residence with a note asking Richard to meet her later that evening at their special rock beside the Longbrook. She had waited a week, choosing to bide her time before speaking to Richard in order to be completely certain of her feelings. She did not allow herself to consider what his response might be.

The wind caused autumn leaves to swirl in the air around her as she made her way down the steep hill. The afternoon rain had made the path slippery, and she trod with special caution to protect the precious life within her. She was conscious of eyes that pierced through the partial darkness, like arrows ready to puncture her, but whenever she turned her head, she could see nothing out of the ordinary. She pulled her cloak more tightly around her shoulders.

At the bottom of the slope, Alice rounded the corner to the Longbrook but stopped at the sight of Richard just a few yards away. She advanced toward him, and her stomach fluttered when he turned to her. She loved his smile so much: how the glow of warmth emanated from his green eyes, creased the little lines around them, and spread across his whole face.

He reached out one hand for her and pulled her close. When he kissed her, she gave herself over to the pleasure of him: the way his tongue moved hungrily around hers and his familiar taste of fine wine. She clung to Richard and sought to persuade herself that she would not speak of her pregnancy, for surely it mattered only that the two of them belonged together.

But she had to speak. She slid out of Richard's arms and moved to sit beside the river, where she invited him to join her. The wind swayed the branches of the oak and willow trees, almost bare now, as Richard walked toward Alice but sat a body's length away.

"I have something I must tell you." Alice rubbed her arms against the chill of the evening. She turned to face the silhouette of her lover.

Richard did not acknowledge her. He continued to stare into the gurgling stream, his shoulders hunched slightly forward.

"I am with child. And am full of wonder. I am certain it is a boy, and already I speak to him." The flutter in her stomach had become so strong that she wrapped her arms around her waist to hold herself steady.

"I was afeared this was your message." Richard spoke in a strained voice that matched the sawing in the trees above him. He grabbed a large stone and sent it crashing into the river.

Perchance I do not know this man at all. This violence is just how he tried to kill that other drake. Who is he?

"But Alice." Richard allowed himself to look in her direction.

The smile that had lit his face was gone, and in its place, the whites of his eyes glowed with a strange luminescence. Her lover had vanished, replaced by some other man whom she did not recognize. The tightness in her chest grew stronger, and she looked away.

"I do not understand," Richard said. He jumped up and took one step back. "I thought, well, that you knew about these womanly things, how to prevent the conception of a child. Surely it is not too late?"

Alice stood up to face him. "It is our child. Does that mean nothing to you?" *What has happened here? He told me he loved me. But I refuse to shed tears before him.*

A nervous twitch crossed Richard's forehead, and his mouth was tight-lipped. "I am sorry for what has happened, but listen to me." He coughed. "Perhaps we have both been foolish, but to my mind, it is most simple."

When he pulled himself up straighter, Alice sensed that he was making a deliberate decision to suppress all trace of his feelings for her and focus only on his rational, ordered thoughts. The grip within her bosom grew tighter and moved up into her throat. She found it hard to breathe.

"You are from a lowly working family, and my father is one of the leading merchants of Exeter." His voice took on the same aloof tone that Father Hobbes used for his sermons.

She sought to look into his eyes, but he scrutinized the patch of earth in front of him as if it held a magical secret. "I have a duty to him, which I must honor. Can you not see, Alice, that whatever we do together must perforce be in secret? It is your duty to rid yourself of this child. I shall not abandon you." It appeared he had completed his speech and had nothing further to say.

Alice stared down at that same piece of ground and watched her fantasy of Richard, herself, and their child slither into the mud and vanish.

"It seems that you have already abandoned me. And you dare to refer to my kin as a lowly working family? You speak so much of family duties, but what of your duty to me and to our child? And what of all the times you declared your love for me? Were they all so that you might have your way with me?"

"Alice! That is most cruel! You know that is untrue."

Alice looked up at him, hopeful for a second that all might be well.

"But my commitment must be to my family."

Alice's chest tightened as a vision came to her mind: the portly figure of Sir William, Richard's father, hovering over them.

Richard's eyes had narrowed into slits, which rendered him a stranger to Alice—a man with the outward appearance of her lover but who was, in all other aspects, unknown to her.

"This is your father, is it not? You lack the strength to stand up to the power of Sir William Greenway."

She sensed Richard bristle in response, but when he said nothing, she knew it was over. Whatever she said would make no difference, for her lover had built a stone wall to separate himself from her and was beyond reach.

"My commitment must be to our child. As yours should be also."

Alice turned and strode off toward the path. She marched over the squelchy mud, her heart and soul on fire, then stopped and looked around. The brilliant half-moon and panoply of stars revealed only a black emptiness in her wake. Richard had vanished, and she was alone with their child.

And she realized that if their love meant so little—a passion that she had thought was profound and intense—then the forces of power and money were all that counted for Richard.

She turned back to her path and pushed herself to march faster and faster up the hill and through the North Gate, each stride thrusting back down within her the need to scream out in fury. Just inside the city walls, she stumbled, tripped over her skirt, and fell into the oozy mud not far from where her father had died. The thought of him and his trust in her, the times she had spoken to him since his death, made her pick herself up and march on. She would find a way to fight back.

Once returned to the safety of her home, she let the torment within her burst forth: Even as her sobs continued, she pounded on her pallet and cursed Richard's name.

Yet the next day, Alice awoke early and knew what she had to do: She would take her case to the church's consistory court, where she might get justice. This she did that very day: She wrote up her complaint against Richard Greenway and delivered it to Father Hobbes, who smiled sadly but assured her he would deliver the document to the Archdeacon, who was in charge of the court.

One week later, Francis Shields, the registrar for the consistory court, paid Alice a visit. He had come straight from the court and still wore his dark robes, a stark contrast to his full head of white hair.

She had been carrying her child for two months, and the urge to urinate and to vomit still overtook her every morning. At least Shields had waited until the afternoon to call on her.

When he told her who he was, she flung down her cards and stood to greet him. "Have you come to arrest me?"

He had a flat, unsmiling mouth and dark eyes. "No. I am here to inform you of the outcome of the case against Richard Greenway that you brought before the church's consistory court, so that you may be the first to hear it."

Her heart hammered against her chest, and she feared it might explode. She forced herself to take longer breaths so as not to harm the child within her.

"Please, tell me everything. Won't you take a seat?"

He shook his head, but dizziness overcame Alice, and she had to sit down.

"I cannot tarry long, so I shall make it brief. Richard Greenway declared in his sworn statement that he never had to do with you and that he has no knowledge of you. He implicated Jeffrey Clepyt as the father of your child."

Alice's mind froze as she stood and pounded her fists on the table. "How can he say such words when he has spoken of his love for me? He lies."

Francis Shields ignored her question, and she slumped back down into her chair.

"John Heron, surrogate for the Archdeacon, had summoned three witnesses to refute your allegations. The first of these, Henry Cornwall, a member of the guild of weavers, entered the room. Greenway stepped out since it is forbidden for a defendant to hear a witness speak on his behalf."

"Another of Sir William's cronies. Why did Heron not call on witnesses who know me?"

"He has the right to call whatever witnesses he chooses."

"But that is completely unfair!"

"Allow me to finish. Cornwall spoke in defense of Richard Greenway, as you might expect. As he finished up, Sir William Greenway burst into the room. He placed himself squarely before the judge, threw down six gold coins, and demanded that Heron declare Richard Greenway not guilty. That is the verdict. And now I must depart."

His tall leather boots resounded on the earthen floor as he marched outside.

Alice stared after him. *How dare these men judge me guilty when they don't even know me? Do I have no rights? What makes the Greenway name so special? I cannot allow one old upper-class man to change the course of my life.*

⁂

The next morning, Alice lay on her straw pallet in the half-gloom when it was no longer night but not yet day. She had been dreaming she was in a cart being driven along a narrow path by a gnome-like man dressed in a brown cloak. On either side of the path rose a high wall composed of sharp, pointed rocks instead of the customary Devon hedgerows. Even worse, the rocks could speak. As she passed, they called out, "Witch! Brazen whore! Cozening bitch!"

The cart rolled faster, but the driver refused to slow down in spite of her pleas. They rounded a corner and were headed for a steep, rocky cliff, down which they would surely fall and die. "Stop!" she screamed, but to no avail. She stood up and hurled herself out of the cart to land on the stone path.

Alice remained on the hard straw and willed her breath to come more slowly. She touched her face and arms to make sure she was not hurt from the fall even though she knew it had been a dream. Was this how her life would be henceforth?

⁂

Once the sun had risen on this cold Wednesday morning, Alice determined she would take the yarn to the market as usual, Richard and his father be damned.

Yet as she entered the market for wool and linen at the New Inn, not far from her home, the spinners slid away at her approach, making sure she heard their exaggerated whispers:

"Whore!"

"Witch!"

"See how she bears an unnatural sign!"

Master Courteney stood with arms folded as she approached him with her basket full of spun wool. "I have no need of yarn today, Alice."

She stopped in front of him. "You owe me four shillings. My family and I have worked hard and need this money." *He knows of the consistory court's decision against me. What will we do if we cannot make a living carding and spinning?*

"I owe you nothing. You should leave now."

She turned and walked away from him. In the past, she had loved to spend time with the other spinners on market day. On this Wednesday, she blinked back tears and hurried straight toward home. *What have I done to my mother and Dorcas? How can we survive?*

As she approached the Molland cottage, she saw someone had scrawled on her front door and made out the word "whore." Once next to it, she smelled the raw stench of horse manure.

Whoever had defaced the door hated her. What would the next attack be? Alice wanted to shed tears but could not. She had dried up inside. She needed to talk to someone, and Susannah lived but a short distance away.

Her friend opened her front door the moment Alice knocked on it and brought her into the kitchen. Alice's thin body trembled, and her teeth chattered as she sat down. She recalled the meeting in this very room when she and her fellow carders and spinners had planned the market raid.

Susannah used a small stick to get a flame from the hearth. She lit a rush candle, sat beside Alice, and waited for her visitor to speak.

"I am sorry that I argued with you. Can you forgive me?"

Susannah did not speak for a moment. Then she touched Alice's left hand. "Of course I forgive you. But tell me, what brings you here this morning?"

"You know about the 'not guilty' verdict. Less than a month ago, Richard Greenway swore his love for me, and now he proclaims to the world that I am nothing but a common whore."

A sudden cramp gripped her right leg, and she rubbed it to ease the pain.

"Listen to me, Alice. It is amazing that you should have had the courage to take your complaint against Richard Greenway to the consistory court. Most women in your situation could not have done this. You should be proud of yourself."

"Thank you. But I lost. And now the city of Exeter turns against me. This morning, Master Courteney refused to pay me for the spun yarn, and I came home to find 'whore' inscribed in horse shit on my cottage."

"Oh, Alice, I am so sorry." Susannah reached out to embrace her friend. "Sir William has had it put about that you are a common prostitute, a witch in league with the devil. He has cast around much money to persuade people to speak ill of you. For he fears dreadfully that you may tarnish the Greenway family reputation."

The idea that she had some power over Sir William Greenway almost made Alice smile. Susannah continued. "But what did you expect? The merchants and the spinners of this city are separated as surely as if there were an iron wall between them."

"I believed in the power of our love, as I told you."

Susannah nodded.

"I must leave Exeter to save Mother and Dorcas and myself and my child. I don't belong here." As Alice spoke these words out loud, she realized she had made her decision.

Susannah reached for Alice's hand. "You are right. I believe your life is in danger if you stay here. You should go away as soon as possible. Do you have relatives who will take you in?"

Alice hesitated. She had been welcomed in Ivycombe all those years ago, but would that still be true now that she was pregnant? "Yes, I think so."

"And if you are concerned about your mother, Dorcas is well able to care for her, and I can also help."

"Thank you." Alice stood up, and the two friends embraced. "I must return home and bid farewell to my family." She spoke with a calmness that belied the turmoil gripping and crushing her innermost soul.

⁂

A pale noonday sun forced its way through gray clouds as Alice set out with her belongings in a burlap bag that hung from her left shoulder. Both her mother and Dorcas cried, but Alice did not.

She passed over the Exe Bridge and glanced at the Seven Stars Inn before she turned left onto Plymouth Road. In two days, she would arrive in Ivycombe.

Alice's mind was numb, and she didn't allow herself to think about the father of her child or how the court had done her wrong. She knew only that she had to get away from Exeter and protect the life that grew within her. Yet she feared that she lacked the courage to raise a child alone. *Can I muster the strength I shall need to face my unknown future?*

BOOK 2

CHAPTER SIXTEEN

Ivycombe, Devon. June 1667.

"Alice!"

The man's shout came from across the meadow. Alice's mind went numb. For almost five years, ever since she had fled Exeter to save her life and the life of her child, she had expected Sir William's men to arrive and announce that they had come to arrest her. She looked down at Tommy. The sun glinted on her son's hair and highlighted the hints of red, the color of his father's hair. Had this man come to take her child away? Did she have time to pick him up and run?

"Alice!" A tall man who wore a floppy hat with a wide brim walked toward her across the meadow. "Goddamn!" He swore as his latchet shoes sank into a boggy patch.

"Who is that man?" Tommy whispered.

Alice put one finger to his mouth. "Shh."

She picked up her son and held his small, sturdy body close.

"Alice! It's me, Jeffrey."

The shortness of breath that had gripped her eased, and her relief at the sight of Jeffrey made her burst into laughter. "What a wonderful surprise!" She set her son down and reached to embrace her old friend. Tears moistened her eyes.

The two pulled apart.

"And this must be the child your mother spoke of?"

"Tommy, this is my good friend Jeffrey. Bid good afternoon to him." Tommy turned and buried his head in his mother's skirt as he twirled a strand of hair between his fingers. Her child had inherited the habit of playing with his hair, exactly as his father used to do.

Jeffrey laughed and fingered the feathery beard that had sprouted on his chin. "Alice! You have a fine young son there."

They sat down on the grass, a few feet apart, and Tommy lay with his head in his mother's lap. His eyelids fluttered and closed.

Alice took deep breaths. "What brings you here from Exeter?" She stared into Jeffrey's clear blue eyes. For a second, she allowed herself to imagine how her life might have been if she had married him. "It must have taken you at least two hours to ride out here from Exeter."

Jeffrey nodded and flung off his hat.

Alice gazed at the man she had not seen for over four years. Aside from the beard and the way his body had filled out, he had hardly changed at all. She felt she had aged a lifetime from working hard on her uncle's sheep farm, living with the constant fear of arrest, and dealing with the hostility of people like Margary Badcombe, the innkeeper's wife. She would not have survived without her son. She also would not have survived without the monthly ritual gatherings under the full moon when she joined her cousin Matthew, his wife, Philippa, their leader, Sybil, and the other moon worshippers in the sacred oak grove.

"You are looking well, Alice. I am here to bring you news of Exeter."

Alice assumed this was news of her mother, but she did not interrupt him.

"The city does well, especially the serge market, and Exeter is considered to be the fifth-largest city in England, excluding London."

"Yet the carders and spinners are still as hungry as church mice."

Jeffrey ignored her comment. "I can tell you a little about London also, where life is not so good. The Great Plague wiped out over seventy thousand souls in the past two years, and last year, a blaze at the King's Bakery ignited a fire, which destroyed much of the city. Meanwhile, although we welcomed King Charles the Second to the throne just a few years ago, his court is now known for its lavish lifestyle, and he himself for his many mistresses."

Alice could only reflect on how little she cared about King Charles and his mistresses. Tommy was sound asleep. She edged her skirt out from under him and stood. "I am sure you have other news to give to me, perhaps of my mother or Dorcas?"

Jeffrey took both of Alice's hands in his. They were rougher and more calloused than she remembered.

"I am sorry to bring you these tidings. Your mother fell asleep last night and never woke up."

"What do you mean? Is she dead?"

"She went peacefully and didn't suffer. Dorcas brought her a posset, and Catherine fell asleep quietly. This morning, she was gone."

Alice pulled her hands away and laid them across her son's back. Her throat thickened so that she could barely breathe. *I didn't even say goodbye to her. She was my best friend, and now she has gone. I should have listened to her more.*

Alice closed her eyes for a moment to conjure up the familiar sight of Catherine seated at the spinning wheel with one foot controlling its movement while she eased the spun yarn through the distaff with her hands. "At least she is no longer in pain. But I must return to Exeter with you and take care of my mother's body."

"No. Sir William Greenway has had it put about that if any citizen spies you within the city walls, they should report it to him and will be handsomely rewarded. You cannot return."

But how can I be sure Mother is dead if I never see her body?

"Dorcas and I will attend to everything. She will be buried in Bartholomew Yard next to your father."

"It seems you have no need of my help." Alice had seen her mother only once since fleeing Exeter, and now it was too late. She could do nothing. She remembered her mother warning her not to commit blasphemy as they lingered beside the Longbrook. Alice had been so proud on that day as she helped her mother heal a sick colt. Much later, on the day of the successful market raid, her mother had greeted her daughter with sorrow and fear in her eyes. With her mother gone, Alice alone held these memories.

She looked down at her child. He was still asleep with his little hands nestled under his chin. Had she sacrificed her mother for the sake of Tommy?

"Are you sure I may not come with you?"

"Trust me, your mother is at rest now, and you made your choice to leave her."

Alice heard the bitterness in his voice and wanted to scream at him that her decision had not been a choice.

"She made me promise to tell you in person when it was her time."

"You are a dear friend, to me and to my mother. Thank you."

"I cannot stay long. I must get back to Exeter." Jeffrey stood. Alice joined him and picked up her son to cuddle him.

Jeffrey grabbed his hat, and the three set out across the field with Tommy still asleep in Alice's arms.

As they crossed the meadow, Alice recounted how she had arrived at Ivycombe after walking from Exeter for two days, wet through from falling into the frigid waters of the River Ivy, only to find her aunt's cottage empty. When Aunt Sarah had returned, she'd welcomed Alice into her home, grateful for her niece's company; her son Matthew had his own family now, and Caleb, her oldest child, worked at a tin mine on Dartmoor and came home only during the weekend.

Alice listened to herself speak these words, but a great weight crushed her inside, and she found it hard to keep up with Jeffrey. Tears blurred her vision. *I have no mother, no father. I am alone. Part of me is dead too.*

Tommy opened his eyes, and she set him down on the grass under the apple trees. *How can I go on without Mother? And my son will never know his grandmother.* Tommy turned from her to walk toward the river as Alice and Jeffrey reached his handsome black horse.

Jeffrey put one arm around her shoulder, and the feel of his touch made her burst into sobs.

"I am so sorry to bring you this news, Alice."

He held her a few moments longer before he mounted his steed and set off at a brisk trot.

Alice wiped her eyes with her fingers and looked around for her son. Tommy stood atop a boulder that was partially submerged in the water, close to the riverbank. He had his back to her and was very still, his golden head bent over to stare at some object in the greenish water that flowed beneath him. She willed herself to move soundlessly across the short grass until she reached her child.

"Ah!" The breath was pulled out of her as her son lunged forward.

He had not fallen but was crouched over to examine more closely whatever so fascinated him. The warm sun vanished, along with the squawk of the crows in the apple trees and the burble of the River Ivy. Alice heard only the blood pounding in her temples as she tiptoed forward. *No, not my son. Don't take my child from me.*

She snatched Tommy's small body and lifted him to her.

"Mummy, what's wrong?" Tommy quizzed her with his transparent blue-green eyes. "Are you crying?"

"Jeffrey came to tell me my mother, your grandmother, died last night. That makes me sad. And I never said goodbye to her."

Tommy brought his lips to her cheek and kissed her. "Sorry, Mummy."

Alice set her son down. "Why don't you show me what you were so interested in?"

He would have stepped back onto the boulder, but Alice held him close. "Look!"

Alice stared at two minnows who chased each other in a tiny underwater pool. She recalled another stream, similar to this one, and the feel of her mother's rough skin against her own palm.

Her mother had been teaching Alice how to tickle trout. She had to be very quiet, lean into the water, slowly work her fingers toward the head of the fish, and tickle its tummy. The fish, her mother explained, would become mesmerized by this, so it would be easy to grab it by the gills and pull it out.

They had feasted on fresh trout for supper that night.

How long ago that seemed, as if she had dreamed it and now woke, only half-remembering what it was she had dreamed.

"Did your friend from Exeter find you? What did he want with you?" Aunt Sarah greeted Alice as she stepped into the farmhouse.

Alice was exhausted. She had carried her son, first on her right side and then on her left when he grew too heavy, as she walked the mile or so back home under the warm sun. The sweat ran down her back, and she was grateful for the cool air within this house with its thatched roof.

"What did he have to tell you?"

Alice placed her son on his pallet, smoothed the woolen dress over his knees, and sank down into the high-backed chair before the gray ashes of the hearth. *Is my mother really dead? I didn't see her die.*

"Mother died last night. She fell asleep and never woke up." Alice pulled off her bonnet and shook her head. Her long black hair reached almost to her waist. She listened to herself speak these words. They didn't make sense.

"Oh, Alice, I'm so sorry." Aunt Sarah leaned over to embrace her niece and then sat in the chair next to her. "My little baby sister." She wiped away tears with the back of her hand.

"We were always together." Sarah grabbed the kerchief from around her neck to blow her nose. "Until your father came along. After that, she wanted only to be with him. Do you know the story?" She blew her nose once more and stuffed the kerchief into her apron.

"I know he came from Plymouth and was proud of the work he did for the Parliamentarians."

"Your father was one of a group of young men who marched from Plymouth to Exeter to join up with Cromwell's army. Ivycombe was just a stop on the way, but Thomas saw your mother up a ladder, picking apples, and he decided to stay a few more days. They were a sight as they threw apples back and forth, chased each other, and fell on the ground together." Her aunt laughed even as her eyes grew moist, and she reached for her handkerchief once more.

"She left with him?" It was hard to picture her parents as young people who frolicked together.

"She did. Our mother warned her not to leave with Thomas—said she didn't like the look of him—but Catherine wouldn't listen. And we didn't see her much after that, as you know."

"And they loved each other!" Alice said. A long-ago memory popped into her head: the time Faith had awoken her in the pitch black one night to listen to the grunts and laughter of their parents' lovemaking. At the time, she had wanted to slap her sister. Now she wanted to hear Faith's soft voice and see the blonde curls that hung in ringlets around her face.

Alice swallowed hard and looked over her shoulder at her son, who was curled up asleep on his pallet. "Tommy will never know his grandmother."

Sarah grasped Alice's hands, forcing her niece to look directly into her gray eyes. They were usually as soft as a dove's feather, but today, they glistened with the tears she had not yet shed. "True," Sarah said, "but Catherine is in a better place now, with God. Her suffering is over. And we are left behind. My tears are selfish, not for my sister—they're for myself."

Alice removed her hands from her aunt's grip and sat back. She hesitated. She loved her aunt, but how could Alice pretend to believe in a God who had robbed her of so many of her dear ones: first Goody Luscombe and then her father, her sister, and her mother?

She stood, walked toward the big oak door, and turned to face Aunt Sarah. "I don't believe in your God." She heard the tremble in her voice. "I wish I did, but I can't. I know what you're going to say, just as Mother did—that it's blasphemy to speak like this—but I cannot lie."

"Oh, you poor thing. I feel so sorry for you. So sorry. And yes, you must keep these thoughts to yourself."

Don't feel sorry for me!

"Can you watch Tommy for me? I have a task I must perform."

Sarah nodded.

Alice shut the front door behind her and set out at a brisk pace, almost a run, in order to block out the muddle in her head. She knew she had to get to the sacred oak grove as fast as possible. She strode over the low stone bridge that crossed the Ivy and headed toward the oak woodland on the other side. It was mid-June, almost the longest day of the year, and the brilliant sun hung high in the sky. All around her, the fields glowed a vibrant green.

"Who was that man I saw with you?" Alice heard a voice from behind and turned to see Margary Badcombe standing on the bridge. "Is he the father of your child?"

Margary smiled but in a strange way, with gleeful eyes and a little rise in the corner of her mouth.

"None of your business!" Alice retorted and continued on her path. Yet even as she spoke, a tremor ran through her. *What does the Badcombe woman want from me? Why does she hate me?*

She walked fast to put these thoughts behind her as she entered the woods. Then she slowed when she arrived at the oak grove where she and her fellow moon worshippers assembled at every full moon, unless the rain was so heavy that the moon was invisible and the passage dangerous.

She pulled off her shoes, tiptoed into the special place, and sank her feet into the soft mush of the oak leaves. She had always liked the mushroom-like shape of the oak tree at the southern end of the grove. Now, she leaned her back against its trunk and slid down to sit beneath its broad canopy.

I must find a way to honor Mother here. But how?

"And how dare you die and leave me alone? Damn!" She flung a buckskin shoe onto the ground and was distracted for a moment as a shiny black stag beetle emerged from under the leaves and hurried away.

Summoned by her voice, a pair of red squirrels emerged on the far side of the open space. They dug into the piles of leaves, quickly discovered what they sought, and scampered out of sight, each carrying an acorn in its mouth.

Acorns! Mother always told me they were magical! They must be left over from last autumn.

Alice reached for the dead leaves, tossed them aside, and discovered a mass of acorns. In no time, she had gathered several handfuls and used them to spell out her mother's name under the oak tree: "Catherine Molland."

Satisfied with her work, she stood before the memorial and called on the four elements to bless her mother.

Ye mighty powers of air,
I summon, stir, and call you up
To bless the life of Catherine Molland
Hail and welcome!

This she repeated for fire, water, and earth.

A rustle of leaves broke the silence. Alice turned to see what creature had caused this noise. She heard laughter and caught sight of someone slipping out of the sacred grove. Alice recognized the intruder by the way her black hair lay in plaits against her back. Margary Badcombe had spied on her. What would this woman do next?

CHAPTER SEVENTEEN

Ivycombe, Devon. July 1667.

Philippa's voice resembled the snapping of a swan's bill. "It's all on account of you."

Alice had hoped that she and her cousin's wife would become friends, but it hadn't happened. She detected a tension in Philippa, something she hid behind her angry words.

"You should never have gone to our sacred gathering place alone during the day. Goody Badcombe is telling the whole village that something ungodly has gone on in our oak grove, that she heard you talk to someone there and is sure you communed with the devil. We will need to find a more distant grove for our monthly moon rituals, if we can even continue."

The two women stood under the canopy of the horse chestnut tree in the graveyard that surrounded St. Michael's church. Above them bloomed the tree's delicate white flowers, which grew pink at their centers.

Philippa's brown eyes scrutinized Alice.

"It's true I visited our sacred grove in the daylight." Alice moved into the shade of the tree to avoid the glare of the bright sun. "My mother had just died, and I needed a place to mourn her. I felt sure I was alone."

"Well, it wasn't enough." Philippa stepped closer to Alice and rested one hand against the scaly bark of the huge tree.

"It wasn't deliberate. And you know how much I value our full moon rituals." *Why can't Philippa understand that I was in shock after Mother's death? Although how could I have been so stupid as to not notice the Badcombe woman had followed me?*

Philippa grabbed Alice's shoulders and held her gaze. "We can surely find another place to come together. But I thought our gatherings were important to you. And yet you keep yourself so aloof. Your reputation as a healer grows even as you hold yourself apart from your own family." She let go of Alice's shoulders and waited for a response.

Philippa's nagging tone made Alice recall those women in Exeter who had shouted "Brazen whore!" and "Witch!" after her. She took a step back from her cousin's wife and almost fell into a hole beneath her feet, the burrow of some animal.

"I am truly sorry I have revealed our secret place. I understand if you and Matthew don't want me at your full moon gatherings any longer. But Sybil, our leader, does trust me and has invited me to her home several times."

Philippa did not respond. She pushed a strand of blonde hair back under her white cap and continued to stare at Alice.

"I love our oak grove." Even as Alice spoke, she knew Philippa would not be convinced.

"But not enough to protect it from curious eyes." Philippa turned away to march through the lych-gate that guarded the churchyard entrance.

Alice watched her leave. *Does Philippa know something about Margary Badcombe that I don't?*

What Philippa had said was true: Alice did hold herself apart from others. Goody Luscombe and her mother had taught her to keep secrets early on, and she wasn't about to share them with Philippa.

She picked up a shiny conker and remembered how the fruit of the horse chestnut tree had given her strength on the long-ago day of Goody Luscombe's execution, when Alice's mother had warned her not to reveal that she was a friend of the accused.

At the thought of Catherine, Alice gulped and let out a long wail. *How can I go on without Mother?*

Startled by a tap on her shoulder, she turned to see Father Hopwood, the vicar of St. Michael's.

"I know you still grieve for your mother, but you must put that aside for now. There's been an accident at the mine. Caleb wants you to come. I think he broke his arm. You must come now. Your skills as a healer are well known."

Alice took a deep breath and pressed her arms against her chest to calm herself. How could she heal someone when she knew only an enormous void inside and felt panic that she would be unable to help Caleb?

"Are you certain he asks for me, not his mother?" Aunt Sarah's oldest son had shown little affection for Alice since her arrival in Ivycombe. He worked all week at the Wheal Jenny tin mine, and even when he returned home at the weekend, he barely spoke to her.

"Yes, it is you he asks for." The priest mopped his brow with a white kerchief, and Alice wondered if he had run all the way from the mine, a good three miles away. He was a heavyset man, and the path to the mine was indistinct and strewn with rocks in places.

Mother never said no to any request for help. I will do this to honor her and hope that she will watch over me.

"Then I shall come at once." Alice had learned from her mother that healers must cast aside any likes or dislikes and simply do what is necessary to hasten the healing process. "Although I must first return home and gather what I need."

She remembered from long ago how Goody Luscombe, white hair tied up in a bun, had applied a paste made from comfrey root to a little girl's broken arm. There had been a brownish liquid, too, and one drop of it had sent the child to sleep. Goody Luscombe had not shared its ingredients with her, but Alice had created her own medicine using a decoction from the bark of the white willow tree.

⁂

Alice soon discovered that Father Hopwood had not walked from the mine. A lad named Michael helped out up there, and it was he who had run down to Ivycombe with the bad news. Caleb had been digging with a pick beneath the River Ivy to divert the waters into a steeper incline so the sediment would run out and leave the tin ore behind. He'd slipped on a rock and fallen onto his left arm. He was in great pain, but no bone stuck out.

Under sunny skies, Alice followed the boy along the narrow footpath. The track wound its way past granite outcrops, brilliant green meadows, and the broad crowns of oak trees.

Michael, a tall, gangly boy who looked to be about fourteen, encouraged her to walk faster but otherwise did not speak, for which Alice was grateful.

She stared down at the contents of her basket, which included boiled brankursine leaves. Just two weeks ago, Matthew's son Henry had fallen from his swing and broken his arm. Alice had assisted her aunt as Sarah used the leaves on the five-year-old, telling Alice they worked to knit broken bones together. But what if Alice were unable to make them work?

I made a mistake. I shouldn't be here. I watched Aunt Sarah set

Henry's forearm, but I have never done it myself. What if I am unable to heal Caleb? Oh, Mother, help me. I cannot do this alone.

⁂

She followed Michael into a tiny stone cottage, grateful for its coolness after the glare of the afternoon sun. She could just make out the shape of her cousin, who lay on a pallet set on a simple platform. His left arm hung down to the ground, and his shirtsleeve had been ripped off to reveal well-defined upper arm muscles. Near the wrist, his arm was a mess of blue and black, but the skin appeared to be intact.

The place smelled of urine. *Has Caleb pissed himself? Is that why he asked for me and not his mother? Did he not want her to see him in this state?*

He groaned as Alice sat on a low stool next to him. Her hands shook when she pulled the small flask of willow bark decoction from her basket. "Here. This will help with the pain. And then I can look at your arm." She forced herself to speak firmly.

Caleb threw the medicine into his mouth and handed back the empty container. Some of the liquid landed in his scraggly mustache, and she reached to wipe it off.

"Just get on with your work." He pushed her hand off his face and groaned. "I'm in pain. Can't you see that?"

Why did he ask me to come? He doesn't seem to want me here.

"Michael, I need your help." Alice was in charge, and Michael acted as her assistant. "Bring me some water to clean the arm."

Beads of sweat appeared on Caleb's forehead, and his face turned an eerie blue when she washed the area around his wrist. She had to work fast.

She said to Michael, "The wooden board you carried up—can you bring it over here?"

She turned back to Caleb. "I feel your pain, cousin. And I'm going to help you." She stroked the top of his head lightly, and this time, he did not object. *Perhaps the willow bark is working.*

Michael handed over the piece of wood. "We must bring the left arm to lie on the board like this." She demonstrated with her outstretched arm, palm up, just as she had seen Aunt Sarah do with her grandson. Michael crouched down next to Alice and did as she directed. Caleb let out a loud scream.

"I'm sorry. Now, can you tell me where it hurts?"

"The wrist. My hand and arm don't seem to be working together."

"Then here's what we must do." Alice was thankful she had seen Aunt Sarah take care of a break just like this. She dug into her basket and pulled out the comfrey paste, the brankursine, and some cloth strips. "Michael, can you lift Caleb's arm at the elbow and hold it there?"

The boy reached forward, and once the arm was held still, Alice gripped Caleb's wrist and prodded his forearm. Caleb grew ever paler and sweat covered his face, but after just a few pushes with two fingers, Alice knew she had found a clean break beneath the ugly colors. She pulled on the wrist to straighten it and was relieved to hear the bone pop back into place.

"Good laud, woman, are you trying to kill me?"

"Michael, get him some water while I bind the wound." Alice placed the large brankursine leaves over the wounded area before wrapping it in the comfrey paste, just as she had seen Goody Luscombe do all those years before. Tears welled up as she covered the paste with layers of cloth strips and fashioned a sling for the wounded arm.

With the dressing completed, she sat back on the stool. She had done it! The color had returned to Caleb's face, and he breathed more easily.

Exhaustion filled her, and the rank smell of sweat surrounded her. She needed to take care of herself.

Two days after Caleb had broken his wrist, the sun dipped toward the horizon as Alice made her way to Sybil Privet's home. The leader of the moon worshippers had sent Rosie, the little girl who helped her out, to invite Alice for a visit at dusk, but Rosie had not said why. Alice was still filled with exhilaration from her success with Caleb's forearm, but she feared Sybil might have some bad news for her.

The first time Alice had visited, she'd discovered, to her delight, that a small stream flowed under Sybil's cottage. Alice had to step over a tiny stone bridge to find the front door. When she opened it and inhaled the sweet, pleasant aroma of gorse bushes burning in the fireplace, she seemed to step into another world.

Sybil had invited Alice into her home on several occasions since then. Each time, the magic of the place drew Alice in; she drank nettle beer, admired Sybil's pet jackdaw, Master Jacko, and listened to the wise woman's stories of her life.

On this evening, Alice wanted to share with Sybil how she had successfully treated Caleb. The old woman was seated in her straight-backed chair beside the hearth with Master Jacko perched on her shoulder. The bird glared at Alice with the pupils of his eyes, but Sybil gestured for Alice to sit on the chair opposite her.

"Here. I have some nettle beer for you." Sybil handed Alice a small mug. "You can drink to your skill in taking care of your cousin."

Alice took a long draw of the sweet, bubbly liquid, and its warmth flowed through her. "I was very nervous—didn't think I could do it—but somehow, the strength and courage came to me."

Sybil sat back, and Master Jacko gave a loud squawk. "You must be wondering why I asked you to visit me this evening."

Alice set her mug on the three-legged stool beside her and looked up at her friend, whose bushy black eyebrows were raised expectantly.

Sybil moved one hand to play with the necklace she always wore: a leather choker strung with a single pearl.

As Alice stared at the jewel, she saw instead the silver heart Richard had given her; she kept it wrapped in his handkerchief, hidden under her pallet. She pushed hard to force the image of the *RG* initials embroidered on one corner of the linen out of her head. "I feel we have a bond, almost as if we were related, and I've learned so much from you."

"I wasn't sure about you when Matthew first brought you to our group all those years ago. But since your return to Ivycombe, you've become an important part of our gatherings."

"No. I have ruined everything. You must have heard: I went alone to our oak grove on the day I learned of my mother's death. I needed a place to be alone, to honor Mother. Margary Badcombe spied on me. Now everyone knows about us and our special place."

"You must learn to always be vigilant for your surroundings and for any strangers close by." Sybil's hazel eyes lit up, belying her stern expression.

"How can I do that?"

"You train yourself to always be aware of your surroundings and of your movements. It's not difficult, but it takes time and continued practice."

"Thank you." It sounded simple, but Alice wondered if she could do this.

Sybil leaned forward and took Alice's hands in hers. "You made a mistake, as we all do at times." The woman's face had lost its fierce look. "Nothing is ruined, but you must take it upon yourself to seek out another oak grove." She sat back and rested her hands in her lap. "I need you to listen well. I am not long for this world."

"What can I do for you? How can I help you?" Alice's heart lurched. She had thought her friend would always be there. She gazed into Sybil's beautiful eyes and swallowed hard to push back her tears. Sybil did not waver in the face of death, and Alice had to show the same strength.

"I am ready to go on to whatever awaits me. I have lived my life to the fullest, and I am not afraid to die. I want you to assure me that you will uphold the traditions of our monthly rituals. Indeed, I believe you might replace me as leader."

Alice's mind went blank. She couldn't imagine that she might take over from Sybil. What would the other moon worshippers think? She stood up and knocked over the stool where she had placed her mug. The remains of the nettle beer formed a small puddle by her feet, which she hastened to mop up, using her apron.

"Are you sure? I am honored by your trust in me but feel I am not worthy."

"No, listen. You are special. I have seen your power to call birds to you, how you are able to heal sick animals and offer comfort to those who seek succor. Your abilities as a healer are earning you a fine reputation in our village, but I believe the power of magic has also touched you. I might say you have a gift for it."

Farmer Fletcher had also used the word "magic" about her when she was just a child, a warning to her mother that Alice could cause trouble.

"I've seen this in you when you call upon the four elements to be present in our circle, how passionate you are." Sybil flung her arms in the air, and Master Jacko cawed and flapped his wings. "Look how you took care of Ursula Wilcox after her tragic miscarriage; you let her stay with her pain for a while when she found life too difficult to be lived. But then you predicted she would give birth to a fine baby girl, and she did."

It was true. Alice had had a clear vision of the young woman with her newborn.

"I have two gifts for you. First, I want you to take the house sign for my cottage. You may find some use for a fine piece of slate." Sybil stood up. "And I have something else for you." From the mantel above the hearth, she removed a wand almost two feet long, carved from an ash branch and tipped at one end with a deer's antler. She handed the precious tool to Alice. "This belonged to my grandmother, and you must use it well."

Alice was astonished and humbled. She took the wand, caressed its smooth texture, and promised to carry forward Sybil's work of honoring the Goddess of the Full Moon. She hoped desperately that she would be able to live up to such a special gift. She also realized that owning this magical gift could bring suspicion upon her.

The day after her visit with Sybil, Alice woke and reached under her pallet to feel the pointy end of her wand. She ran her fingers down the length of her precious gift, and a warm glow filled her. She had decided to keep it a secret, unsure of who to trust with the news of Sybil's gift or what power she had been given with the wand. *What if I can't live up to Sybil's belief in me?*

That morning, she took Tommy to a disused limestone quarry just outside Ivycombe, where she hoped to find the mugwort her aunt was sure grew there. They needed it for young Ethel Ridge, who was heavily pregnant with her first child.

Aunt Sarah had assured Alice that an infusion of mugwort with some other herbs would speed the birth of Ethel's baby and help bring down the afterbirth. This would be the first time Alice had assisted at a childbirth; she feared she would find it hard to watch and might let Aunt Sarah down.

With the sky overcast, Alice hoped it wasn't going to be one of those dreary days where it drizzled and then stopped and then started again. Tommy was not happy to accompany his mother, and Alice had to persuade him with the promise of hot cider when they got back home.

Once they were at the quarry, Alice searched for the plant and Tommy set off to explore the nearby rocks.

"Don't go too far! I need to be able to see you."

At the sound of his mother's voice, he turned and waved, then crouched down to examine a boulder.

Alice walked beside the small stream that flowed through the quarry, the most likely spot to find mugwort. It was an oddly shaped plant with a long stalk and leaves that were big near the ground but diminished in size toward the top of the stalk, where small yellow flowers appeared in the summer. Alice knew the plant well since it had grown profusely in front of Goody Luscombe's cottage. She remembered how she and her mother had gone in search of the plant the day before John Colbert and his men barged into the Molland home. *That was the beginning of the end for Father.* She stopped for a moment and realized the mugwort was right in front of her.

Just as she went to pick it, she heard someone yell, "Watch out!" She looked to her right. A large boulder had dislodged itself from the rock face of the quarry and was tumbling toward Philippa and Tommy.

CHAPTER EIGHTEEN

Ivycombe, Devon. July 1667.

As an enormous boulder descended toward her son, Alice raced to save him, but it was Philippa who pulled Tommy out of the way just as the rock crashed behind him.

The pair took a few more steps and collapsed on the ground just as Alice reached them.

"Tommy!" Alice knelt beside her son and held him tight. His heart pumped fast. "You're alive! I thought you might die!"

The child burst into tears and rubbed his right hand against his knees. "It was Philippa." He could say no more, as the sobbing overtook him.

"She saved your life."

Philippa leaned over and patted Tommy's back. "Any decent human being would do what I did. These limestone quarries can be treacherous with their crumbling rocks."

"Thank you."

A faint smile crossed Philippa's face.

"Tommy," Alice said, "why don't you and I stand up so I can see if you are hurt?" Aside from a few scratches on his arms and legs, she found nothing wrong with her son. Then she addressed Philippa. "How are you?"

Philippa jumped up and shook herself. "Good as new!"

"We go home?" Tommy tugged on his mother's sleeve.

"In a moment, love." Alice's hands shook and her heart raced so fast she could hardly breathe. *Tommy almost died. Philippa saved him. I had Father on my mind, and I neglected my son for a moment.*

"Philippa and I need to speak. First, let's get out of danger's way."

The light rain had ceased, and the three of them moved to sit on the trunk of a fallen ash tree.

Philippa looked directly at Alice. Her eyes had lost their beady look. "Now you know you can trust others."

Alice wondered why Philippa's tone was almost friendly. It was surprising since Philippa always seemed ready to criticize her, especially after the way Philippa had chastised Alice less than a sennight earlier.

Tommy wandered off to examine something on the ground a few feet away.

"What are you doing here?" Alice asked. Her hands shook as she realized how close Tommy had come to dying. "Are your children here too?"

"No," Philippa smiled. "I like to come here alone to sketch."

"You came here to draw?"

"Yes. I can show you, but it's not very good." Philippa stood, walked over to a wooden box, and pulled out a sheet of brownish paper, which she handed to Alice.

"It's a field mouse! You have captured its very long tail and large back feet perfectly."

"I was lucky." Philippa sat beside Alice. "It stayed still for several minutes as it sniffed at something."

"It's wonderful!" Alice handed back the paper. "I am sorry for how I have behaved," she continued. "As you know, my mother died last month, and I wasn't even there for her. I abandoned her and grieve for her every day." She looked up to see how Philippa would react.

"At least you had a mother who loved you, and you loved her." Philippa bit her lower lip and shifted along the log, away from Alice. "You cannot know what it is like to grow up with a father who holds you responsible for his wife's death. My mother died giving birth to me, and for many years, Father let me know he wished it had been me that died and not my mother."

"Oh, Philippa, that's horrible!"

"It took me a long time to stop blaming myself for my mother's death." Philippa choked up.

Alice didn't know what to say. *No wonder Philippa seems strange and often rude. I don't know how I would have survived what she has endured. She must be very strong.*

Alice's heart filled with the realization that she was grateful for the love Mother had shown her. And Father too.

"It was Matthew who saved me. He taught me to believe in myself, comforted me when I spoke of how hard it was to grow up with a father who criticized me constantly. Matthew praised my skills in painting and drawing, which is what brought me here today, and I began to spend more time with him, away from Father."

The two women stood together.

"Thank you for sharing so much with me." Alice extended her arms toward Philippa. As the two women clasped each other tightly, Alice thought how fragile Philippa's small body was.

"Mummy! Look! Mugwort!"

Alice moved toward her son, but Philippa stopped her. "I am sorry if I have used sharp words with you. Now that I have spoken plainly, can you not open yourself? We wanted to welcome you into our lives here in Ivycombe, but you always behave as if you need no help from others. Do join us at the first day of the corn harvest next week. It's hard work, but always a jolly affair."

"Of course! I would love to."

"Mummy! Come on!" Tommy yelled. The three of them dug with their fingers and used a small knife to extract the whole mugwort plant, including the roots.

As they worked, the sun broke through the clouds, and they were able to walk back to Ivycombe under a miraculously bright sky.

Alice thanked Philippa several times for saving Tommy's life and for the openness she had shown. Yet Alice worried because she hadn't spoken to Philippa about the magic wand Sybil had given Alice, nor had she spoken of Sybil's suggestion that Alice might become the leader of the moon worshippers. And she still had to find a replacement for the original sacred grove, a place that Philippa had loved.

Alice stooped to pick up three ears of corn from the ground where the reapers had cast them. Trying to ignore the prickly feel of the grain on her hands, she raised one knee on which to rest the ears and withdrew some strands of corn silk from her apron, just as Philippa had instructed her the day before. These strands she wrapped around the ears to tie them together. Then she threw the bundle onto a pile of sheaves, as these bundles were known.

She laughed out loud and waved to Philippa, who had watched her. "I did it!"

It was a glorious summer's day, the first Tuesday in August and the first day of the corn harvest. Most of the adult population of Ivycombe had come to help out at William Blagdon's estate. He owned the biggest farm in the area, and years of tradition dictated that the harvesting of the year's corn begin here.

All around, Alice heard rasps of the men reaping, interspersed with loud whoops and the laughter of the women who followed well behind, out of the way of the swinging sickles, tying up the ears of corn. She recognized some of the women in front of her: Esther, with a mass of auburn curls framing her small face, who had come to Alice to ask for a love potion to draw Caleb to her, and Christina and Daphne, both of whom worked at the local inn, The Cross Keyes.

When she stood tall, the ache in Alice's lower back and legs grew stronger. But she had to go on. By the time she had secured five bundles, it became easier, and after she had tied another ten, the leg pain was gone.

The laborers had to work fast, for even though the sky was a clear blue with just the occasional cloud, there was always the fear of a sudden summer storm, which could flatten the crop. It became a race: As each woman completed one bundle, she added it to the nearest collection of sheaves and then leapfrogged forward to find the next ears to tie.

Alice stopped for a moment and looked around. *All of us women united. We are powerful together.*

She was determined to keep up with the others and gradually found the physical labor so engrossing that her mind and body became as one, completely focused on the task at hand. She was also mesmerized by the red soil. Aunt Sarah had told her the color was due to the presence of iron oxide in the earth, but today, it appeared bloodred as she had never seen it before.

When a loud gong sounded to signal the end of the day, Alice could barely stand upright, and yet she smiled and laughed. With Philippa and Esther, she joined the crowd that gathered for the traditional feast, and they pushed their way into Farmer Blagdon's lofty barn.

The air inside was refreshingly cool, and the long tables were laden with jugs of cold drinks. Alice poured herself a mugful of hard cider and swallowed it in just two gulps. She grabbed the jug, poured another mugful, and dispatched it immediately before taking a seat next to Philippa.

Reverend Hopwood said grace and carved the first joint of mutton, a large leg.

As the feast began and the chatter grew loud, Alice wondered what Tommy was up to. Just before she left, he had asked her why he didn't have a daddy like other children did. She had informed him that his father lived in Exeter, where he needed to stay for his business, and that had appeared to satisfy her son.

As she spoke, she had understood that she could never forget Richard, and she could also never replace him. And yet she found that when she thought of her lover, a dull ache came into her body, but not the sharp pain she used to experience.

A deep baritone voice sang out the praises of the corn dolly, a symbolic figure fashioned from strands of straw, and interrupted Alice's thoughts. "'Tis the ripening of the corn!" To her surprise, Alice saw that Caleb stood at the piano and held up the corn dolly as he sang.

At the conclusion of the song, he looked toward Alice, seated two tables away. "And I want to give thanks to my cousin Alice, who deftly healed my broken wrist." He displayed his left arm to the group, which burst into spontaneous applause.

Surprised, Alice looked over at Caleb and smiled. She noticed the women seated at the table behind him did not applaud but rather seemed to glare at her.

The day after the corn harvest began, Alice stood before a circular grove of tall oak trees whose rounded crowns reached for the sky. In the middle of the circle lay a flat, oblong stone that was perfect for an altar.

"Yes, this is the place!" When Sybil had passed away a fortnight earlier with Master Jacko still on her shoulder, just as she had predicted, Alice knew it was all the more urgent to discover a place for their small group to continue its monthly rituals and thus honor their leader's memory.

Now she had found it. She was sure Sybil would have approved of this magical spot and hoped that Philippa, too, would agree that Alice had made a fine choice.

She sat down cross-legged at the edge of the circle. It was sunny, but not hot, and she stayed very still as a light breeze ruffled the leaves above her. From close by, she heard the faint babble of water. She fell into a meditation where she was no longer a separate body but just one element of the whole, along with the wind, the sun, the water, and the trees.

When she emerged from her trance-like state, she felt strong, like one of the oak trees that surrounded her. She took slow breaths. Perhaps she could replace Sybil and become the leader of their group. A chill ran through her. *I am a mere child compared to Sybil. Yet it was she who suggested I might take over as leader. So perhaps I must do this.*

If only her mother could be with her. *Would she be afraid for me? But this is real, Mother. I feel I am in touch with a deeper power. But can I take it over? I don't know.*

A wave of grief overcame her and gripped her throat. A few tears escaped her eyes, but she understood she should embrace her sadness.

She decided the moon worshippers should have a simple ceremony to begin their work anew. They would set four candles on the stone, one for each of the four elements, along with the willow wand and the water and salt. The next day, when she explained to Philippa that Sybil had given her the wand, Philippa seemed surprised but did not object.

The ceremony happened two days later, on the full moon. There were only six of them: Alice, Philippa and Matthew, Philippa's friend Esther, and another two women whom Alice knew only by name, Judith and Gwen.

First, Alice used a broom to sweep around the circle. She concentrated on her actions, and just as Sybil had instructed her, a stillness entered Alice with the rhythmic swishing of the broom. The world outside no longer existed.

Next, she set the four candles in their places, each ensconced in a small clay pot so that wax did not drip onto the stone slab. The group watched as she offered the crucible of water for consecration by the Lord and the Lady, poured the salt into it, and sprinkled drops of water around the edge of the circle. Finally, she used one finger to place a drop of water on the forehead of each group member and then on herself.

She had seen Sybil perform these rituals so many times and sought to emulate her actions as precisely as possible.

She used Sybil's wand to cast the circle and chanted, "I call upon the spirits to create a circle of power as a meeting place of love, joy, and truth."

Alice then moved to the first candle, lit it with a taper, and said, "I light this candle in the east, and I invoke the powers of air. Hail and welcome."

She moved to the south, west, and north, lighting the three candles and invoking the powers of fire, water, and earth.

In all the previous rituals, she had been a participant, but today, she was a leader. Her hands trembled, and a tremendous surge of excitement passed through her.

Next, Philippa invited them to meditate on the power of the moon and its four phases: "She waxes, is full, wanes, and then disappears."

With the meditation over, Philippa rose to pass around the mug of small ale. When it came to Alice, she took a sip and looked up at the moon. Energy surged through her body, down her spine, and into her legs and feet. Sybil had explained that a person's physical and magical abilities are at their greatest at the full moon.

Finally, it was Philippa's task to close the ritual. Beginning as Alice had, with the east, she intoned, "I thank you, powers of air, for your presence here, and I bid you hail and farewell." She blew out the candle and repeated the chant for the south, west, and north, and thus the gathering came to an end.

Alice remained behind as her fellow moon worshippers left. She wanted to hold on to her excitement, to the sense that she had moved out of her everyday world and had touched a life force much bigger than herself.

She continued to gaze up at the brilliant moon but was shocked when she found herself transported to Exmouth Beach with a brilliant sun setting over the ever-churning waters. And as Richard's tender touch became fiercer, she cried out for joy.

Alice stood up and shook herself. How dare Richard smash into her thoughts like that? And how could she make sure he never came back?

***

Love of my life, come to me.
My heart burns for thee.
Love, I await your coming.

Esther chanted the love spell, her eyes fixed on the red candle. A golden sunset broke through the overcast sky on this late August evening.

Alice and Esther knelt behind a hedgerow just outside Ivycombe. Alice directed her thoughts to the image of Esther and Caleb and prayed that this magical spell would bring them together. She had used such a spell to invite Richard to come to her, but would it work for Esther?

"It is important that you concentrate on your desire so the energy of your thoughts can reveal itself in the world outside. And be sure to guard those strands of Caleb's hair close to your person." Alice remembered how her cousin had allowed her to pull the comb through his thick hair the morning after harvesting. She had saved a few individual hairs to pass on to Esther.

"And the rose oil?"

"Take it with you, to dab on your wrists." Alice passed Esther the tiny jar. "These are all vital parts of the spell. By the time we next see the moon in its waxing phase, Caleb will feel the power of your love and be drawn to you, I am sure of it. He simply needs some persuasion to see where his true path lies."

Esther rose from the ground.

Alice blew out the stub of the candle in its small copper container and picked it up. She stood up next to Esther. "And do not speak of this spell to a living soul."

They started out in silence on the path toward Ivycombe, but Esther stopped and turned to Alice when they approached the stone bridge. "Oh, thank you. I do believe this spell will work! But tell me, dear Alice, why do you not work this charm for yourself? Are you not lonely for a man?"

Alice paused. For a moment, the river grew silent, and in the gathering darkness, she could just make out a skein of geese flying over distant treetops. "No. I have Tommy, and that is all I need."

"But surely, that is not the same—and besides, you are a comely woman."

"Truly, I am kept well busy with my child, my uncle's sheep, and those who come to me for help. And I do not wish to tic myself to any man." In the almost five years since she had made her way from Exeter to Ivycombe, she had lain with only one man, a handsome peddler passing through the village.

Paul Baker had appeared in The Cross Keyes just a few months ago after a day of selling the wares he carried in giant baskets strapped to a donkey: brightly colored cloths, metal combs of all sizes, sharp knives, a variety of haberdashery items, and even some pots and pans.

He was tall with a bushy beard and hair almost as black as Alice's. As he'd approached Alice at the shiny wooden bar, ale in hand, and sat beside her, he had remarked that they must have some handsome distant relative in common. She immediately warmed to his brilliant smile and flirtatious voice as her cheeks flushed. She realized she missed physical intimacy with a man and wondered what it would be like to lie with him.

It had been a beautiful spring eve, and after a while, she suggested they step outside. She led him to the other side of the tall hedgerows that surrounded her uncle's farm, and when he kissed her, a wave of warmth had moved through her body. She returned his kiss and pushed her body against his, feeling his firm manhood between her legs.

It hadn't taken long before they lay down together on the rough grass and he pulled down his breeches, lifted her skirt, and thrust himself inside her. His heat had filled her, and she'd known the explosion of great relief at a physical need being met, although it bore no resemblance to the passion she had known with Richard.

The two had continued to take much pleasure in each other's bodies, but the next morning, she was glad of it when Paul left, for she had no intention of ever coming to depend on a man again.

Esther's voice brought Alice back to the present. "Perchance it would be better for you if you had a man to protect you. And take care not to spend too much time with Margary Badcombe and her friend Lucy Harbuckle. Perhaps no one has told you, but those two were the ones who accused Tabitha Smith of witchcraft a few years back. She wished the pox on Josias Wall and his wife, Charity, when they did not provide her with bread. The two fell ill and died a few moons later, and Margary and Lucy put it about that it was Tabitha who had killed them."

"What happened next?"

"Father Littlejohn, the Puritan minister who was here then, ordered that Tabitha's ankles and wrists be bound and that she be thrown into the river. If she had come up, he would have declared she had been rejected by the water, a symbol of holy baptism, and so must be a witch. And he would have had her hanged. But she didn't. She sank like a stone, and eventually, they brought her up and declared her innocent. Much good that did her. She was dead."

Alice could barely breathe, as though someone had punched her in the gut. "Did no one think to stop this obscenity?"

"Matthew tried to, but his mother cautioned him to be silent."

"And Margary and Lucy had no remorse for their words?"

Now it made sense that Philippa had been so overwrought at the notion that Margary had spied on Alice.

The warm, stuffy smell of wood smoke, wet wool, and mutton stew greeted Alice when she returned home.

Her uncle dozed by the fireplace. His sinewy arms rested atop the arms of the big chair and his head leaned to one side, almost against his shoulder.

Alice closed the door, and the sound made Uncle Henry sit up.

In the adjacent bedroom, Aunt Sarah and Tommy slept side by side on straw pallets.

"Uncle Henry, there is something I would ask you."

"Ask away." Henry leaned back in his chair once more.

Alice began slowly. She recounted to her uncle how Caleb had spoken to her and let her know she was an unwelcome guest when she first arrived in Ivycombe. "Why did he despise me so for having a child out of wedlock? Of what import could it be to him?" Her question hung in the air, and the only sound in the room was the crackle of the fire.

"The answer is simple. Your cousin was often teased as a child, for he was born but two months after his mother and I were married. He never grew accustomed to the jibes, and it seems he still bears a grudge, which he unfortunately decided to take out against you. I am sorry that he spoke so to you."

"But he has changed. He even thanked me in front of the crowd gathered for the harvesting of the corn for how I healed his arm." Alice relived that moment, and a burst of happiness filled her.

"I am glad to hear that. But you should know your son has been asking all day about his daddy: who he is and why he is not here with the two of you. I put him off as best I could, but you must answer him, Alice. He deserves to know the truth."

CHAPTER NINETEEN

Ivycombe, Devon. May 1668.

Alice's hands shook. Hot sweat ran down her back as her fingers reached inside the soft flesh of Mabel Cook's birth passage and touched the edge of the door to her womb, not yet open.

Alice had helped birth four babies in Ivycombe. She had been so proud when Aunt Sarah used a decoction of the mugwort Alice had picked to help Ethel Ridge deliver her baby boy. And relieved when Dora Smith gave birth after almost a full day in labor.

The miracle of new life thrilled her, but she had always been the assistant to her aunt. On this warm Friday at the end of May, she was in charge since Aunt Sarah lay ill in her own bed. Alice withdrew her hand and heard Sarah's voice in her head: "Make Mabel get off the mattress and walk."

Alice stood. "Mabel, I think you have an hour or two to go still, and it would help if you could stand and move around, encourage your baby to make his appearance."

The young woman sat up and emitted a loud groan. Her blonde hair was plastered to her head and shoulders, and her face shone.

"Annie, can you help your sister over here?"

The sixteen-year-old grinned as she took her place beside Alice, and the two of them lifted Mabel off the straw-filled mattress. Alice inhaled a strong odor of garlic. Mabel must have taken this to ward off any evil spirits, and it mixed oddly with the acrid smell of Mabel's sweat.

The small room was hot and dim with the shutters closed, forcing Alice to take short breaths. She and Annie stood on either side of Mabel and walked her around the bed, first toward the right several times and then to the left. After some time, Mabel shrieked and declared she could no longer walk. She crumpled to the floor, but when Alice and Annie raised her up and sought to help her back to her bed, she resisted.

"No, no. Let me stay here. It feels better to stand." She grabbed the edge of a table and leaned against it before she was taken over by another strong surge.

"The pains are getting closer. Your time is almost here." Alice hoped her voice had the right blend of authority and compassion. "But can you not let us help you to lie down?"

Mabel's hands were clamped onto the table, and when Alice tried to lift them, she could not. "You are very strong!"

A smile crept across Mabel's face before she moaned as another surge came. Annie leaned over to pat the top of her sister's head.

What am I supposed to do now? She should be on her back, but I can't get her to move.

"Let's see if all that walking did the job." Alice knelt down, sat back on her legs, and gently inserted her fingers inside of Mabel once more. This time, the womb was wide open, and Alice trembled with joy when she touched the top of a tiny wet head. "Remember how we did those breathing exercises? I want you to take those deep breaths, just as you practiced. Don't push yet. Just breathe, nice and slow."

"Could you say a prayer for me?" Mabel's voice came out in a hoarse whisper.

"Of course!" Alice sought to recall the words Sarah used. "O merciful God, look down and protect Mabel as she brings new life into the world. Lighten her infirmity in the time of travail and grant her fortitude and strength for giving birth. Blessed be."

Annie stared at Alice but said nothing.

"I can't do this anymore! The pain is too much!"

"Keep going, Mabel. This is nature's way of telling you not to push too hard but to let your birth canal expand of its own accord to make room for your baby." These were the exact words Aunt Sarah had spoken when Alice was in labor. Tommy was five years old now, but Alice still recalled vividly how she had endured the worst physical pain of her life when she gave birth to him.

"We're almost there!" Alice turned to Annie. "Get that bowl of hot water from Roger. And tell him he's about to be a father."

Annie scuttled out of the room and returned immediately with a large wooden bowl filled almost to the brim. She set it down beside Alice.

As Mabel took deep breaths, Alice sensed the slippery head making its way out. "Start pushing, but not too hard."

Mabel complied, yet Alice could feel the baby struggling. For some reason, it was unable to move any further down the birth canal.

"Push a little more." *What if the baby gets stuck partway and I can't get it out?* And this time, there was no friendly advice from Aunt Sarah, just silence. The baby was motionless, and Alice wasn't sure if she could remain on her knees on the hard floor much longer.

"Now you can push harder. Your baby needs your help." And then the tiny body fell into her hands.

"You have a beautiful baby girl!"

Alice almost cried as she brought Mabel's babe into the warm water and washed off the blood and the whitish fluid. Next, she got to work with the sphagnum moss. She remembered how her aunt had used it on Ethel Ridge's baby. At the time, Alice had no idea what it was, but she had since learned that the plant was invaluable at childbirth.

She grabbed a handful of the light, dry substance and rubbed it all over the baby, who gurgled when Alice placed her on a woolen cloth. She summoned Annie to kneel beside her and hold the newborn. Mabel still leaned against the table as Alice grabbed the long scissors and a piece of thread, and in no time, the navel cord was cut and sewn up. This seemed to bring on Mabel's afterbirth, and Alice wrapped it up and put it aside.

When Annie stood and showed her sister the baby, it burst into loud crying, which brought the father into the room. He gaped in silence at his first child, then embraced his wife and lifted her onto the mattress.

Next, it was Alice's turn to move. She stood up slowly, for her knees and back ached so, took the newborn from Annie, and placed it in Mabel's arms. She needed the sphagnum moss again, this time to clean out Mabel's birth passage, and this Alice did as gently as she could while assuring the new mother that it would not take long.

But she didn't need to be concerned. Entranced by the miracle of life he had helped produce, Roger stroked his wife's cheek and then fingered the baby's tiny hands. He and Mabel paid no attention to Alice.

Alice motioned to Annie, and they left the airless room. When they stepped outside into a bright, sunny day, Annie turned to Alice. "Why did you add 'Blessed be' to the Christian prayer?"

"It's just an old saying that your grandparents and their grandparents used to bring good luck. And I think it worked."

"But what about that strange mark I saw on your left hand?"

"It's a birthmark. Many people have them." Alice smiled and reached to hug Annie, but the girl turned and walked away down the path that led to St. Michael's church.

"When will I see my daddy?"

Two days after Mabel gave birth, Tommy and Alice stood next to the physic garden that Alice had taken over from her aunt, although the well-laid-out rows of parsley, eyebright, pennyroyal, chamomile, and dozens of other plants, divided by carefully placed stones, looked to have been in place long before Sarah's time. Tommy had declared he had no interest in the various plants his mother nurtured there but instead wanted to grow food they could eat. The two dug into the hard ground as they prepared to plant carrot seeds.

"I want to see my daddy!" Tommy flung his trowel down next to the small hole he had dug. "Henry and Stephen have Uncle Matthew for a daddy. Why don't I have a daddy?" He planted his hands firmly on his waist and glared at his mother.

Alice set her trowel on the ground. Her son had asked her this question several times before, but she had always been able to put him off. Today, his tone demanded an answer.

Over the past year, the villagers of Ivycombe had come to her with their ailments. Alice was happy to offer her advice: decoction of dandelion as a sleep aid, eglantine to stop defluxions of the stomach, nettle beer to calm troubled nerves.

They also shared other problems with her. Alice had listened when Martha Sowden confided that she had never forgiven herself after her child fell into the fire and died. Ruby Hemer spoke of how she worried about her son. The two had argued, and he had left Ivycombe, swearing to never return.

But now she was the one who needed help.

"You do have a daddy. Everyone has a daddy." She sat down on the red earth and tried to pull Tommy to her side, but he resisted.

"So, where is he? Doesn't he want to see me?"

"Your father and I were deeply in love. He even gave me a silver necklace, which I still have."

Tommy plopped his small body on the ground and pushed his fingernails into his palms.

"But your grandfather, your father's father, didn't like me, and I had to leave my home in Exeter before you were born."

"You lied to me! You said my daddy had to stay in Exeter for his work, but I would see him one day. I hate you."

Tommy's transparent blue-green eyes were moist and his mouth drawn down. Alice desperately wanted to pull him to her and tell him everything would be all right, but she knew that would be a lie. Even if he was only five, Tommy had to face the truth about his father on his own.

"I wanted to protect you. And your daddy does live in Exeter, where his business keeps him." Alice realized she had been forced to keep secrets all her life, and she didn't want to pass that burden on to her son. She would answer all his questions truthfully.

The two sat in silence, and Alice watched the tears pool in her son's reddened eyes.

"Tommy, none of this is your fault. Your father would love you if he could see you. It's all his father's fault. But I love you, and Auntie Sarah and Uncle Henry love you. This is our home. We are happy here."

Then she did reach over and embrace Tommy, who cried and declared that one day, he would go to Exeter and find his father.

⁂

That night, Richard haunted Alice's dreams. She relived her first visit to the Greenway home, where Richard had led her mother and herself up the wide staircase and into Florence Greenway's bedroom. She saw again the four-poster bed encased in gold damask curtains. When she stepped onto the rug that lay beside the bed, with its patterns of vines and lions, the lions snarled and snapped at her. Catherine didn't seem to notice, but when Alice attempted to run away, she could not move, and Richard watched her in silence. She woke up in tears.

⁂

On the last Tuesday in October, Uncle Henry suggested that Matthew could use an extra pair of hands to prepare his sheep for the Martinmas market, which took place every year on the eleventh of November. Alice was delighted. Nowadays, her cousin was so busy with his farm that she only saw him at their monthly moon gatherings.

Over the past year, the group had continued to celebrate the full moon at the grove of oak trees chosen by Alice, save when a Devon rainstorm made it impossible. They honored Sybil's memory by enacting the rituals they had learned from her, but Alice introduced some new elements. She had discovered through meditation that she could go deep inside herself and feel the essential power of the natural world. And a strength always filled her when she emerged from this state. Since then, Alice had led the group in silent contemplation for several minutes to open each moon ritual.

On this morning, she set out with Tommy to walk to the outskirts of Ivycombe, where Matthew and Philippa had their sheep farm. Tommy would spend the day with their children, Henry and Stephen, and Alice would work with Matthew.

It was a cool morning; the sky was a solid gray, and there was no sign of the sun. They walked across a lush green meadow, avoiding the bumps created by voles and other rodents, to reach a small tributary of the River Ivy, which led them directly to the farm. Around them, the trees were almost bare, their dark shapes outlined against the sky, and the air was strangely quiet. Alice missed the loud calls of the brightly plumaged chaffinches and the noisy chirp of the shiny black starlings, now departed for the winter. Tommy sang to himself as they walked beside the stream and followed a solitary swan. His golden blond hair was turning a darker reddish-brown, closer to his father's color. While she was in the village last week, Aunt Sarah had overheard that Richard was married to the daughter of a wealthy banker, and they had two children. Alice's heart had stopped for a second when Aunt Sarah told her, and she had listened to the thoughts that refused to leave her head. *It's Sir William's doing again. Richard obeys his father's commands. The family of a wealthy banker should form an alliance with a rich merchant's family.*

The news of Richard occupied her mind for a few days, but she told herself she was responsible for Tommy and needed no other man in her life. She had her freedom and would never again suffer as she had for Richard. Alice wanted only to become the best healer in Devon and create a community of healers.

They drew close to the farm. Although Alice was thrilled to spend time with Matthew, she was less excited about working so closely with the sheep. She had helped clean rams when she visited Ivycombe after her father died and had found it hard to get them to keep still long enough for her to do anything to them.

Matthew embraced Alice when she walked into the big barn and led her over to a hayrack where three Dartmoor rams were tied up. He handed Alice a damp cloth and a small wire brush and told her it was their job to prepare the sheep for market.

She would clean their legs and faces, and then he would use the hand shears to clip under the belly of each animal and get rid of any unsightly wool.

Alice approached her first white-faced sheep. The creature *baaed* at her and burped, which made her laugh out loud. Maybe this wouldn't be so bad after all. She grabbed its jaw in one hand, and with the other, she wiped its face. At first, the animal struggled to get away from her, but it soon relaxed, seeming to like getting so much attention. Once she had finished her cleaning job, Matthew stepped in with the shears and she moved to the next sheep.

One by one, Matthew's shepherd brought in the rams, tied them up, proceeded to untie the cleaned-up animals, and led them away.

They continued their work for over an hour, when Matthew suggested they take a short break. Alice threw herself down onto a pile of hay.

Matthew joined her. "Thank you for your help today. You are looking well. You and Tommy must stay and sup with us. Philippa would like that."

"Thank you."

"I'm so happy you two have become good friends."

Yet there was something about Matthew's tone that worried Alice. He had seemed to force the words out against his will. "What is it?" she asked.

His soft gray eyes were focused on her, but he bit on his lower lip. She settled deeper into the hay and waited for his response.

"Alice, I asked you here today because I needed to talk to you in private, to tell you what they are saying about you."

What they are saying about you. The words echoed in her head, and she was swept by the memory of her mother's words: "They say Goody Luscombe has caused the harvest to wither and die."

"You know I only want to protect you. But Mabel's sister, Annie, has put it about that you spoke heathen words over Mabel at the birth of her child."

"I simply added the old saying 'Blessed be' to a Christian prayer that I learned from your mother. Is there more?"

Matthew pulled back and sat up straight. "Yes. You have surely made an enemy of Margary Badcombe. She speaks ill of you often: that she heard you commune with the devil several times in the oak grove, and you have cast spells over the people of Ivycombe to make them come to you and reveal their innermost secrets. Then Lucy Harbuckle chimes in and says she's heard you talk to the plants in your physic garden. Is that true?"

"Not talking, but singing. I sing when I work in the garden because it gives me so much pleasure." Although she sought to dismiss Matthew's concern, Alice recalled Esther's advice to stay away from these two women, whose accusations of witchcraft had caused the death of a young woman.

"Well, Lucy thinks you are concocting some magic with your plants. But that's not the point, dear Alice." He grabbed her right hand, forced her to look at him. "Ivycombe is a small place, and if people suspect you have power they don't understand, you may not be safe. You must take care."

For two days after Alice's visit to the farm, a windstorm sent pelting rain onto anyone who ventured out. Usually, she loved the rain. She and Tommy would skip, dance, and jump in the many puddles that appeared. They both loved to climb to the top of the big oak tree in front of the farmhouse and open their mouths to catch the raindrops.

But this storm was different. The skies were dark, even at noon, and the wind shrieked and blew so fiercely that Alice was afraid to venture out. Inside, the wooden shutters rattled interminably, and the rain lashed against the walls of the farmhouse. When a flash of lightning lit up the skies and the crash of thunder rent the air, Tommy and Alice huddled together by the hearth.

During this time, Alice did not visit her physic garden at all. Finally, on the third day, she awoke to a brilliant sunny day with just a few clouds in sight. She skipped and ran the short distance to her special garden but stopped close to the entrance. Something was wrong. Instead of her garden's usual orderly arrangement, with each row of plants separated from the next by carefully placed stones, Alice saw chaos. All her medicinal herbs had been pulled from the earth and lay like tiny orphans on the ground. The stones, too, had been smashed up. In the middle of the garden, someone had set a large spade.

This place was her child, and it had been ripped from her. She knelt before the remnants of her physic garden and wept. Who could hate her so much as to destroy her precious plants?

CHAPTER TWENTY

Ivycombe, Devon. October 1669.

"Caleb, is it not time you were wed?" The family had just returned from the Holy Communion service on this first Sunday in October and were seated at the breakfast table when Aunt Sarah posed this question. Alice held her breath and waited for the response from her cousin, who had spent many spring and summer weekends helping Alice recreate her physic garden.

"Mother, you know Esther and I take much pleasure in each other's company."

He blushed a deep red, and Alice was overcome with a wave of happiness.

"But I am a miner. What can I offer her?"

Aunt Sarah stood and walked over to her eldest son. "You can offer her your heart and your promise to always take care of her. I have seen how you have grown warmer, blessed by the love of a good woman. Together, you can determine where you might live, whether up on the moors or here in our village, but these are small matters. It is Sunday. She will be home with her family. Why not go to her father now and ask for her hand?"

Caleb waited a fortnight to follow his mother's advice.

As Esther accepted Caleb's proposal of marriage, she suggested they might have a handfasting instead of a church wedding. To her surprise, Caleb agreed, and they decided to perform this rite in the oak grove close to Ivycombe, where the full moon gatherings had once been held. They settled on the first Saturday in November at sunset and asked Alice to officiate their ceremony.

On the appointed day, Alice, Matthew, and Philippa arrived early at the oak grove. The trees raised bare branches toward the sky, and coppery brown leaves lay strewn across the ground.

Alice had not returned to this place since the day she'd learned of her mother's death, over two years ago. She stepped over to the spot where she had spelled out Catherine's name in acorns. At once she found it hard to breathe. She was alone, and she had no witness to what she and her mother had shared.

"Alice! Stop daydreaming! You have a job to do!" Matthew's voice broke into her sadness. She grabbed her broom and swept away the fallen leaves to create a circle.

Matthew found an enormous log, which he and Philippa dragged to the middle of the circle. On it, they placed three candles: one large white one and two more slender candles, already lit, one on either side.

Just as they finished, Esther and Caleb entered the grove, followed by their families and a small group of people from Ivycombe who were curious to watch the ceremony. Handfasting had been popular when there was no priest in the village to perform marriages, but ever since Father Hopwood had arrived a few years ago, he had discouraged couples from performing this ancient custom.

At Esther's request, Alice was to be the one in charge, and now she stood before the couple in the pink glow of the sun as it set behind her. She wore a white robe and had woven a simple wreath of daisies to adorn her long black hair. She smiled at the sight of the petite Esther, resplendent in a fine red dress with a wreath of colorful poppies and harebells in her auburn hair. Beside her, Caleb wore dark breeches and a matching waistcoat.

"Esther and Caleb, you have chosen the ancient rite of handfasting, a rite to show the world that it is of your own free will that you choose to marry. Do you agree?"

"We do."

The three of them had sat down with Martha Sowden a week earlier to devise the exact wording of this ceremony. Goody Sowden had performed many such rituals as a young woman, long before Father Hopwood became the vicar of St. Michael's.

"Know that within this circle, you are stating your intent to hold fast to each other in the sanctity of marriage and that you are declaring this intent before your neighbors gathered here as witnesses. Please take a candle."

The two stepped forward together. Each of them grasped a lit taper and brought its flame to the big central candle.

"By lighting this candle together, you manifest your belief that you are stronger when united."

With the big candle lit, the two blew out their smaller tapers and placed them on the ground.

A light breeze rustled the oak leaves, and Alice heard the insistent *whoo* notes of a long-eared owl. The circle held within it a deep silence.

"Esther and Caleb, please look into each other's eyes." Just as they had practiced, the two turned to face each other and clasped their right hands.

Alice looked to her notes again.

"Esther, will you share in Caleb's pain, in Caleb's laughter, his burdens, and his dreams for the rest of your life?"

"I shall."

"Caleb, will you share in Esther's pain, in Esther's laughter, her burdens, and her dreams for the rest of your life?"

"I shall." Caleb's voice echoed in the enclosed area.

At this prompt, Philippa walked over with several brightly colored ribbons twisted into a braid that she used to bind the couple's right hands.

"And so the binding is made. Esther and Caleb, just as your hands are bound together today, so your hearts and bodies are joined together in love. May your hands be blessed this day, and may they always hold each other."

With the ceremony complete, Caleb bent toward Esther to kiss her when the loud voice of Father Hopwood shattered the magic of the moment.

"What is going on here? A handfasting? This is a heathen practice." He marched over to where Esther and Caleb stood. "A true marriage takes place in church, in the presence of God. You act against God's wishes."

Although he stood next to the newly handfasted couple, the minister stared at Alice, his eyes filled with fiery warning.

Alice did not look away, for she would not let Father Hopwood intimidate her. Yet an unwanted shiver ran down her spine as she watched him turn and stride off, his black cassock flapping behind him.

She glanced toward Esther and Caleb, right hands still tied together. How dare Father Hopwood attempt to destroy the beautiful union of two of his parishioners? Surely, she could make him understand that a handfasting was just as binding as a church wedding.

On a bitterly cold December afternoon, the first Saturday in the month, Alice made her way to the parsonage, just behind St. Michael's church. She had waited almost a month to speak with Father Hopwood in order to let her anger dissipate. She hoped he might regret his spiteful words and actions.

She had also worried that her connection with a handfasting could lead to her being labeled a witch. She had heard that the number of witch trials in Exeter had decreased and that even when women accused of witchcraft were brought to court, they often received full pardons. She knew of two such cases from a few years ago: Bridget Wotton had been presented at the Exeter Sessions as a witch but was acquitted, and Joan Furnace had been charged with witchcraft at the city court but was found not guilty by the trial jury. Would the justices in Exeter continue to give fairer treatment to those accused of witchcraft?

In addition, Esther had come to her, worried that perhaps her marriage was invalid. Alice assured her that handfasting was an ancient ritual that carried as much weight as a church wedding. Still, Esther didn't want to make an enemy of Father Hopwood and suggested she might ask him to give her union with Caleb a church blessing. Her husband would go along with whatever Esther wanted.

Cecily Howard, the parsonage servant, brought Alice into Father Hopwood's musty study and instructed her to take a seat on a small stool. The reverend would be with her shortly. In addition to the stool, the room contained a desk, a high-backed chair, and a shelf with a few books. Alice smoothed out her woolen skirt, pushed a few strands of loose hair under her winter bonnet, and took a deep breath.

In front of her hung a tall wooden crucifix. Christ's hands and feet were nailed to the cross, and his head was bent over, which made his hair fall to one side. One tear escaped each eye. Alice reflected, as she had before, that the Church of England was a miserable religion, its worshippers always feeling guilty and having to make up for the state of sin into which they were born. For the moon worshippers, by contrast, rituals honoring the moon and the universal connection to the land were joyful events.

"Good day, Alice." Reverend Hopwood stepped into the study. He took his chair but did not offer Alice his hand. "Have you come to discover the latest news of our fair land? It seems the people of Ivycombe have little interest in such matters, but perhaps you are the exception?"

Alice managed a smile.

"Our Merry Monarch, King Charles, has taken a wife, a Roman Catholic. Imagine that! She is the daughter of the King of Portugal and brings with her a great dowry. And have you heard about Charles's designs in America? He has issued a royal charter to gain possession of a section of the province known as Carolina, south of the colony of Virginia, and a group of English plantation owners has established Charles Town there, named in honor of our king. This is wonderful, is it not?"

Alice shifted on her stool. A long-ago memory flitted into her mind: her father showing his family a pipe filled with tobacco from Virginia before lighting the pipe and smoking it.

"But I assume you have come to apologize to me?" The priest sat back and raised the left side of his mouth into a half smile.

Father Hopwood appeared to smirk at her and enjoy his superiority. She would not let her anger or her fear show. She smiled sweetly at him. "Not to apologize, but to clear the air between us." She spoke deliberately and calmly, for she had rehearsed these words several times. "I understand why you were angry to discover our handfasting, but surely you know this practice was common in Ivycombe for years before you arrived here."

Father Hopwood had lost his half smile. He leaned forward but did not speak.

A pain gripped Alice's chest, but she had to keep going. "Esther came to me. She had decided she wanted a handfasting and asked me to be the officiant. She did not seek to cause trouble but rather to carry on an age-old tradition. I wanted to help her. It is what I do."

"It is time to get rid of the old pagan ways and embrace Christianity. You cannot go against the words of Our Lord," the priest declared without raising his voice.

Alice hoped perhaps she was winning.

The reverend continued. "You and people like you cannot sanction marriage, for the ceremony must take place in the house of God."

"The oak grove, the hills of Dartmoor, the River Ivy—these are the churches of God." Alice's heart raced. "We can worship outside in God's nature as well as in any church."

Father Hopwood sat back in his high-backed chair, upholstered in a reddish leather, and stared at Alice.

She did not look away.

"You must know I am still angry with you, Alice, but I acknowledge your willingness to discuss this matter. Perhaps if Esther and Caleb were to receive a blessing for their union in our church, I could forgive you. Your passion for our lovely countryside is admirable, but the sanctity of marriage requires a church service." The priest stood, and this time he did hold out his hand. "Please pass this message along to your cousin and his betrothed."

Alice rose and shook his proffered hand.

"You are a strongheaded woman, Alice, but sometimes too strong for your own good." With that, he dismissed her.

She emerged into the crisp, frosty air with its smell of wood smoke and pulled her long woolen shawl tight around her shoulders. Aunt Sarah had sought to persuade Alice not to confront Reverend Hopwood, but Alice knew she had to. She had succeeded in that he had listened to her, but she had not won him over. She hurried forward. Was Father Hopwood her enemy or her friend?

***

As Alice drew nearer to the farmhouse, she sensed something was amiss. She quickened her pace.

She opened the front door and swiftly closed it. Aunt Sarah stood next to the hearth holding a handkerchief and a necklace, Richard's gifts to Alice.

Tommy sat on a chair beside his great-aunt. He cried and cradled his face in his hands. "You told me once that my father had given you a necklace, and you still had it. I just wanted to see it."

"Why didn't you ask me to show it to you instead of snooping around to find it?" Alice took the handkerchief and necklace from her aunt and sat beside her son. She glanced for a second at the tiny heart dangling from the delicate silver chain. She recalled the brilliance of Richard's eyes and her belief that he would stay with her forever.

"I knew you would say no, that you wanted to keep it a secret."

Alice swallowed. "Then let me show it to you." She placed the necklace into the smooth palm of Tommy's hand.

He barely examined it but turned instead to touch the handkerchief. "What are those letters in the corner? Is that my daddy's name?"

Alice stared at the letters *RG*, embroidered in blue on the white linen. "Yes."

"What do those letters mean?"

Her chilled hands trembled as she pointed. "The *R* stands for Richard and the *G* for Greenway."

"Richard Greenway, Richard Greenway. What does he look like?"

Alice's throat tightened. "That's enough talk of your father."

"But why do you want to keep us apart?"

Alice turned to look into her son's clear, sad eyes. Her heart ached for him, but she had sworn to tell him the truth. "I am not the one who keeps you from your father. I wanted him to have you in his life, but he chose otherwise. It appears that your father is married to another woman and that he has two young daughters."

"I have two sisters! I want to meet them."

Alice's mind went blank. She couldn't promise to grant her son's wish, but she dared not reject it outright. She looked up to her aunt for help, but the woman patted Tommy on the head and left the kitchen.

Alice trembled. How could she ever hope to placate her son without endangering both of their lives?

CHAPTER TWENTY-ONE

Ivycombe, Devon. May 1670.

The orange glow of the sun was peeking over the horizon, sending rays to brighten up the sky, when Alice heard the strange, uneven bleats of a ewe. May was peak lambing time, and on this last Sunday of the month, Alice had agreed to take turns with her aunt and uncle staying awake at night in case one of the pregnant sheep needed help giving birth.

She had watched the stars fade as the gray of the sky shifted to the palest blue, and she thought about Esther and Caleb. The two had received a blessing for their wedding from Father Hopwood, but he had warned them that Alice could not be trusted, and they should stay away from her.

She must have fallen asleep. At the sound of the ewe, she pushed off her blankets, flung open the farmhouse door, and shook her uncle awake to let him know one of his animals was in trouble.

Together, they ran to the far corner of the sheep enclosure and found the source of the noise. Henry had separated Maggie, his favorite ewe, from the rest of the flock because they had crowded her as she drew close to her time. She walked around her pen, *baaing* and snorting, while her companions slept outside.

"Alice!" Henry laughed and slapped her on the back. "Those are not sounds of distress but the natural noises of a ewe in labor."

Alice stared as the mother, freshly shorn to make giving birth easier, threw her head back and emitted a series of loud groans. The animal licked all around her mouth, lowered her head for a moment, and took a few steps forward.

"Oh, no, you don't." Henry stepped over the low wooden bar and pulled the animal up when she tried to lower her backside to the ground.

She burped in response, and Alice saw a large bubble emerge from her rump.

Henry held on to the sheep. "That's her water bag. Once it breaks, she'll be ready to give birth."

"Look! There it is!" The bubble burst, water poured onto the straw, and two minuscule hooves appeared. "Should we help her?"

"Have you done this before?"

Alice shook her head. "Not with a pregnant sheep!"

"I'll tell you what to do."

Directed by her uncle, Alice knelt down, grabbed a wet toe in each hand, and pulled. Henry cautioned her to wait a bit between tugs, and this gave Alice the chance to wipe her damp hands on her apron. After each contraction, she was able to slide the legs out a little further and move her hands to grasp higher up until the lamb's head emerged and it whimpered. "It's breathing!"

"One more time."

She yanked hard, and suddenly the whole body emerged, sending Alice flying backward onto the straw. She lay there for a moment, exhausted.

Henry picked up the newborn and placed it in front of its mother. The little creature fiercely shook to get rid of the afterbirth slime, and soon its mother made loud slurps as she licked her baby clean of long strands of white mucus.

"You did a fine job. We can leave her." Henry stretched out his hand to help Alice stand.

Exhilaration at the wonder of this birth filled Alice, and she was sure she would be awake forever. She entered her bedroom and saw in the pale morning light that Tommy lay asleep on his pallet but twitched and muttered to himself. He was seven years old and seemed to love life on the farm. What could be wrong? She knelt beside her son and caressed his right cheek. "What? What's happening?" she asked.

Tommy sat up and dissolved into tears.

Alice pulled her son to her and held him tight.

"I had this bad dream. My little horse, Rocky, the one Uncle Henry carved for me, came to life. He breathed fire at me. I closed the door so he couldn't get in, but he pushed and pushed, and the fire and smoke crept under the door toward me. It was scary." Tommy's shaky voice came out between sobs. "Can I sleep on your pallet, Mummy?"

"Of course. I shall protect you." Alice stood up and carried Tommy to her pallet. He lay beside her, and she pulled a blanket over the two of them.

He soon fell asleep, but as she listened to his faint snores, she was wide awake. *Why is my son so troubled? What does this nightmare mean?*

When Alice woke to the soft light of early morning, she was alone. She caught her breath. Tommy was required to stay in their bedroom until his mother woke. He had never disobeyed her before.

She ran first to Aunt Sarah to check on her son's whereabouts.

"No, I haven't seen him. I thought he was with you. But he's more than likely outside with Henry. He loves to assist with the lambs."

Uncle Henry was busy with another ewe that was about to give birth when Alice hurried over to him. "Have you seen Tommy? Do you know where he is?"

"No, but I could use your help again."

"Perhaps later. I must first find my son."

With blood beating in her head, Alice ran back to her bedroom. A corner of her pallet was disturbed, the one where she kept the necklace and handkerchief Richard had given her. She lifted the edge of the pallet, and they were both gone.

When Tommy realized I was fast asleep, he must have pulled out the silver necklace and stared at the Greenway family crest emblazoned on the handkerchief. With that and Richard's initials, he must have decided he had enough information to lead him to his father.

Her wand lay undisturbed at the other end of the pallet. She grabbed it and raced back to her uncle to explain what had happened. Within a few minutes, Uncle Henry decided that they must send out a search party to look for Tommy. He himself could not leave with lambing in full swing, but all the men of the village who were available assembled at the farmhouse: Matthew, Philippa's father, Roger Badcombe, the cooper Alfred Knox, and the Oddfellow twins who ran the bakery. Even Father Hopwood joined the group. The men set out on the road to Exeter brandishing long sticks. Uncle Henry instructed Alice that she could not come with them but must remain at the farmhouse in case her son returned.

Though they had been gone only a short time, to Alice it seemed like many hours as she stared at the spot where the searchers had disappeared like a procession of soldiers off to war.

She knew she had work to do. She needed to prepare the dried leaves and flowers of the vervain plant to make an infusion for the sore throats that plagued several of the villagers. Her supply of willow bark, which she had used so successfully on Caleb, had run low, and she needed to get more. But for now, she could not move from her spot on the low bench in front of the farmhouse.

"Tommy is lost. Tommy is lost." She clutched her wand and repeated the words to herself, but each time, the blackness inside her expanded, ready to swallow her up. A procession of white clouds trailed across the powder blue sky like newly shorn bundles of fleece tossed into the air, mocking her pain.

Have I failed at being a mother? Shall I ever see Tommy again?

Alice closed her eyes and worked to visualize her son so that the darkness would not engulf her. It was hard, but at last she could make him out, crouched under an enormous yew tree.

She forced herself to keep very still and focus on her breathing as she sought to make this image more distinct. She remembered when she had discovered she had the power of vision. It was when she had seen her father as he lay dead on the ground not long before he was murdered. She could see Tommy just as clearly as she had seen her father, but he was motionless. He was safe but could not move.

She strained to see more, but the darkness welled up in her again, and she could not shift it. It wasn't about Tommy anymore. No, this was about her, and she knew a sense of despair, a great loneliness.

A shiver passed through her, and she gripped the edge of the bench.

"Mummy!" She opened her eyes to see Tommy running toward her.

"Tommy! Where have you been?"

"Did you miss me?" He leapt onto her lap, and she was overwhelmed by his familiar grassy smell mixed with the smell of sweat. She pulled him to her. He seemed bigger than she remembered. The darkness fell away, and it mattered only that Tommy had returned to her. She took a deep breath to calm her shaky hands and rocked her child back and forth.

"We didn't have to go far."

Alice looked up. Matthew stood in front of her with the rest of the search party just a few feet behind him.

"Only about a mile down the road, this little rascal was cowering under a yew tree, scared of a bull in the next field."

"Thank you." Alice swallowed hard and addressed the gathered group. "I am sure some of you judge me to be a bad mother if my son seeks to run away from me, yet it is truly more complicated than you know. I shall explain it to all of you in due course. But thank you so much. I am most grateful for your help."

Matthew reached down and tousled Tommy's hair. "You gave us a fright, young Tommy. Your mother will have words with you."

The men nodded and moved away, eager to get back to their day's work.

Tommy struggled to break free of his mother's arms and stood up. "Is there a new lamb? Can I go see Uncle Henry?"

"Not yet."

"But I want to see the lambs."

"First, you need to explain yourself to your mother." She grabbed his left arm and forced him to sit beside her.

"I found a frog." The words tumbled out of Tommy's mouth. "But there was a bull on the other side of the hedgerow. It had this big face, and it snorted out of its white nose, and its horns were aimed right at me. I ran away and tried to hide. And it was really stinky, like moldy grass."

"That sounds horrible. But, Tommy, listen." Alice saw that the corners of her son's mouth were turned down, and he refused to look at her. "What you did this morning alarmed all of us. You are just seven. You could have been killed."

"You worry too much, Mummy. It was only when I saw that mean bull that I got scared. I want to see my daddy, but you won't take me. So I decided to go to Exeter on my own." He kept his eyes fixed on the ground in front of him, and his voice was tight and brittle.

"And you took that handkerchief from under my pallet again?"

Tommy nodded. "I thought I could go find my daddy. If I showed him the necklace and the handkerchief, he would know who I was."

"That necklace and handkerchief are mine. You need to give them back to me."

Tommy pulled the special gifts from his breeches pocket and handed them over to his mother. He shifted his gaze to stare at her. "If you don't take me, I'll run away again, and this time, you won't catch me."

How dare my son talk to me like that? And yet I fear that he means what he says.

"Then I promise you I shall take you to meet your daddy within the next month. Although I cannot be sure he will agree to see us. But you must assure me there will be no more running away." Alice listened to herself utter these words, but she had no idea how she could fulfill this commitment. Tommy was the most important person in her life, and she would do anything to protect him. But how would Richard react when he met his son?

CHAPTER TWENTY-TWO

Ivycombe, Devon. June 1670.

Alice ran as fast as she could along the path beside the River Ivy, desperate to reach Caleb and Esther. She stopped for a moment to catch her breath, and instantly, her stomach clenched. Tommy might be in danger, but how could she protect him? Surely Caleb could help.

On this Whit Sunday, Caleb and Esther strolled hand in hand not far ahead of her.

Alice resumed her pursuit of her cousin and his wife, and her heart ached as memories of walking with Richard at the Green Pool and at the boulder by the Longbrook filled her mind. She had loved Richard so much and had once believed he would always be there, but he had abandoned her. Now she dreaded the thought that she might have to confront him once more.

"Caleb, I need your help!"

Caleb stopped and turned at the sound of Alice's voice. "What is it? What's amiss?"

Alice allowed herself to take a deep breath and gaze at the hay meadow beside them, rich with purple musk thistles. The buzz of bees and the clicks of crickets filled the air while overhead came the loud, beautiful trills of a chaffinch, returned for the summer.

"You heard—" Alice's voice came out in short bursts. "About when my Tommy ran away."

"That must have been ghastly for you." Esther let go of Caleb's hand to pat Alice on the shoulder. "Has he disappeared again?"

Alice rubbed her sweaty palms against her skirt. "No, no, it's not that. My son wants to see his father. That's why he ran away. To make sure he would not leave a second time, I promised I would take him to Exeter within the month so the two of them could meet. That was a fortnight ago, and I haven't slept through the night since then."

"You did what?" Caleb's brown eyes opened wide. A group of starlings in the gnarly ash tree that towered above them burst into loud chirping.

"I couldn't think what else to do. I had to promise him. And I cannot bear the thought that my son could disappear again. I want nothing from Richard but for Tommy to know his father exists."

"What you are saying is impossible." This time, it was Esther who protested, her soft voice rising in tone. "Sir William will have you arrested once you set foot inside the city walls."

Alice's eyes grew moist. She could not lose her son, but she worried something bad would happen to him. Over the past two weeks, she had weighed the fear that Richard might harm his child against her concern that Tommy might feel less than complete for all his life if he never met his father. She couldn't take that risk.

How had she come to this point? She loved Tommy and wanted to do all she could for him. If only she could make Sir William go away. "That's why I need your help. I have two ideas: Someone else takes Tommy to his father, or I get a message to Richard asking him to meet us in one of the villages between here and Exeter. What do you think?"

No one, not even the moon worshippers, had been privy to Alice's anxiety about Tommy's wishes. She inwardly judged herself for once naively believing Richard would take care of her. Now she wanted everyone, including Tommy, to see her as strong. How could her peaceful life with her son be ripped away so violently?

Caleb placed his right hand on Alice's shoulder. "He may well refuse to see either of you. Has he ever acknowledged he has a son?"

Alice shook her head. "I don't believe so, but I promised Tommy I would try to introduce him to his father. Try I must."

Caleb moved his arm around Alice's shoulder, and a wave of relief swept over her. "Cousin, you healed my broken arm and brought me to my wife. Tell me how I may repay my debt to you. Shall I introduce Tommy to his father?"

Esther pushed her auburn curls off her face. "Taking Tommy to Exeter is a bad idea. He will be in danger. Better to have my husband carry a message."

Caleb nodded in agreement, and Alice decided to compose a letter for her cousin to deliver in person the next Sunday.

It took her several attempts before she was satisfied.

Richard,

Please accept this message, which I have asked my cousin Caleb to carry to you.

I have not troubled you these eight years, and I shall not trouble you again. But I have one request. You have a handsome son who is determined to know his father. He even tried running away to Exeter to find you.

I ask nothing more than for you to meet him once. He is seven years old and absolutely insistent that he wants to know who his daddy is. You will recognize him as kin, I am sure.

I can bring him to you myself or ask that Caleb bring him. Please give your answer to my cousin.

Alice

On the following Sunday afternoon, the malty smell of boiling nettles pervaded the farmhouse kitchen. To calm her nerves as she awaited Caleb's return, Alice had decided to brew nettle beer. She remembered when she had tasted the thirst-quenching drink for the first time at Sybil's cottage. She had listened, enraptured, as the old woman spoke of the practice of "sitting out," something Sybil had learned from her grandmother. It was very simple, she had explained, but also very important. You needed to find a quiet place outdoors, sit there for a long time, and use your magical mind to commune with the power that ruffles the water in the brook, that billows the clouds and glides them along their path, that opens to the world of the spirit.

A knock on the front door interrupted her thoughts. She opened it. Richard stood before her.

"Hello, Alice." His voice was warm, and he smiled.

Alice stared at the man she had not seen for almost eight years. His flaming red hair reached over his collar, and he sported a mustache and goatee to match. His chest filled out the handsome golden waistcoat he wore. Alice's heart pounded so hard she feared he might be able to hear it, and her face grew hot. "What are you doing here? I asked you to give Caleb a message, not to come here yourself." Yet as she spoke, the familiar sight of Richard's emerald green eyes took Alice back to the beach at Exmouth the night her son was conceived: the brilliant orange sunset and the ever-moving waters, Richard's hands as he caressed her body at first gently and then more fiercely.

She took a deep breath to clear her head and repeated her question. "What are you doing here? Where's Caleb?"

"He's on his way. Once I knew where you were, I wanted to see you and my son for myself as soon as possible. And you are still so beautiful! Will you not invite me in?"

Alice realized Richard had never been inside her home before and knew he would compare it unfavorably to his own splendid abode. In Exeter, he used to send his servant, Walter, with messages or deliveries such as a side of beef or a sack of flour. She didn't want Richard to poke around inside her home. On the other hand, if he was going to play the flirtatious role, she could be the welcoming hostess. "Of course."

She opened the oak door wide to allow his entrance. "You must be tired. Come take a seat." She indicated the high-backed chair that stood to the left of the hearth, the newest and most comfortable piece of kitchen furniture.

"Thank you." Richard stepped in, and at once his presence seemed to take up all the air in the kitchen. He picked his way over the straw-covered floor with careful steps.

Does he fear his boots with those impressive buckles may be damaged?

He allowed his short black coat to brush against Alice as he passed her, which made her skin tingle and her cheeks flush again. *How can I still find him attractive when he has treated me with such cruelty?*

When he reached the seat, he pulled a white handkerchief from the breast pocket of his waistcoat and used it to wipe down the chair before he sat.

"You can be sure this kitchen is clean. No chickens leave their droppings here."

Richard did not respond but leaned forward and sniffed loudly. “What is in that pot over there? It smells like a brewery in here.”

What has happened to the man who was once my lover? He never spoke to me in such an ill-mannered way but delighted to share his poetry and books with me.

The memory of Richard reciting a Shakespeare sonnet ambushed her:

Like as the waves make towards the pebbled shore,
So do our minutes hasten to their end,
Each changing place with that which goes before,
In sequent toil all forwards do contend.

Where is that gentleman now?

Alice stepped over to the other side of the hearth. She grabbed the handle of the red earthenware pot from the flame and placed it on the ground. “These are stinging nettles, which need to be boiled as the first step toward the preparation of nettle beer. It is delicious. Have you never tried it?”

“You know well that my father’s Bordeaux wine is my preference.” He gave her a slight, sly smile, which made Alice feel he was toying with her.

She dismissed her memories of the smooth, rich liquid she had sipped from Richard’s silver flask. “I have no wine but can offer you a small ale. Would that suit you?”

At that moment, Caleb stepped into the room, moved forward, and banged his fist on the long kitchen table. The two brown chickens that had followed him scurried outside.

“Richard! What possessed you to ride so fast? I told you to give me some time with Alice before she saw you.” He moved over to where Alice stood and put one arm around her.

Alice looked into Caleb's chestnut eyes. Normally quiet and pensive, they were now on fire.

With Caleb by her side, Alice felt she could stand up to Richard. "Cousin, you are an angel. Thank you so much for bringing Tommy's father here." She stood on tiptoe to brush her lips against Caleb's cheek. "Could you do one more thing for me? I think Tommy is out with your father. Tell him his daddy is here to see him."

Caleb stomped out of the room while Alice poured the small ale from a jug on the table into a pewter mug and handed it to her guest. He ran his fingers over hers before he clasped the mug, and she quickly withdrew her hand.

He took a deep swallow and plunked the mug down on the table.

In a flash, Alice recalled the Greenway kitchen with its gleaming pots hanging in long rows and a silver candelabra on the beautiful polished oak table where she had sat years ago after taking care of Richard's mother. She examined this wooden table, not shiny at all but marked by scratches from years of use. Her gaze wandered around the kitchen: the spinning wheel weathered with age, the burned pots hanging near the hearth, the straw that covered the dirt floor.

"Do you still live in the house where I came to tend to your mother?" Alice struggled to keep her voice steady as she poured herself some ale and sat on the bench on the opposite side of the table from Richard. "And is your mother well?"

"Mother died several years ago, and Father suggested I should move my wife into our family home after the marriage so she could run the household."

Richard's tone made Alice think of how a merchant might discuss a business proposal. She yearned to let Richard know that she, too, had lost her mother but sensed he would show no interest.

Is your wife blonde and pretty? Yet I might have been that wife. How would it have been to live in such a fine house and be in charge of a number of domestic servants? She allowed herself to dream for a moment, then gazed from Richard's fine waistcoat and embroidered breeches to her own faded green skirt. *No, we could never have been married.*

"I got your message, and I came here at once because I could not abide the thought that you might seek me out in Exeter."

First he says he came here to see me and Tommy, but now he gives a different reason for his visit. What is the truth? We both know his father would have me arrested if he found out I had returned to Exeter.

Alice took a long sip of ale. The two chickens strutted back into the kitchen through the open door and pecked at the ground. "Albert! Molly!" She stood up, shooed the birds outside again, and turned to face Richard with an unwavering stare. "Are you ashamed of me that you fear to see me in Exeter?"

"You know that is a lie. I knew not if you were dead or alive. You disappeared, and it is true I never sought for you. But what is all this up here?" Richard stood and strode over to the many plants Alice had laid out to dry on a shelf to the right of the hearth. He picked up the closest and held it to his nose.

"Please do not touch the herbs. Those are mine. Leave them alone." *How dare he be so presumptuous as to decide he can handle my plants without my permission. He doesn't own me. These healing herbs are my soul; they are who I am. Why does he seek to violate me?* "Put the lavender back on the shelf. You have no right to meddle with my plants."

Richard studied her for a moment before he did as she requested.

He is an intruder in my home. He should leave. Yet I must be polite, for I do not want to anger him. "This plant is lavender, good for all pains of the head and brain, including fainting. Next to it is pennyroyal, a great help for women and their courses, and—"

"So you use them to make potions and cast spells?"

"I am a healer, Richard. You know that, for it is how I first met you. These plants are my healing tools."

He came to stand close to her.

She prayed he would not touch her again.

"I am kept very busy. My father grows old, and I shall soon take his place in the Merchants' Guild. I came here to protect you. The citizens of Exeter still hold you responsible for the death of Agnes Furze and believe you are a witch. You would not be safe there." As he completed his declaration, he took his seat once more.

So now he puts forward yet a different reason for coming here. "And you? What do you believe?"

"We might have continued as we were, but you chose differently."

"You haven't answered my question. Do you agree with the people of Exeter that I am a witch, in league with the devil?"

Richard leaned back in his chair and was silent for a moment. "You are not the Alice I knew. You've become much more forward."

"Thank you. I shall take that as a compliment. But answer my question." She grabbed the bench and sat down.

"I certainly did not consider you a witch all those years ago."

I don't believe him. He holds something back.

"Again, you are avoiding my question. Yet how can you speak of my having chosen differently? Richard, I became pregnant with our child, and you abandoned me, and allowed your father to buy off the consistory court." Alice fought to maintain her voice at a level tone.

"I had no choice. My father would have disowned me entirely, and I would have been out on my ear, left with nothing."

"That is exactly what happened to me. You say we could have continued as we were. With a child? You with a wife and family, the respect of the citizens of Exeter, and me, the mother of your bastard child? I chose to provide for myself and our son with my healing knowledge. And now you blame me that I started out alone, with nothing?" Alice's heart raced, but she did not yell at Richard. He must see that she no longer needed his approval.

"You appear to be thriving in this little village. Whereas I am wed to a wife who cares little for me but more for the position I hold. A marriage arranged by my father."

"Mummy! Look what I found!" Tommy burst into the room. His turquoise eyes sparkled with excitement. In his hands, he held a long wriggling snake, yellow-green in color and with dark markings. He stopped when he saw Richard. "You are my father! You look just like me! Do you want to touch my new friend?" Tommy moved toward Richard and held out the creature to his father, who leapt to his feet and stepped away.

"Get that venomous thing away from me! It's evil."

Alice laughed. "That's what you said about my birthmark all those years ago. You were wrong then, and you are wrong now. It's just a harmless grass snake. Tommy, put the poor snake back where you found it."

Her son bobbed his head but hesitated.

"Go fast and come right back. Your father will still be here when you return, and you two can have a proper introduction."

Tommy ran out, and Richard sat down again. "My son. No doubt about it: my hair, my nose, my look." He twiddled a strand of hair between thumb and forefinger. "Why does he have a snake?"

"Tommy has a passion for crawling creatures, especially reptiles. He loves the lizards, the slow worms, and the grass snakes.

And he knows to leave well alone when he spots an adder." She did not add that she herself did not share this passion but was determined to let her son pursue his own interests.

"Vile. Tommy with his snakes and you with your healing concoctions."

For the first time, Alice recognized she might be in danger.

Richard shoved his chair back, and the wooden legs screeched against the hard dirt floor.

He jumped up, stamped his square-toed boots on the ground, and pointed at Alice with long, elegant fingers. "Perchance the citizens of Exeter have it right, and you are a witch."

Alice gripped the edge of the bench.

Before she could respond, Tommy stepped back in, hands empty, and stood next to his father. His eyes had lost their glow. "Why did you never come to see me?"

Alice held her breath.

"Your mother ran away—she disappeared."

"Tommy, it is true that I left Exeter and did not speak of where I was headed. We can talk about this later. Why don't you take your father around the farm, show him where the lambs are?"

Richard gave a wan smile and followed his son outside.

I should never have let him know my whereabouts. But Tommy begged me. I couldn't let him down. Now that Richard has discovered where I am, what will happen to us? Has he come to destroy us?

The June sun beat down on the farmhouse, and Alice mopped her brow with her apron as she strode up and down the small kitchen. She picked up the pot of nettles and replaced them over the flame to cook a little longer before adding the sugar. At once, the distinctive sweetish smell of stinging nettles emerged. On any other day, this would have brought her comfort, but today she heard Richard's dismissive tone about her favorite drink and knew absolutely she was in danger. How could she protect herself and her son? She sensed the walls of the kitchen closing in on her.

Soon, father and son reentered the kitchen, but they looked downcast and walked several feet apart, like strangers.

Tommy ran to his mother's side. "My daddy doesn't like the smell of the lambs. He made me leave them. And then he asked me lots of questions about you, whether you go to church on Sundays, and what potions you make. He scared me."

"I'm sure he didn't mean to frighten you, did you, Richard?" She tousled her son's hair.

Richard gave no response but glared at Tommy. "Why don't you go back outside again and help Uncle Henry? Your mother and I must talk alone."

Tommy looked at Alice, and she saw how his beautiful eyes had glossed over. Tension gripped her, but she reached to hug her child. He turned away from her and walked out. A hand of panic squeezed Alice's heart as she watched her little boy disappear through the doorway.

"Tommy tells me you often spend time alone, with your eyes closed, and that you do not attend church regularly. Does he speak the truth?"

"He does. I learned from a dear friend, a wise woman, that meditation is essential to my life. As for the church, I find no comfort there."

"And is it true you go out every month at the full moon and perform pagan ceremonies?"

Alice wished she could shake Richard hard. How dare he address her in this patronizing manner? "You cannot understand these things because our lives are so different. You, with your important business in Exeter, the heir to a fortune, while I live in this 'small village,' as you put it. And if you want to hear the truth, the church reviled me when I first arrived, a pregnant woman with no husband. But what can it matter to you how I choose to live?"

"So Tommy spoke truthfully? You are a witch." Richard's face flushed, and he wrung his hands.

I was right. We are in danger, and he is threatening our lives.

"Richard, you are very overwrought. Perhaps I might prepare a decoction of chamomile to help you relax?"

"I want none of your magic potions. You are a bad influence on my son. Pack up his belongings, and I shall return from Exeter early on the morrow to take my child away to a place where he will be safe."

Richard strode out without saying goodbye.

Alice sank back down onto the wooden bench.

BOOK 3

CHAPTER TWENTY-THREE

Ivycombe, Devon. June 1670.

Half an hour after Richard left, Alice remained on the kitchen bench. She rocked back and forth, arms wrapped around her waist, and wept softly. She knew she should move, take some action, but her body was numb. *How dare he? He hasn't thought about me or whether he might have a son for almost eight years. How dare he step into my life and my son's life and demand to take Tommy away?* She rubbed the tears off her face with her hands. "He cannot do that. I shall not let him."

A burnt smell distracted her. She rushed over to the hearth; although the flame was still alight, the outside of the pot had turned black, and the water had boiled dry. Alice blew out the fire. The embers below still glowed, but her nettles lay in a black pile of cinders at the bottom of the earthenware bowl. "Damn you! My favorite drink turned into a black mess, just like my life." She dumped the cinders onto the embers and moved back to sit on the bench.

Richard cannot take Tommy to Exeter, for it will be obvious they are father and son. He lied to me. He seeks to destroy my inner soul and my son. A terrible emptiness filled her. *What do I have to live for if Tommy is taken from me?* Images of her son flooded her mind: the sight of her newborn with his shock of blond hair, his beautiful translucent eyes, his brilliant smile when he picked up a newborn lamb. Sobbing overtook her once more, and she collapsed, shoulders slumped, as she stared at the scratched wooden table.

"Alice! Where is Richard? What has happened?" Caleb barged through the doorway, his long black tunic flying behind him.

Alice stood to greet her cousin. As she drowned in the darkness of her own mind, she wasn't sure if she could pull herself out. "He left but threatened to return tomorrow and steal Tommy from me."

Caleb held her in a tight embrace and drew her back to the bench.

She could barely breathe, but the force of Caleb's arms made her sit up straighter, and the warmth of his body comforted her.

"This is all my fault." Caleb's voice was shaky. He pushed the mousy brown hair from his forehead and stood to pace up and down the kitchen. "Richard at first refused to admit me into his home but soon changed his tune. It seems he had decided you had disappeared forever and never considered seeking you out. When he learned you were still alive and that you had a son, his eyes lit up like beacons, and he smiled so broadly I knew he had something bad in mind. I should never have told him where to find you."

"I asked you to go to Exeter, and that's what you did. You are not to blame." Alice clutched her stomach and gasped for air.

Her cousin reached for the jug on the table, poured the small ale into two mugs, and handed one to Alice. "Tell me what happened."

Alice looked up at Caleb, who was chewing on his right thumbnail. She recounted how Richard had seemed friendly at first, even flirtatious, but grew hostile. "He showed little interest in Tommy, other than to remark how much the child resembled his father. That's when I knew we were in danger." Her final sentence came out in a raspy tone. "Richard proclaimed I was a bad influence on the child and that he intended to return tomorrow morning to take his son away. I fear he means to kill my Tommy."

"What on earth makes you believe Richard wants to murder his own son?"

For a second, Alice recalled the moment when Richard had hurled a stone directly at a duck, as if to destroy it. "Sir William would never tolerate having the bastard child of his son in his household, especially one whose mother he has condemned as a witch and forbidden to set foot in Exeter. That's one reason for Richard to get rid of Tommy."

Caleb nodded.

"But do you recall the story of Joan Taylor, an unwed mother here in Ivycombe who had to give up her child? Your mother told me about her and a few others. She had to take her baby daughter to a beggar woman and pay the woman five pounds to raise the child and keep her away from Ivycombe. Joan never saw her baby again, and the child died within a year. Even if Richard didn't literally kill his son, he is certainly capable of giving Tommy away to an ignorant woman who would neglect my son and let him die."

This time Caleb nodded with more vigor. "You might be correct, Alice."

"Your mum told me bastard babies are often assigned to the care of their local parish. The parish resents such a burden and neglects the poor infants so that they subsequently perish. Your parents took me in with no hesitation, Caleb. I was lucky. Other women in my situation are forced to give up their newborns."

She didn't wait to hear Caleb's response. She knew she must leave this stuffy kitchen, if only for a moment. "Forgive me. I have something I must do." Alice pulled herself up from the bench. "Can you take care of Tommy if he returns?"

Alice ran outside, away from where she knew her uncle and Tommy would be. The sun burned the top of her head and sweat ran down her back, but she didn't care. Her mind was an empty blur as she ran through the long grass, vaguely aware of her surroundings: chirruping grasshoppers, numerous cabbage white butterflies, displays of tall white yarrow and yellowish lady's bedstraw. Soon she reached her destination, the furthest meadow beyond her physic garden.

She flung herself down on her knees into the long grass dotted with purple loosestrife, lifted her face to the clear blue sky, and howled as loudly as she could. Then she placed her hands on the rough ground, bowed her head so low that she touched the earth, and let out a series of full-throated screams. Exhausted, Alice raised her head up. Drops of sweat had gathered on her forehead. She sensed the build-up of saliva in her mouth and a queasiness rising from her belly. She swallowed hard but couldn't stop the flow of bile out of her mouth. It landed in an ugly mess on the tall grasses. She pulled the apron from her waist and used it to wipe away her tears as she coughed and spluttered.

Yet as she rose from the earth, she understood that she had spewed Richard out of her system. Now that she was rid of him, she could focus on saving Tommy.

"What man seeks to separate a mother from her child?" Uncle Henry spat on the ground. "He is half man, half devil. But I have a plan. My brother Gilbert lives in Bideford, where I grew up. He will gladly take you in, and you will be safe from the heinous desires of your son's father." Uncle Henry leaned forward in the high-backed chair that Richard had so recently occupied.

Alice shuddered.

She had returned to the farmhouse kitchen to find her aunt and uncle, along with Caleb and Esther, gathered together. Alarmed by the news of what Richard Greenway planned to do with their beloved Tommy, they were planning his escape.

"Bideford is a good day and a half's journey from Ivycombe, and in the opposite direction from Exeter. Caleb can take you there in the horse trap, and you can stay as long as you need. But I shall miss my Tommy."

Alice sat on the bench in front of her uncle. He patted her on the shoulder and tried to smile, but his mouth drooped at the corners, matching his shaggy eyebrows.

Tension gripped Alice's heart. She could not allow Richard to drive her out again, nor would she even consider such a cowardly act. Her cheeks flushed bright red as she explained to her uncle that she had been forced to flee Exeter on Richard's account, but she would never again give him such power over her. She and Tommy would stay in Ivycombe.

She spoke in a fiery tone, but the moment she finished, misery crept into her heart again. What good were such words without action? Was she being selfish, putting the whole family in danger? The acrid smell of ash and embers lingered in the air and made her cough.

"Then we must fight this man! I can summon all the men of our village to be prepared when this disgusting specimen of a human approaches." Caleb leapt up and wiped his brow against the heat of the room. He plunged his arm forward into the air and twisted it back and forth.

Alice watched Caleb, but instead of her cousin, she saw Richard brandishing his sword toward a terrified Tommy, who cried out, "No! Don't kill me!" She clutched her stomach and feared she would vomit once more. How had she failed so completely as a mother? What could she have done to protect her son?

Aunt Sarah wrung her hands. "And Sir William Greenway will send all his men here to destroy Alice, Tommy, and all of us. That is no solution."

Caleb glared at his mother. "We are faced with evil and must fight back. What do you suggest? Would you rather Tommy be taken away from us?"

Pain gnawed at Alice so that she could not think, but her brain was ready to explode.

"Tommy can hide in the barn beneath the hay." Aunt Sarah sniffed and rubbed the tears from her puffy eyes. "Or we can put him in disguise, or he could live at the mine with you and Esther for a while."

It came to Alice then what had to happen. "Richard must see that Tommy is dead."

A collective gasp escaped the group as Caleb took his seat next to Esther. They all directed their attention to Alice.

"It will not suffice for my son simply to be missing. Just before she died, my dear friend Sybil gave me many of her dried herbs, including a small amount of deadly nightshade. Tommy can take a few seeds of this plant and will appear to be dead for at least a day. But in truth, he will be in a deep sleep and will awake refreshed."

Alice had to believe in Sybil, who had given her strict instructions on how to administer this concoction. She could not allow herself to doubt even for a second.

Aunt Sarah was on her feet and shouted at Alice. "But what if something goes wrong? What if he doesn't wake up?"

"Nothing will go wrong." In spite of her heart pounding against her rib cage, Alice spoke in a confident tone. "I am a trusted healer, and you have taught me well. Tommy will swallow a decoction made with a few seeds, and Sybil gave me the antidote for deadly nightshade to use as necessary. If I had the slightest doubt about this, I would not do it. This is the only way to save his life."

⁂

At suppertime, the family sat down to a delicious meal of carrot, onion, and potato soup prepared by Aunt Sarah, and with the sun still high, they disappeared outside to enjoy the summer evening.

Alice asked Tommy to stay behind for a moment.

He yanked off his floppy hat, revealing damp red-blond hair stuck to his head and neck. "Where is my father?"

She swallowed hard and put one arm around her son. "He has left."

"Good!"

"But he promises to return tomorrow and take you with him. Would you like that?"

"You mean take me away from you forever?"

Alice nodded. Her vision grew blurry with unshed tears, but she refused to cry.

Tommy sat on his mother's lap. "No. I have met my daddy, and I don't like him. He was scary. He asked so many questions about you, wanted to learn all your secrets."

Alice hugged her son tightly. Aunt Sarah had suggested that Alice should not tell Tommy about her plan with the deadly nightshade, but Alice could not hide such a thing from her son. She had made a commitment to herself that she would never again hide the truth from Tommy. She would honor that promise.

"I have a plan. Tonight, I will give you a sleeping draught, and when your father arrives tomorrow, he will believe you have died, for you will be deeply asleep. Then he will leave without you, and all this will be over."

"But what if I never wake up?" Tommy's high-pitched voice came out between sobs.

"Of course you will wake up, but only after your daddy has left. You must trust me, Tommy. You know I would never hurt you."

"Can I go outside to play now?"

Her son jumped out of her lap and disappeared through the front door.

Alice was left alone. The rich smell of soup still filled the air, but she turned her attention to preparing a decoction from the tiny black seeds of the deadly nightshade. These she had stored in her small ceramic jar, Catherine's gift to her.

Alice placed just a few of the round seeds into a pan and added a good amount of water. Although she had prepared hundreds of decoctions and infusions before, her hands trembled as she set the pan over the fire. *Do I have the right number of seeds? Sybil instructed me that it would be dangerous to use more than a few. But I must have enough.* Her right arm gave a sudden involuntary twitch, and she cried out in pain. *No. I am in charge. I can do this.* Once the water had boiled for some time, she strained the brownish liquid through a linen sieve into a pewter cup. It gave off a pungent, earthy smell.

When Tommy returned as the sun was setting, he rubbed his eyes, clung to his mother, and asked her if he still had to take the medicine.

Alice's heart pounded as she held her son. She wanted to tell him she believed his life was in danger, that his father might kill him, but knew she could not. But what if something went wrong and her beautiful child never woke up?

She walked toward the bedroom they shared, and Tommy followed. He pulled off his breeches and jacket so that he was clad only in his nightshirt, and he lay down on his straw pallet.

Alice wrapped him fully in a blanket, so that it resembled a shroud, except that Tommy's face was uncovered. His eyelids drooped over his eyes when she raised his head and brought the pewter cup to his mouth. Her hands shook so fiercely that she feared she might spill the liquid across the blanket. *Am I murdering my own son?*

He swallowed the liquid, brought his head to lie on the pallet, and was asleep within a few minutes.

Alice sat beside him, the son who was so precious to her. Nothing had changed. He was a young boy tired out from a horribly long day, and he slept. Working slowly, she wrapped ribbons around his body at the elbows, wrists, and ankles to hold his limbs straight, something she had seen her mother do years ago.

What if I have made a mistake and Tommy dies? Will he just fall asleep and never wake up? Or will he suffer terrible pain first? I cannot bear to think of this. Surely, Sybil has told me the truth? But I can use the activated charcoal if I see Tommy is struggling. Richard, be damned that you put me in this situation. Sybil was not afraid to die, but she had lived a long life. Tommy is seven and has his whole life in front of him. What if his body is not strong enough to withstand this sleeping draught? He trusts me and believes I will always protect him. But something could go wrong. What if the antidote doesn't work? I must trust in the power of nature and the universe and in Sybil's word that all will be well.

A final query presented itself: *What if Richard doesn't appear tomorrow?*

CHAPTER TWENTY-FOUR

Ivycombe, Devon. June 1670.

Catherine cradled Alice's hand as they swung arms and sang, "I will give my love an apple." Alice welcomed the dream of her mother, so alive, with her pale blue eyes, her long hair streaked with gray, and her strong hands. In the early morning mist, the two had stepped outside the North Gate of the Exeter City Wall to gather the smooth, hollow stems and hairless leaves of the dandelion plant.

Alice walked in the long, dewy grass, and the tiny drops brought energy to her feet as she and her mother crossed a meadow that resembled the Northern Hay. Yet it was not, for here were brick cottages where none had existed before. An unfamiliar silence hung over the grassland; gone were the ravens with their loud caws and the tiny squeaks of the spotted flycatchers.

After her mother almost tumbled onto the slippery ground, Alice warned her to be careful. Catherine laughed, pulled her bony hand away from Alice, and strode over to a cluster of bright yellow dandelions. Catherine reached down with her trowel to dig up their roots, but her feet slid out from under her, and she fell flat onto the damp grass.

Alice rushed over to offer support. But when she peered into her mother's face and reached out both hands to help Catherine stand, a skull looked back at her with empty eye sockets and an eerie grin. Alice shrieked and jumped back.

She woke with a start and shook her head from side to side to dislodge the terrifying image. In the past, dreams of her mother had always brought the assurance that Catherine's spirit still lived within her. This nightmare made her want to vomit. She had lost her bearings.

Although it was early, dawn light already bathed the room, and Alice could make out the shadowy outline of her son's body. "Tommy!" She pushed back her linen blanket and leaned toward her son's pallet, which lay next to hers.

He looked exactly as he had when he had fallen asleep. She inched over to examine him more closely. With his eyes still shut, his face had no color except for a slight purplish mottling. Preparing a body for burial included the placement of pennies over the eyelids, something Alice had done long ago with her mother, but she didn't do this now. *What if my sweet Tommy wakes up but can't open his eyes?*

When she touched his cheek with one finger, it felt waxy and cold. *Is he dead? Did I kill him?* Her breath came faster and faster while her hands grew clammy. Tommy lay motionless, covered by the woolen blanket she had wrapped around him, as required by law for all burials.

Tremors shook her body, and she found it hard to breathe. If Tommy was dead, she would kill herself, too, for she could not imagine life without her son.

Alice recalled that Sybil had told her the deadly nightshade would induce a coma with a heartbeat so slow it could be mistaken for death. At once, Alice remembered what to do.

Earlier in the year, on Ash Wednesday, John Caton had been repairing the roof of St. Michael's when he fell off and hit his head on a gravestone in the cemetery surrounding the church. Father Hopwood summoned Alice and Aunt Sarah to examine the roofer and see if he was still alive. When they arrived, a small group had gathered around John's body near the entrance to the church.

Blood had dribbled in a steady stream from a crack in his head, and Alice saw again her father collapsed on the ground all those years ago, the empty space where his left ear should have been, and the blood that flowed from his mouth. She had known Father was dead, murdered by one of Cromwell's men. This time, she was unsure. She took the piece of flat glass that Aunt Sarah handed her and held it under John's nose for a few moments. The glass did not fog up. John Caton had stopped breathing.

She brought the same fragment of glass under Tommy's nose. Nothing happened. He still appeared stiff and cold.

She feared she might injure her son, but she moved the glass ever closer to his cold nose.

She wished she believed in a God she could pray to as she waited. And then, a miracle. Ever so slowly, the glass fogged over. Tommy still lived.

⁂

Alice dozed off and on for a while, but once the sun had risen above the horizon, she no longer tried to sleep.

With Midsummer Eve just over a week away, she knew she could not make a bonfire, leap over it, and dance with the Morris dancers. Her body ached with the fear of what would happen when Richard appeared, and besides, what if Tommy never woke up?

She decided to dress as simply as possible and chose a plain linen bodice and an undecorated brown wool skirt.

Once more, she eased over to her son and brought the glass under his nose. Again, nothing at first, and then a slight misting.

I must stop my constant checks on Tommy. She had set two white candles in the family's beautiful silver candlesticks and positioned them just behind Tommy's head. Now she lit them. They brightened up his face, but it still appeared waxen and ghostly. She had cried so much that she had no tears left to shed, but her eyes remained moist, floating in their own pain. *Damn that man. Richard has forced me into this horrible position. He still has control over me.*

When Aunt Sarah brought her niece a breakfast of buttered oat bread and a mug of small ale, Alice thanked her and assured her that Tommy still breathed. Alice feared that the smell of the breakfast ale would make her nauseous, so Sarah set the food and drink on a small table on the other side of Tommy's pallet. The sun brightened up the bedroom, and its rays on the curtains brought out the slightly fishy smell of linseed oil.

Once her aunt left the room, Alice slid out the tiny ceramic jar of activated charcoal from under her pallet. She removed the cork and sniffed even though she had done this twice before and knew the antidote had no odor. The fine black powder looked nothing like charcoal, but Sybil had explained to Alice how she had created the antidote. First, she burned wood at an extreme temperature. Next, she washed the resulting charcoal and ground it into a fine powder. Lastly, she cooked the powder in a special solution. Sybil had explained that this final step created a spongelike substance that sucked poison from the body.

The old woman had also warned her that the activated charcoal should be ingested with a good amount of boiled water since it tended to make the body dry up. A full ewer stood ready on the chair next to Tommy. Alice replaced the cork and pushed the jar back into its spot under her pallet, next to a small spoon.

She sat on a stool next to her pallet. *Shall I be able to do this? How can Tommy possibly swallow any liquid?*

A light knock on the bedroom door sent Alice's mind into a frenzy, and she fell from her stool onto the ground. *No! Richard cannot be here yet. It takes more than two hours to ride from Exeter.*

Esther pushed open the door. In her delicate white hands, she carried a small jug filled with pink and white peonies. "I picked these for you." Alice stood up, and Esther passed her the flowers.

Their fresh, sweet aroma brought Alice a measure of peace, and her mind ceased its agitation as she inhaled their fragrance. "Thank you. They are lovely." She placed the jug next to her still uneaten breakfast.

Esther reached down to embrace Alice, who didn't know whether she appreciated more the flowers or Esther's kindness in thinking of such a gesture.

"How is he?" Esther came over to Tommy's side and laid her lips against his right cheek. "My dear Tommy."

"He is alive, though just barely. I learned from Sybil, who gave me the nightshade seeds, that they could put a person in a deep sleep, which would make him look dead. But my son still has a heartbeat and does breathe."

"That's wonderful!" Esther stood, pushed her auburn locks behind her ears, and came to embrace Alice once more. "And I have woven a wreath of oak twigs threaded with harebells and daisies and hung it on the farmhouse door to let people know there has been a death in the family."

"Thank you, Esther. I am so grateful to you."

"Caleb stands guard at the entrance to the farmhouse. He feared your son's father might round up all the servants of the Greenway house to accompany him. I assured him that wouldn't happen—he would come alone. Richard Greenway doesn't want anyone to know he has a bastard son."

***

Over an hour later, Alice listened to the chatter of warblers and goldfinches outside her window as she gazed down at Tommy. *I must compose myself, yet no, for I am in grief. Richard will surely see my sorrow.* Her mind raced from one unrelated thought to another while she wrung her damp hands and sought to remain calm.

When Aunt Sarah burst into the room, Alice thought she might faint.

"He's here. He saw the wreath and demands to know the truth. Caleb spoke with him, and I brought you this fine black shawl to signify you are in mourning."

Alice thanked her aunt for the delicate woolen shawl as Sarah placed it around her shoulders, but her stomach knotted up at the thought of laying eyes on Richard again. *Make him go away. I don't want to see him. I cannot bear to see him. But I must believe that my son is still alive and maintain my strength for him.*

"You can do this, Alice." Aunt Sarah leaned over to embrace her niece. "Remember all the ways this man has done you wrong. This is your chance to take charge. And your family stands firmly with you." With that, she left the room and closed the door softly behind her.

A loud rap made Alice sit up, alert.

Richard didn't wait to be invited but barged in and stood before her. "What is this trick you seek to play on me? Caleb told me I didn't need to be concerned about my son anymore, that he died last night. What is this devilment?"

He no longer sported the fancy embroidered waistcoat he'd worn the day before but had donned a long-sleeved white shirt under a black cape. The silver buckle that cinched his leather baldric over his shoulder and around his waist glistened.

The baldric rested vacantly against his hip, for he carried no weapon today, but Alice knew he meant to frighten her. She would not allow that to happen. She sat up straighter in her chair.

"No devilment. I am in mourning for our son. Does that mean nothing to you?" Her voice trembled, and the taste of last night's soup came into her mouth. She swallowed.

Richard's holly-green eyes glared at her from a reddened face. *How could I ever have fallen in love with those eyes?*

In spite of her sorrow, Alice noticed the musky scent Richard brought with him. She remembered how Catherine had told her, when they first visited the Greenway home, that rich people rarely bathed but covered their smells with other perfumes. She disliked this odor and wondered if he sought to impress or overpower her.

"We were talking last night when I noticed black smudges around his mouth." Alice sobbed into her handkerchief. She didn't have to pretend to cry, for she feared greatly that she might have killed her child. "Then he fell to the floor, his legs jerked, and I knew I'd never talk to him again, that he had gone. And I realized those black marks meant that he had eaten the berries of the deadly nightshade." Alice choked as she finished her speech. She had promised herself in the past that she would always speak the truth, but her son's life lay in the balance.

Richard flung his wide-brimmed hat onto a chair. "You lie. I don't believe you."

He marched over to where Tommy lay on his own pallet.

Richard wore heavy jackboots, such as a soldier might wear, nothing like yesterday's boots with their fancy buckles. His stomping filled the small room and made Alice put her hands over her ears. *He treats me like an enemy he must destroy.*

"Ugh! What have you done to him?" Richard poked the

boy's forehead. "His skin is rigid, cold. And why have you tied him down with ribbons?"

Alice uncovered her ears. "You would do well to stay away from Tommy. Deadly nightshade, or belladonna, as it is also known, is highly poisonous and he may still have berry juice on his face. It could be dangerous for you to touch him."

Richard stared at her for a moment and then took one step away from Tommy. "Why does it stink like fish in here?"

"The faint odor you speak of comes from the linseed oil used to waterproof the curtains." Alice brought her handkerchief to her nose, but she could not stanch the flow of tears. "Did you not witness your own mother's body laid out for burial? The ribbons are there to hold Tommy's limbs in place. Do you not feel sorrow at the death of your child?"

"There is villainy here." Richard stamped one jackboot on the floor. "With your magic powers, you have bewitched my son."

"Our child is dead, but you seem not to care. I am sorry you have made this journey for nothing. You should leave us with our misery and go back to your wife and children. I shall never bother you again."

"You shall hear more of this from me." Richard picked up his hat, banged it against the chair, and set it on his head. He exited the bedroom and slammed the door shut behind him.

⁂

Alice dozed intermittently for the rest of the day. She did not move, other than to check on Tommy's breathing once in a while. Sybil had told her the deep sleep could continue for as long as a day and a half, but it might last only twenty-four hours. Should she try to get Tommy to ingest the activated charcoal even though he still breathed?

As twilight set in, she blew out the two candles and brought the glass to Tommy's nose one more time. Alice could just see the blur on the glass, but her son lay inert. *If Tommy dies, I shall swallow a larger number of nightshade seeds and die with him.*

When Aunt Sarah and Esther visited her, anxious to learn about Richard's visit as well as Tommy's condition, Alice shared with them her concern that it might be time to administer the activated charcoal.

"No, do not try this yet." Esther came to sit on the floor beside Alice's pallet and took her hand. "We watched as Richard left, but he could well have ridden only a mile away from Ivycombe, dismounted, and already come back and be close by, ready to spy on you."

A weariness had taken over Alice, and she could no longer think straight. "What do you mean?"

"Do not alarm yourself. Your aunt and I will keep watch for him until nightfall and report back to you. I am certain such a fine gentleman would fear being out here alone in the dead of night." Esther let go of Alice's hand and stood up. "We shall take up our positions immediately."

After the two women had left, Alice removed the shawl and lay down on her pallet, too exhausted to pull up the linen coverlet. She slept for a short time, but loud voices that cried out in her head made her wake up in a panic.

It's been too long. He trusted me to take care of him. He's been asleep almost all day and night. I must give him the antidote at once.

Wide awake, Alice reached under her pallet for the ceramic jar that held the activated charcoal. She thrust her right hand forward to the place where she was sure she had left the jar but found nothing. The activated charcoal was gone.

CHAPTER TWENTY-FIVE

Ivycombe, Devon. June 1670.

A short time after Alice discovered that the charcoal was missing, Aunt Sarah rapped on the bedroom door and flung it open. "Alice! What are you doing? St. Michael's clock has already struck ten. The sun has almost completely set, and I can barely see you!" Sarah crouched down beside her niece, who knelt on the floor.

Alice did not look up. Her hands scrabbled beneath her pallet but encountered only crumbs and tiny stones. "The antidote—I cannot find it. I know I put it here, under my mattress cover, but it's gone." The dead weight of her insides filled her with gloom, and her body shook. "Please help me."

"Of course we shall help you." Esther stepped into the room and placed the rushlight she carried on the table next to the peonies. "There. Now we shall be better able to see. And you should know there was no sign of Richard out there."

"I care not about Richard. It is Tommy I must save. Perchance I pushed the little jar with the antidote through a hole in the canvas cover of my pallet and into the straw." A few tears spilled from her eyes, and the void within her grew deeper.

"We shall find that antidote." Aunt Sarah stood and tried to yank the pallet off the ground, but it fell back down with a thud.

"Esther, stand beside me. We are two strong women; we can do this. We need to move Alice's pallet to see what lies beneath."

"Of course." Esther turned to address Alice. "But first, this room has a musty smell for lack of fresh air. Why don't you stand up and push the door back so that it's wide open?"

Alice obeyed her friend's command, and fresh air entered her bedroom. When she looked into the darkened kitchen, she could just make out the ghostly shape of the hearth and the kitchen table. How long ago it seemed that she had sat with her family and consumed Aunt Sarah's tasty soup. So much had happened in little more than a day.

She turned to watch as the two women stood on either side of her heavy pallet and shifted it sideways, away from where Tommy lay asleep on his mattress. "Take care! Do not disturb my child."

"Trust us, Alice." Esther reached to the ground and, together with Aunt Sarah, strained to lift Alice's pallet, carry it forward, and drop it on the ground. The bare floor where her mattress had lain revealed nothing. No antidote. Next, Aunt Sarah and Esther turned the mattress over and discovered a hole in the cover where a long, wriggling tail stuck out. Esther grasped the tail and pulled hard to reveal a brown house mouse. Between his teeth, he clasped the jar containing the antidote. Esther shook the creature, which made him drop the tiny container. This she handed over to Alice before tossing the rodent from the front door of the farmhouse.

"Where am I?" Tommy's voice came out in a high-pitched squeak. "What is happening? Why have you tied me up?"

Alice and Aunt Sarah rushed over to where Tommy struggled to sit up.

"Tommy, my Tommy. You came back to me! You're here!" Alice sobbed as she knelt beside her son, and the two women worked to loosen the knots in the ribbons that held him down.

His normally smiling face glared at her, and his eyes narrowed into slits. "What do you mean, I came back to you?" As he spoke, Alice and Sarah slid the ribbons away from Tommy and helped him sit up.

Alice placed her arms around her son and brought him to stand beside her. Weeping overwhelmed her as she hugged him hard. The familiar scent of his hair, slightly grassy, and the warmth of his back assured her that he was indeed alive. She touched his face; the cold waxiness had vanished.

Tommy pulled free from his mother's embrace. He stamped his feet and shook his arms. "My mouth is dry. I must drink!" He gulped down the mug of boiled water Alice handed him and demanded more.

"Tommy!" Esther came back to the bedroom and threw her arms around the boy. "I am so happy to see you!" She wiped the tears from her eyes as she stepped back.

"What is going on? Why is everyone crying?"

Alice stepped over to her son, who no longer glared at her. "Tommy." She put one hand on his shoulder. "What is the last thing you remember?"

"You told me my daddy wanted to take me away forever." Tommy scratched his head.

Esther touched Aunt Sarah's arm. "Perhaps we should leave these two together."

After they had left, Alice turned back to Tommy. "We made a plan. Do you remember?"

"You would give me a drink to make me sleep for a long time, and Daddy would think I was dead. That drink tasted terrible!"

The boy sat down on the edge of his pallet and stared up at his mother.

"Our plan worked. I told you the truth." Alice came to sit next to her son. Her brain scrambled as she decided what to say to her child, but she knew she had to tell the truth this time. "Your daddy came back, saw that you looked dead, and left. But he may return. How would you like to live with Matthew and Philippa for a while and spend time with their children?"

"Play with Henry and Stephen?" Tommy reached up and embraced his mother. "I would love that!"

"A false death requires a false grave. And it's not going to dig itself." Caleb had to shout to make himself heard over the pounding of an unexpected June shower on the farmhouse roof. The family had gathered for the midday dinner, and the pungent smell of a pottage of mutton cooked with cabbage and leeks filled the kitchen.

Alice stared at her cousin. The weight in her stomach persisted, as did the moistness in her eyes, and her body ached with tiredness, for she had slept only a few hours before she delivered Tommy to Matthew's farm. She couldn't imagine how she might find the energy to dig a hole. She wanted only to sleep.

"Tommy's father, that scoundrel, will surely return one day," Caleb declared. "If he finds no gravesite, he will explode in fury, and Alice will be in danger once more."

Alice swallowed a spoonful of the pottage, hoping to quell the distress rising within her.

"Caleb may be right." Esther leaned over to embrace Alice.

"And he may be wrong." Aunt Sarah stood up and walked around the table to refill mugs with ale. "How on earth do we explain such a grave to the people of Ivycombe when they can see Tommy is alive and well? And how to dig a grave without anyone spotting us?" She plonked the jug down in the middle of the table and sat beside her husband.

"It will take but one person, myself. And a grave for a seven-year-old is a small thing." Caleb lifted his right arm and flexed it.

"Son, I know you are strong with all that work you do at the mine." Uncle Henry grinned. The rain had ceased to lash and now fell onto the roof in a soft pitter-patter. "Perhaps if you'd been fighting against the Dutch back in 1667, the English fleet would not have lost so disastrously."

"What I heard was that the sailors fought hard. Many of them died, but our king was broke and had no money to pay his sailors or his dockworkers. I am glad I wasn't there."

"Can we please decide where this grave should be?" Alice spoke up even though dizziness had overtaken her and she thought she might faint. "And how can we hide it from nosy neighbors?" The image of Tommy wrapped in his funeral shroud appeared in her head, and she remembered the feel of his damp, cold forehead. She shuddered.

"The false grave will be within the family plot at the outskirts of our farm, where generations of Powells have been buried and where nobody goes." Henry paused. "And where you and I will be buried one day." He winked at Sarah, who looked away.

"I have not stepped outside these past two days. Has anyone in Ivycombe visited us?" Alice stirred her pottage. "Or seen the wreath on the door?"

"Only Richard. We are safe," Esther assured Alice.

Alice wanted to be comforted by her friend's words. She took a sip of ale and smiled as she stared at Esther's auburn hair and deep blue eyes.

"Decided!" Caleb looked at Alice. "I shall dig a hole this very evening, and we shall need to find a branch about the size of Tommy to fill that hole."

"I shall be ready with the gravestone." Through her weariness, Alice recalled how she had lied to Richard and told him to step away from Tommy. The emptiness within her grew smaller as she determined to carry out this final act of defiance. "Years ago, my father taught me how to carve into stone, and I still have his chisel. I even have a piece of slate I can use."

Caleb stood. "Good. Everything is decided. And since the rain has ceased, let's get to work outside. I can help you today, but tomorrow, Esther and I must return to the mine." Caleb pushed his light brown hair away from his face and strode out of the kitchen.

After she and Aunt Sarah had cleared away the dinner dishes, Alice reached up to the shelf where she dried her herbs. The piece of slate Sybil had given her lay next to the plants; it weighed no more than a full pot of stew. Alice easily slid it over and brought it to rest on the kitchen table. On one side was carved "Sybil," for this had been the sign that hung in front of Sybil's cottage, which she had presented to Alice as a gift. Alice ran her fingers over the smooth bluish-gray stone and wondered where the old woman's spirit was now, for she had been dead for over two years.

The other side of the slate was blank. Alice estimated it was about three feet tall and perhaps two feet wide. This gravestone would lie flat on the ground. It did not match the height of Tommy, who was at least half a foot taller, but it was the only such stone she possessed. She removed a small knife, her chisel, and a hammer from the kitchen drawer and got to work.

With the knife, she etched her son's name, date of birth, and date of death on the stone, which was easy. Her next step was using the chisel and hammer to go over the letters she had marked to make them stand out. This was more difficult. "Father, is this how to use the chisel?" Alice heard no response but was able to dimly recall how her father had started out with the chisel flat and made steady clicking noises as he banged on it with his hammer before turning the instrument sideways and using its pointed edges to scrape around the letters. Just the letter *T* made Alice's fingers burn. It took such a long time that she decided to carve only TOMMY and the date of his death.

A loud rap on the door made her heart beat faster. She picked the slate up and turned it over so that only Sybil's name was visible.

CHAPTER TWENTY-SIX

Ivycombe, Devon. June 1670.

"Alice! Are you there?"

Alice recognized Father Hopwood's voice.

"Where have you been these past few days?" he asked. "Wilmott Snowe has fallen sick and his wife, Joane, asks for you."

Alice hesitated to open the door. *Is this a trap?* Yet she was a healer; if someone requested her aid, she had to answer the call. She opened the door to see the clergyman in his black cassock and stiff square hat wiping the sweat from his face. When she invited him in, he refused.

"Old Wilmott is most unwell. You should come at once." Father Hopwood paused and removed his hat to reveal a bald pate shiny with perspiration. "The pipemaker has a persistent dry cough and finds it hard to swallow. Can you help him?"

"I most assuredly can." Alice forced herself to give the man a wide smile even while the unfinished gravestone with a *T* carved into it emerged in her head.

"I shall hurry down to the Snowe home and let them know you are on your way. They will be glad since they have been asking for you." The clergyman held his hat against his chest and strode away down the narrow trail.

Alice pushed the door shut. She still feared this might be a trick, that someone had seen Richard visit on two consecutive days and wanted to learn the identity of this fine gentleman and what business he had with Alice. She picked up the piece of slate and stared at the "Sybil" on the reverse side. She had to keep her promise to Father Hopwood. Surely she had enough time to take care of Wilmott and return to finish carving the gravestone before nightfall.

She remembered that Goodwife Harris, who lived in the nearby village of Ashleigh, had told her an infusion of thyme, a harmless plant, helped a cough and any pains in the head. Alice stood on tiptoe before the kitchen shelf to gather dried thyme leaves. These she placed in her basket, along with her pot of honey, and hastened on her way.

Wilmott Snowe lay sideways on his pallet and rested his head on a sack of hay. His wrinkled left hand, with its long, elegant fingers, covered his eyes. Alice moved toward him but stopped when the old man sat up abruptly and a loud hacking cough shook his body. His skin bore a strange greenish tinge, and she knew at once that the pipemaker suffered from more than a simple cough. For now, she would start with the thyme and honey, but on the morrow, she would bring something stronger.

The small, stuffy room held the unpleasant odor of urine. Alice breathed through her mouth as Wilmott lay his head back on the sack, which served as a pillow.

"He's been like this for two days." Wilmott's wife, Joane, stood by the doorway and poked a loose strand of gray hair under her linen coif.

She does not question why I have been absent these past two days. She must be so wrapped up in her own misery that she pays no attention to the doings of others. The tension in Alice's head eased.

"What can you do for him?" Joane set a small wooden chair next to the pallet. Alice placed her basket on the ground beside her and sat down, grateful to rest her body after so few hours of sleep the night before.

She continued to breathe through her mouth and leaned over the old man. When she lay one hand against his forehead, it burned under her touch. "How are you feeling today, Goodman Snowe?" Alice knew Wilmott had earned the respect of the people of Ivycombe for his skill as a pipemaker. In the corner of the room, she spied an iron mold and a pile of clay.

"Terrible." He forced the word out, barely able to speak.

"You will feel better soon." Alice hoped she spoke the truth and placed one hand on his bony shoulder. "I shall first give you something to ease the cough. Are you in pain?"

"It's his chest. That's where it hurts. I've been keeping him covered with a warm, dry cloth." Joane stepped into the kitchen and returned with a piece of woolen material, which she placed across her husband's bare chest.

"An infusion of thyme will help the cough and clear Wilmott's head." Alice reached into her basket and removed a small amount of dried thyme. She inhaled its strong, earthy aroma, which she loved, and passed the leaves to Joane. "Put these into a mug and fill it with hot water. Cover it over, and let the infusion steep for about an hour. Once strained, you can give it to your husband to sip twice a day. And here is something to soothe his sore throat instantly." Alice lifted her one-handled honey pot from the basket and placed it on the small table beside Wilmott's pallet. "You can give him a teaspoonful two or three times a day, and it will bring him comfort."

By this time, Alice could barely focus on her tasks as a healer and wanted only to return home to finish carving the gravestone. She took her leave of Wilmott and Joane, promising to return the following day.

⸻

"Is it never going to grow dark?" That evening, Caleb threw himself down on the kitchen bench next to Esther, who kissed him on the cheek and massaged his back. "I have done my job and dug a grave at the far end of the Powell family plot, under an ash tree with plenty of wide branches reaching out. Tommy's grave will be well hidden. And I saw no one. But now we should return. Not a soul is abroad at this hour."

Alice peered out of the open front door. She had finished her work on the gravestone and massaged her stiff, achy fingers. With the sky darkening, the air grew cool after such a hot day. She gazed up; a half-moon revealed itself above her. "We must wait." She turned to address Caleb. "Let's give the moon time to rise so that she may guide us."

Caleb grunted his agreement, and Alice continued her contemplation of the twilight. The sun had dipped below the horizon. Wispy pink clouds expanded across the sky before being pulled into its grayness. Alice's weariness had disappeared, and instead, the energy to complete the creation of a false grave for Tommy filled her. When she left her son at Matthew's farm this morning, Tommy's delicate turquoise eyes had danced with pleasure as if he had not just undergone a terrible ordeal. *Shall I tell him about his grave?* Even while she considered this idea, she knew the burial place should remain a secret.

⸻

The two gravediggers set out after Caleb's parents had returned from tending to their sheep and lambs. The whitish-yellow moon loomed high in the sky, and the cool night air held a refreshing sharpness. All around them came the incessant chirp of crickets. Alice carried Tommy's gravestone along with the wand she had received from Sybil. Caleb led the way, for he knew this track well. He held the sturdy branch of an oak tree, about the size of Tommy, to replicate the child's body. The bough was wrapped in a woolen shroud, for the law decreed that all who died must be buried in wool.

They had to walk the length of the farm, about a half mile, before reaching the Powell family plot. At first, Alice loved being out under the dark sky with its brilliant pinpricks of stars, feeling the power of the soft moon light their way. She clutched the wand and the gravestone to her side, staying behind Caleb and listening to the melody of "Greensleeves" repeat itself in her head. Alice smiled as she inhaled the fresh, earthy scent of the grass after the midday rain shower.

The breathy shriek of a fox shattered Alice's peace.

She shivered and clutched the slate and the wand closer to her body. *What if Richard finds the grave and digs down to search for Tommy's body, only to discover a tree branch? What if we are not alone after all?*

"Alice?" Caleb spoke in a whisper.

"It's that fox. Do you think someone is spying on us?"

"Only the ghosts of our ancestors. We have arrived at the Powell family graveyard."

Alice took a deep breath, willing herself to stay calm. No wall surrounded the cemetery. Yet as Alice moved into the area where she could glimpse haphazard rows of gravestones, the air turned eerily chilly. The dank, musty smell of mildew surrounded her and made her cough. By the light of the moon, she made out two tall tombstones. Near these hefty pillars, she spied smaller slabs close to the ground; one of these had cracked and lay in two pieces. She leaned over to read its inscription and caught the woody odor of the lichen covering the tombstone.

Caleb pulled her up. "We must hurry. We are almost at the ash tree."

Alice continued to walk behind her cousin. In the darkness, she heard a chorus of tiny squeaks.

"Those are bats you can hear. We have dozens of them at the mine, and they only come out at night." Caleb stopped short to allow Alice to catch up with him. "Have you not heard them before?"

"I have, but not so many." Alice peered at Caleb. "Are you sure?"

"Yes, I know those cheeps well. But look, we have arrived." Caleb raised his arms to indicate the dark canopy of the ash tree overhead.

Alice looked up into the darkness. Her body shook, her heart beat faster, and she found it hard to breathe. A sour, dry taste filled her mouth. *This is a mistake*, a voice in her head screeched. *Go home.* What if someone had come behind them?

"Over here." Caleb beckoned to Alice.

Too late to change my mind. Hands shaking so that she feared she might drop the gravestone and the wand, she followed Caleb as he led her around the ash tree, its branches silhouetted by the glow of the moon.

"This is our grave spot." He pointed to indicate the place where he had excavated close by the base of the trunk.

Alice made out a pile of damp earth and fresh grass beside the hollow. She could hardly bear to watch as Caleb lowered the oak branch wrapped in its woolen shroud into the hole. Instead of seeing a piece of wood enclosed in the winding sheet, Alice envisaged the body of her son. She squeezed her eyes shut to rid herself of this dreadful image and placed her gravestone and wand on the ground.

The damp handfuls of earth and grass Caleb had dug up gave off a sweet, almost fragrant aroma as the secret gravediggers eased them around and over the woolen shroud. Alice muttered "Blessed be" as they worked to protect the secret of Tommy's gravesite.

Once they had filled the hole, Alice lifted her gravestone, knelt down, and laid the slate over the covered hole, where it fit perfectly. She stood, picked up Sybil's wand, and raised it into the air. "By the powers of air, fire, water, and earth, I bless this sacred piece of ground." She hoped that by pronouncing this incantation, she would rid herself of the terrible image of Tommy's body. What would happen to her if someone uncovered this deceit? Her heart beat faster, and she rubbed her clammy hands together.

Caleb stared at her. "Alice, quiet."

She disliked his tone but said nothing, and they moved to make their way home.

An uncanny silence hung in the air, for the high-pitched cheeps of the bats had died out. A gray cloud partially obscured the moon, and the two had to pay close attention to follow their own footsteps as they left the graveyard. When they stepped back onto the track, faint rumbling and rattling erupted in the distance.

She and Caleb stopped and waited. The noises grew louder. Who could be about at this time of night and making such a racket?

CHAPTER TWENTY-SEVEN

Ivycombe, Devon. June 1670.

Alice spent the night dreaming of her son: Tommy lying in his grave, Tommy playing with his lambs, Tommy climbing a tree and falling to his death. She woke late, close to the dinner hour, to discover Caleb had already left for his tin mine on Dartmoor. The two gravediggers had hastened home after the clatter in the night, not eager to find out who or what was the source of those noises.

Alice sat in the kitchen with her aunt and scrubbed potatoes for dinner, but Tommy's false grave occupied her thoughts. *What if an animal comes around, a hedgehog, perhaps, who snuffles under the gravestone and dislodges it? Or a red deer who pokes his mighty antlers under the stone and pulls it out of the ground?*

"Alice." She looked up as Aunt Sarah placed her fists on the table. "You have done well to accomplish what you and Caleb set out to do. Whatever happens next is in the hands of God."

Alice stared into her aunt's soft gray eyes and, for the first time, noticed the dark shadows beneath them. *How much has she suffered over Tommy's false death?* From the hearth came the bubbling of water, where the pot rested on a trivet, ready to boil the potatoes. The heat from the pot, along with the noonday sun, made the kitchen feel oppressive, and she could barely gather her thoughts. She knew Sarah was right, except for the part about God. "But those sounds—I think a carriage was passing by. Could that have been Richard?"

"Instead of Richard, you should turn your attention to poor Wilmott. Didn't you promise to visit him today? And the people of Ivycombe need to see you. They are surely suspicious as to why you have been absent these last few days."

Aunt Sarah's scolding tone made Alice squirm. She had wondered if Tommy missed her; she thought she might visit him today. Midsummer Eve fell in just a few days, and Alice knew her son would want to take part in the celebrations. She also knew her aunt was right about having to attend to Wilmott.

"I shall go directly. I can gather mallow and mint along the way to help his cough. Can you manage without me?"

Her aunt nodded, and Alice hauled herself up. Once she had gathered more thyme from her special shelf and grabbed her bonnet with the wide brim, she left to walk the short distance to Wilmott Snowe's house.

A few yards along the trail, she spotted Margary Badcombe coming toward her. Alice's heart raced. She remembered the tale Esther had told her of this woman who had accused Tabitha Smith of witchcraft and caused her death. Through her muddled thoughts, Alice also recalled how Goody Badcombe had spread the rumor that Alice cast spells on people so they would come to her and trust her with their secrets.

Goody Badcombe stopped about six feet from Alice and mopped her face with a kerchief against the heat. Her black plaits lay against her ample bosom, and her face held a sardonic smile.

"Good morrow, Alice."

The woman's shrill voice entered Alice's head like a musket shot and forced her to halt. "Good morrow." She clutched her basket. *Why has this woman chosen to address me here? Why does she not continue past me?*

"Were you awakened by the sounds of a carriage passing last night?"

Alice pulled off her bonnet to fan herself as she considered how to respond to Margary. "I heard sounds, yes, but did not pay mind to them since they soon grew fainter."

Goody Badcombe's expression had changed to a smirk. "A carriage traveled north, mayhap to South Tawton. They say the witchfinder is out to scour the countryside for women who have been practicing witchcraft."

Alice's heart thumped even more fiercely. She thrust her hat back in place, for the top of her head seemed to be on fire. Sweat trickled down her back. Even the sheep in the field next to her lay down on the grass, wilted by the heat.

"Good day, Alice. I must be on my way."

Goody Badcombe stepped forward, and Alice pulled back to give her plenty of room to pass. Yet as the woman drew closer, she brushed against Alice's basket and laid one hand on her arm.

"You should take care, my friend," she said before continuing on her way.

Alice shook her arm. She felt she had been touched by the devil and needed to exorcise him. Dread flooded through her body. What to do now?

Three days later, on the twenty-third of June, Alice stood at the edge of Ivycombe's market square and watched the Midsummer Eve festivities. She reckoned by the size of the crowd around the impressive bonfire that much of the population of Ivycombe was present, as well as visitors from the nearby villages of Ashleigh and Woodland, and maybe even some outsiders.

She hadn't expected so many people since this festival had only been revived a few years ago, after the Cromwell years.

When she had returned home after Margary Badcombe's warning, Uncle Henry had first embraced her and next told his niece she had to stop living in fear.

"You are a courageous woman, Alice. Even though some in this village are wary of you, do not give them reason to be suspicious of you. Do not hide; do not run away. You are a healer and a midwife. Stay strong."

With a jolt, Alice had recalled Goody Luscombe's admonition: "Stay strong for me." She thanked her uncle as she remembered her long-ago pledge to never show fear.

Later that day, she had returned to visit Goodman Snowe. To her delight, she found him smiling and sitting up on his pallet.

Dusk had almost fallen on this Midsummer Eve, and the sky was dark. Silhouetted against it, the huge bonfire in the center of the square sent bright yellow flames and sparks flying upward, illuminating all who stood around it. The jostle of people close to Alice made it hard for her to stay upright.

She planted her hands over her ears to lessen the deafening music of the fiddles, pipes, and tabors playing at the other end of the square and reflected on her visit to her son earlier that day. She had embraced Tommy, and the smell of grass, which always surrounded him, almost brought her to tears.

"I understand you are intent on coming to the Midsummer Eve festivities, but it would be most dangerous." She stepped back. "Your father may be there to look for you."

Tommy said nothing, merely stared at her with his beautiful turquoise eyes.

"And you also cannot return home for a while in case your father decides to pay us a visit." Alice forced herself to say these words, although she hated the idea of a separation from Tommy.

"Good. I like it better here. Maybe I'll stay forever." Tommy had turned away from her and left the room. She gazed after him, and a deep hollow filled her.

"Alice!" Philippa appeared next to her.

She jumped back, afraid some stranger had spotted her. Philippa's children, Henry and Stephen, followed behind their mother and brandished long sticks.

"Come on. Let's go chase out the devils and the sprites." They waved their poles in the air and disappeared into the crowd.

"Thank you for taking care of Tommy." Alice embraced her friend.

"Your son is a delight! It is an easy task." Philippa pulled away. "How are you? You have dealt with a lot these past few days." She raised her voice to be heard against the crackles and hisses of the fire and the loud chanting all around.

Margary Badcombe and her suggestion of the witchfinder slid into Alice's mind. She dismissed those thoughts. "I am well, thank you." A procession of young men who clutched mugs and sang "Long Live the Sun" danced their way past the two women. "These youngsters sing loud enough to wake the dead." A thick branch fell from the summit of the bonfire, and Alice jumped back. She glanced at the fire once more and realized someone was staring at her from the other side. Could it be Richard? Her body shook with a violence that scared her. She looked away and prayed for her tremors to stop. When she looked back, the eyes still stared, but this man had puffy cheeks and a long, prominent chin. He looked nothing like Richard.

Philippa seemed not to notice any change in Alice. "Farmer Blagdon's endless supply of ale gets the revelers going. Come!" She took Alice's hand and led her over to where three casks stood next to a table laden with bread and cheese. "Here." Philippa dipped a wooden mug into the first cask and passed it over to her friend.

The shakiness had eased, and Alice took a small sip of the ale. Then the trembling started up again, and she thought she might faint. She handed the mug back to Philippa and sat on the ground. A cloud of smoke made her eyes sting, and she coughed.

"What's wrong?" Philippa sat next to her. "Are you ill?"

"I saw a pair of eyes staring at me across the bonfire," Alice explained in a muffled tone. "At first, I thought it was Richard, but I was wrong."

Loud cheers and claps filled the air. To the left of them, young men stripped off their shirts, ready to jump over the bonfire, a tradition at the Midsummer Eve revelry. The flames grew smaller and had almost burned down to a red glow when the leaping began; the figures who bounded over the fire appeared like ghostly apparitions. Each one jumped backward and forward twice.

"Why not go back and look again?" Philippa patted Alice's shoulder. "The fire is less fierce, and everyone's attention is on these half-naked lads."

Alice pulled herself up, and Philippa followed her. With her heart pounding, Alice returned to the place where she had spotted those eyes. There they were still. She had seen this man before, but it took her a few moments to remember where. Then he raised his right hand to his face, and she spied the ruby ring on his pudgy little finger. It was John Heron, the man who had presided over her consistory court hearing. The man who had ruled against her and chosen instead to believe the lies of Richard Greenway and his father, William Greenway.

"We have to leave." Panic rose in Alice, and she clutched her throat. She grabbed Philippa by the arm. "At once."

"I must needs find my children first. Then we can leave."

"I cannot wait." Alice turned from Philippa. *I should walk, not run.* She forced herself to take deep breaths as she made her way through the chanting crowd. Chills overtook her in spite of the fire, and she thought her head might explode.

"Alice Molland." Before her stood John Heron, and she saw that two constables followed behind him.

"Alice Molland, you are under arrest for witchcraft on the bodies of Agnes Furze, Wilmott Snowe, and Joane Snowe."

The claps and cheers faded, and Alice's mind froze. "Wilmott and Joane are alive. I visited them just three days ago."

"They died yesterday. Wilmott went to his maker first. His wife declared she could not live without him and drank poison supplied by you. I believe they were under your care?"

"You lie!" A knot of sorrow at these deaths almost choked Alice, yet it also forced her to speak. "I visited the Snowes thrice only and treated the pipemaker with thyme, honey, and some mallow. These did not kill him. God called him. It was his time. As for Joane, I know nothing of poison." Although Alice spoke in a defiant tone, a hammer within her head drove all thoughts away and blurred her vision.

"Leave her alone!" Philippa's scream drew looks of interest from a few of the nearby spectators.

Heron made no response. He pushed his tricorn hat back. "There is another matter. Your son, Tommy Greenway, is alive and well. You lied to his father, Richard Greenway, when you told him the boy had died."

"Tommy Molland is his name. His father had nothing to do with him all these seven years."

"No matter. You are under arrest."

The two constables marched forward, wielding their truncheons, and seized Alice by the arms. "You are under arrest. You will come with us," they barked in unison.

"She is innocent! Leave her alone." Alice heard Philippa's cry.

Alice did not resist. It would serve no purpose. She would

save her strength for her appearance in court, where she could convince the judge she was innocent. Yet as the constables clutched her arms and led her away, a violent pain gripped her gut and bile filled her mouth.

"Beggarly whore! Witch!" She heard the shouts all around her, familiar names from the times they had been yelled at her in Exeter. Her eyes filled with tears, but she focused her gaze forward and refused to look into the faces of her enemies.

CHAPTER TWENTY-EIGHT

Ivycombe, Devon. June 1670.

Alice continued to stare straight ahead. The two constables led her away from the noise and bustle of the market square, up the main street, and toward a tumbledown chapel behind St. Michael's church. She had seen this building before but had paid no attention to it.

Once there, they pushed open a heavy door with rusty iron handles and hinges and shoved her into the chapel. Alice felt she was entering a dank cave where strange creatures of the night might dwell. She stopped to adjust her eyes to the grayness and made out the remains of an altar rail and, in front of it, a straw pallet and chair.

"Welcome to the Ivycombe lockup."

The constable's voice echoed around her. "You will remain here until you are summoned before a judge. If you are lucky, someone will bring you a jug of water and perchance a morsel to eat."

They slammed the hefty door and locked it. The fusty air smelled of decay, and Alice's heart pounded at an increasingly rapid pace. She crept forward and brought herself to sit on the iron chair. *I must stay strong. I promised Goody Luscombe and my father and my uncle. Surely, the judge will see I am no witch, but a simple healer. I must stay strong.*

⁂

The next morning, Alice woke to a loud "Open up!" followed by a fierce hammering. She willed herself to rise from her pallet just as the door burst open and the two parish constables stepped in. The bright morning sun flooded in, revealing a stone font by the door and three rows of wooden chairs within the chapel.

Behind the men stood two women, a girl of perhaps twenty who stared at Alice with heavy eyelids and, next to her, a white-haired woman who was bent over. Alice had seen her before but couldn't think of where.

"These women are here to search you. Do not try to escape, or it will go worse for you. Do you understand?" The taller of the two men barked his command and handed Alice a mug of water and a hunk of rye bread.

Alice did understand. She had heard from several women that a search meant looking for a teat in a woman's private parts where her imp had supposedly come to suckle. According to this theory, an imp was a familiar spirit, often disguised as an animal and sent to a witch by the devil to seal their pact. Alice shuddered, swallowed most of the water, placed the mug on the ground, and devoured the bread. She resolved that she would find a way to escape. But first, she would work to put herself into a state of inner meditation, which would make it easier to get through this ordeal.

The two women walked forward, and Alice recalled that she had seen the older one when the woman had been sent to wash the body of Jane Upjohn shortly after her death. It seemed some women would do anything for a coin, whether searching a witch or washing a corpse.

The constables left, and the older woman commanded Alice to remove her clothes.

Alice had expected this order and hoped they would carry out their search quickly since the smell of rot grew stronger with the heat of the day. She knew no shame when she pulled off her bodice, blouse, and long skirt, followed by her shift. She was proud of her body.

The younger woman commanded her to squat and produced a long needle. "What are you going to do?" Alice asked, though she already knew.

The woman made no response but hunched down in front of Alice and stretched out her right hand. Alice cringed when she saw the broad, stubby hand with dirt packed under the nails.

The woman inserted her fingers into Alice's private parts and poked around inside her, but Alice had taken herself back to the time of Tommy's birth, when Aunt Sarah had instructed her to take deep breaths and encouraged her to move around. She was reliving this when a painful prick between her legs made her cry out. She looked down to see blood on the tip of the needle.

"Nothing to find here," came the declaration. "No teat, no numbness within. Yet as I search further, I see the outer lips are long, and they sag."

"I gave birth to a child. You must know pushing a babe down through the vagina and past those lips changes how a woman's body looks down there." The pain in Alice's back grew greater. "May I not stand for a moment?"

"No. I must apply the needle to those lips."

As her tormentor did so, Alice let out a scream.

"Or perchance they are lips where the devil has taken his pleasure, for the needle draws no blood." The younger woman spoke with a sneer. "You may stand up now."

Alice rose and almost fell over because her body was stiff from crouching for so long. She slipped back into her clothes.

The younger woman pointed at Alice's neck. "Look! So many red spots. They, too, must be the work of the devil."

"Surely you see these are flea bites." Alice tied her bodice. "There is no one in the county of Devonshire who does not suffer the plague of flea bites."

The two women did not respond but brought a stool over to Alice and commanded her to sit. The younger woman brought her face close to Alice's. The woman's lips were pinched together and slightly raised on the left side of her face.

"Bring your feet onto the stool and your knees to your chest." When Alice obeyed, her searcher produced a short rope, which she used to bind Alice's wrists and ankles together. "We can see if your imp comes to suck at you. I shall watch you until darkness falls."

It was harder to distract herself in this extremely painful position. Alice gasped and shifted about to ease her joints. She tried to rock back and forth, which helped.

The white-haired woman swept the floor continuously. She told Alice she acted under instructions to kill any spiders or flies. If they refused to die, that would be solid proof that these insects must be Alice's imps.

Alice didn't know how long she had been forced to sit in this torturous way, but for a short time, she succeeded in drawing herself into a trance, and this lessened the pain. Late in the day, the two men returned, untied her, and left her alone. She fell onto her pallet and wept.

⁂

The following day, the constables unlocked the heavy door and escorted Alice the short distance to the Village Hall.

Alice's guards chuckled and muttered to each other as they led her forward, although it all seemed to be happening at a great distance. They developed a game between them where they prodded her back from alternate sides. She refused to respond, but when they rounded the corner to the Village Hall, her steadfastness of will slipped away like the ice floes dissolving on the River Exe, for Aunt Sarah and Uncle Henry, along with Philippa, stood beside the building and smiled at her. She smiled back and told herself she must stand strong. She spoke to no one as she entered a large room, and a barrage of noise reached her ears. She heard "Murderer!" and "Foul creature!" followed by "Devil's whore!" and "Unnatural witch!"

She took a deep breath and visualized herself outside under the waxing moon as she had last seen it. How she longed to be with Matthew and Philippa as they celebrated the full moon worship in the ash grove.

In her long hours alone in the chapel, she had sought to concentrate only on her inner thoughts so that she might remove herself from her immediate surroundings. She had eaten little in the past two days and hoped this would help her accomplish her task more easily.

"Are you Alice Molland?" a voice boomed out from a gray-wigged man. The benches around the edges of the room were packed, and people leaned forward, anxious to get a good look at her.

"Answer Goodman John Hill, the magistrate!" This command came from a man seated at a desk to her left, his hand poised over a fat volume, quill pen in hand.

"I am Alice Molland." With her left hand, she pushed back her long hair. It was greasy and limp, but when she brought her hand back to her side, she noticed her birthmark had grown more distinct.

"Sit down!" Strong arms gripped her shoulders from behind and dragged her into a wooden chair opposite the clerk.

Alice focused her eyes on the wall in front of her, where her gaze was drawn to an escutcheon bearing the image of a golden lion that she knew was intended to represent the Royal Family of England.

She recalled asking her mother "What is it?" the first time she had seen such a beast, terrified at its ferocity and terrified too by the sounds of the people of Exeter who demanded Goody Luscombe's death.

". . . and it is said that Agnes Furze stated that Alice Molland appeared to her in the shape of a red pig," Alice heard. The man who spoke had a bulky frame that was resplendent in a green silk waistcoat and deep blue cape with fur collar. "We can determine that Alice Molland holds the blame for Agnes Furze's death in 1661, although no charges were laid at the time."

"These are lies!" Alice stood up to face her accuser. "I visited Agnes several times and gave her comfrey root, which helped her." Alice heard boos from the gathered crowd as she spoke. "She died because it was her time." She sat down.

No response came from her accuser. Alice looked at the lion again and recollected how that very same animal had appeared in a design on the carpet in Florence Greenway's bedroom. All these lions defended the hierarchy of an England where the Greenways achieved all they desired.

"And furthermore," a different man, clad in a Brandenburg coat and black patent shoes, stood up, "when Wilmott Snowe lay ill, hearing somebody at the door, his wife, Joane, did open the door and found Alice Molland standing with a broom in her hands. She had come with the sole intent to torment Wilmott Snowe and to put him out of his life."

Alice jumped up again. "More lies! I brought the old pipemaker some thyme, along with mint and mallow to soothe his chest. I am a healer." Some in the audience hissed at her, and she glared back at them.

The man continued. "The following day, Alice Molland did return to the house of Wilmott and Joane Snowe in hope that there she should have some meat. But Joane not being within her house, Alice Molland could get no meat or bread, so she cursed the Snowes. Wilmott died the next day, and shortly after the death of her husband, Joane was taken ill and died, victim of bewitching by the said Alice Molland, discontented that she had received no meat."

"None of this is true! How can you believe this man? You people of Ivycombe—you know me. You know I would never do what I am being accused of." Alice reached out her hands in supplication and saw that some of the crowd nodded in agreement while others called out "Evil!" and "The devil in our midst! Kill the witch!"

She sat down and fought to remove herself again, but when she looked at the lion, it opened its mouth to bare its teeth, snarled at her, and took on the likeness of Sir William Greenway. She closed her eyes and sought to invoke a different image, this time the meadow where she had taught Tommy how to tickle trout on the day Jeffrey had brought the news of her mother's death. She could picture her son's blond hair with those reddish tints as he leaned over the stream, and she heard again the gurgle of the water as it moved past her.

"Open your eyes, woman, and stand up when the magistrate addresses you!"

She looked up to see John Hill's smallpox-pitted face glaring down at her. She rose slowly, for a deathly weight pulled her down inside. The crowd no longer called out but stared at her in expectant silence.

"These are the charges," Goodman Hill pronounced. "You stand accused of witchcraft on the bodies of Joane Snowe, Wilmott Snowe, and Agnes Furze. How do you plead?"

"Not guilty." Her words came out clear and strong, but the weight within grew heavier. Alice looked around for her aunt, for her uncle, for Philippa. Instead, she glimpsed Margary Badcombe, whose face bore a slight grimace. Alice looked away as the two constables led her out of the Hall.

CHAPTER TWENTY-NINE

Ivycombe, Devon. June 1670.

Alice sat up when she realized Philippa stood over her. She had collapsed onto the thin straw pallet when the two constables delivered her back to her prison. Too exhausted to cry, she had fallen into a series of vivid dreams: her mother at the spinning wheel, Agnes Furze lying in her bed, and Tommy with his precious lambs. One by one, they floated through her head. When she reached out to catch them, they vanished, mocking her.

"I bribed that fat constable with a fresh apple pie," Philippa whispered. "He allowed me to visit you for five minutes."

Alice grasped her friend's outstretched hand and pulled herself up. The two women fell into each other's arms and held on tight.

"They will take me to the Castle Gaol in Exeter to await the Assizes Court." Alice trembled, still clasping Philippa. "How shall I bear it?"

Philippa grasped Alice by the shoulders. "You will bear it because you are strong and because you must. Your family believes in you. We shall always stand by you." Philippa pushed strands of blonde hair from her face and wiped away her tears.

"Two minutes more," a voice bellowed from the chapel door.

"Philippa, I have a request." Alice's voice shook. "If I am to die, I must choose my own time. I have prepared a decoction of henbane and hemlock. Aunt Sarah knows where to find it. Can you bring it to me? And Tommy, what about Tommy?"

"You must leave at once." The constable's words echoed through the chapel.

"I shall return shortly." Philippa embraced Alice and slid away. She stepped out of the chapel, and the constable slammed the door shut and turned the key.

Alice sat on the iron chair. The June sun beat down on the small building, and sweat ran down Alice's back. She slumped forward, hands on her knees, and her stomach caved in. What if Philippa never returned?

After less than an hour, the constable pushed open the heavy door enough to allow one person to enter, and Philippa appeared. As he watched her, she walked along the short nave toward Alice, who was still seated on the iron chair.

Alice stood. Neither woman spoke, but as Philippa embraced Alice with one arm, she pushed a small packet inside Alice's bodice.

"I shall take care of Tommy until you return." With a kiss on Alice's cheek, Philippa pulled away and left at once.

Alice stared after her friend. Her insides were frozen, and she seemed to be outside of her body, looking down at herself.

The sunlight still shone through the chapel window when Alice looked up from her pallet to see the parish constable, clad in woolen trousers and tunic, push through the chapel door as he patted his midriff and whistled. He strode toward her. Her stomach grumbled in fear, and she hoped he might bring her a morsel to eat.

He reached a fat, grubby hand toward her but would not touch her. "Your carriage awaits," he pronounced with a snicker. "Get up and follow me."

Alice struggled to pull herself up and follow her guard as he led her out of the chapel. An animal cart stood outside the door with a young mare in place to pull it. At the front of the cart sat a man in a floppy hat who held the horse's reins, and next to him was a sergeant-at-arms on his own steed. Alice had thought she might run away, but the sight of this man on his horse made her wither inside.

The constable instructed her to get in, and she clambered over the back of the cart and fell to the floor. One hand grasped the side of the cart, and with the other hand, she touched her breasts to feel the small bundle hidden there.

Once crouched in the bottom of the wagon, Alice spent the rest of the journey in a dazed trance. Surely, this was not herself being hauled in a flimsy wooden cart on the bumpy road from Ivycombe to Exeter? She refused anything but water, and her mind wandered off so that she kept reliving the execution of Diana Luscombe. At times, she believed she was Goodwife Luscombe herself on the way to her death; at other times, she became little Alice Molland, begging her parents not to make her attend the hanging and then knowing herself to be alone in the midst of a crowd determined to enjoy the celebration of death.

The brisk young mare needed no encouragement to keep up a steady pace along the muddy path, and the sergeant-at-arms rode beside her. Every rocky bump in the road vibrated through Alice's thin bones as she bounced up and down on the wooden planks, like a sack of cornmeal. The hot June sun burned into her, and she kept her head bent low, curled up like a cat.

When the man driving the horse announced that they drew near to Exeter, Alice could no longer lose her mind in imaginings.

From her position in the corner of the cart, she saw the great walls of the city rise up, and the North Gate, through which they must pass, at the top of the hill.

By the time they entered the city, the sun had begun to set, and they passed few people as the cart made its way along North Street and up into High Street. Most of the cobb cottages down her own small lane had been torn down, replaced with even smaller ones. She had left this place eight years ago, and many of the people she had known must have perished. Only the rich, like King Charles II and his wife, Catherine, survived beyond the age of fifty-five.

The vehicle moved along High Street and turned left onto a narrow lane. At the top of the lane, the dark forms of the three towers of Exeter Castle stood out in a gray sky as the sun set behind them. The cart swung to the right before it reached the castle gatehouse at the end of the hill and pulled up with a jerk.

They had stopped in front of a tavern from which the silhouette of an emaciated old man emerged in the twilight, a thick bunch of keys and a candle in hand. "Come over here!"

The sergeant dismounted, tied up his horse, and stepped over to Alice. He prodded her in the back. "Get out!"

Alice looked up at the man whose eyes glinted at her in the half-light. She scrabbled over the side of the cart and slipped down to land on cobblestones. Her body shook with a powerful ferocity, but she knew she had to do as she was commanded, or it would go worse for her.

The two followed the old man around the red sandstone building. At the back of the tavern, they descended a series of uneven stone steps. A heavy wooden door studded with rusty spikes and nails guarded the cellar entrance.

"The Castle Gaol lies in the ground beneath the tavern. 'Tis pretty sport for my customers." The old man sneered. "They do like to see a filthy prisoner or two when they have taken a pot of ale. Give 'er to me."

The sergeant pushed Alice toward the gaoler, then turned and made his way back up the steps.

The old man set the candle down and unlocked the door, unleashing the fetid stink of urine and excrement.

He grabbed Alice by her right elbow.

Howls came from beneath her, like a dog in pain.

"Must needs be that Carol Twist complaining again." The man's grip on her arm was like an iron vise. With his thin candle lighting the way, Alice accompanied him down another series of steps. As they descended, the odors became stronger. At first, she recognized only human droppings, but soon her nose made out the distinctive smell of rats and their feces. And she had to remain in this foul pit for up to a month before the judges would arrive from London for the Summer Assizes.

Worse, the place was totally dark except for the candle the gaoler held, and each prisoner was chained to the ground, unable to move more than a few feet. In the obscure light, two pairs of eyes gleamed at her, but then her feet reached the bottom of the stairs, and the ground sank and squelched beneath her.

"Here!" The old man, surprisingly strong, threw her against a wall and pushed her down into a squatting position. He grabbed a chain from the ground and locked it around her ankle. "A witch, are you? Well, see if you can work your charms on that one!" He cackled as he moved away and left her in the dark. Within a minute came a loud thud and the clink of a key being turned above her head.

But she would not let herself weep. In the darkness, Alice reached her right hand into her shift and pulled out the mixture of henbane and hemlock she had hidden there. Somehow, she would guard these two herbs close to her body for as long as needed.

Alice estimated that she had been in this place for a fortnight. She shook as she kneaded her legs to keep away the cramps, and she had to endure the harangues from her fellow prisoners: "Evil woman! Unnatural whore!" The screeches of Carol Twist, who had been arrested for deserting the King's Army and was therefore certain to be executed, interrupted her attempts to meditate or to sleep. Most of all, Alice hated her own dirt.

The prisoners received each day a wooden bowl of water and a hard lump of bread. While the others gulped their water down, Alice drank only half of hers, in small sips, and used the rest to cleanse herself. She dipped the end of her sleeve into the cold liquid and wiped it over her face, neck, and ears, trying to imagine she was at the Longbrook and still just a child.

Yet the filth remained: the fleas on her head and neck, the excrement-clotted straw she had to sit on, the rats that scurried around her in the dark. She was obsessed with the battle to keep her spirit clean, for she had to remain proud when she was finally brought to trial. She would not let the people of Exeter see her heart so they might trample on it.

At times, the images of her sister and her mother on their deathbeds floated before her: Faith with her swollen face covered in blisters and her mother, who died in her sleep. At least for them, the suffering had ended within a few short days.

A further indignity was inflicted by the visitations of the gaoler and his drunken companions. Periodically, when the thump of a key being turned broke into their perpetual nightmare, the prisoners looked up: Three or four faces leered down at them, each lit by a candle.

"Where lies the witch?"

Alice shivered at the raucous laughter that echoed around the cavernous hole following this question.

"Here!" A pair of heavy boots clomped down the stairs, the others coming right behind him. "See!" Over the top of the candle flame, Alice could make out several sets of eyes, which appeared to be red in the eerie light.

"But come not too close, gentlemen, for fear she o'erlooks you." As the gaoler spoke, his beer-laden breath oozed all over Alice.

She peered at each pair of eyes until they turned away to look for more sport elsewhere.

On the twentieth of July, twenty-five days after her arrival at the gaol, Alice Molland was delivered to the Assizes Court at Exeter Castle, the site designated for dealing with offenses committed by people who lived within the boundaries of the county of Devon but not within the city of Exeter. She was brought before the two judges assigned to the Western circuit of the Assizes Court for 1670.

When she entered the courtroom, Alice did not struggle in her attempt to distance herself from all that was going on around her. With scarcely any nourishment for over three weeks, she let her mind wander and allowed herself to embrace whatever beautiful scene her imagination gave her. She struggled to keep her body upright; neither Richard Greenway, nor any of his family members, if they were here, nor the citizens of Exeter, would see her bowed down in any way.

"Alice Molland."

She heard her name called, and the guards on either side of her gripped her arms as she perceived the great wooden bench before her.

Two elderly gentlemen sat behind it, both in long gray periwigs and lace neckcloths. The man on her right wore a short jacket with deep cuffs while his companion was clad in a more conservative long waistcoat of blue silk. In front of the bench sat the clerk of the court in a plain gray shirt and breeches, and to his left sat the petty jury, twelve local dignitaries selected for their honorable reputations.

After assessing the bench, Alice swept her gaze to look out around the vast room but saw only a blur of faces and heard angry calls: "Unnatural witch!" "Hard cozening bitch!" She looked down, ashamed of her dirty state.

"Alice Molland, hold up your hand." The clerk of the court gave the command, a gesture required by law to make sure that the correct prisoner was being tried.

Alice did as she was requested and saw that the oak leaf birthmark on the back of her left hand gave off a faint glow. She wondered if others saw this too. "You are here indicted by the name of Alice Molland, late of Ivycombe, single, mother of a bastard child, owning no property." The clerk read from the thick brown volume that lay on the desk in front of him. "For that you are guilty of death by witchcraft on the bodies of Joane Snowe, Wilmott Snowe, and Agnes Furze." He looked up from the book. "How say you, Alice Molland? Are you guilty of these felonies, as it is laid in the indictment whereof you stand indicted, or not guilty?"

"Not guilty." Alice's voice rang out clear and steady.

At once, an uproar broke out in the mob.

Alice stood and faced them. Her body ached with weakness.

The clerk read out the testimony of the witnesses from the statements they had made at the hearing in Ivycombe: Alice's ability to transform herself into a red pig and thus ensure the demise of Agnes Furze, how she tormented Wilmott Snowe to death, and her intent to kill Joane Snowe when the woman denied her meat.

Next, the clerk described how he had heard it plainly from one George Barten how Alice Molland had confessed to him that "she had caused several ships at sea to be cast away, and she confessed also that the devil lay carnally with her for six nights together."

She forced her mind away from these lies to the last time she had seen her mother, who had been so frail and yet so anxious to hide her weakened state for the sake of her daughter.

A searing pain gripped Alice's chest when the clerk turned to her once more. "How can you defend yourself?"

"I am not guilty. There are others in this room more guilty than I, and God willing, they will be punished."

It took less than five minutes for the jury to pronounce their verdict of guilty on all charges, and she was led back to the Castle Gaol to await execution the following day.

Tied to an old mare, in the same fashion as her two fellow prisoners, Alice was led out along the Magdalen Road toward Heavitree. She had been forced to wait to ingest the poison until shortly before leaving the gaol, when she was presented with her final portion of bread and water. Without some liquid, the poisonous concoction might require a long, torturous day to take effect. While the gaoler tossed crusts to the other prisoners, she threw her head back and swallowed the contents of her little packet.

She waited, and after a couple of hours, Alice's legs grew numb, and her body shook. Still, even in her dazed state, Alice heard the cries of the rabble along the way. An easterly wind cut through her thin shift, but she passed over the Wonford

Brook and remembered when, as children, she and her mother had sat beside the Longbrook after Catherine had healed Farmer Fletcher's horse. That was the day she had first known she would be a healer. She saw herself: thick black hair, pale skin, little heart-shaped mouth, and . . . she clutched her belly, gripped by an excruciating pain that burned her innards. She bowed her head low against the nag. The agony had passed, but her arms had lost all feeling, and she had to lie down against the horse's mane and neck in order to stay mounted.

Her mother had still been young herself, though her face was lined and tired from the exertion of dealing with the sick colt. With the splashes of water from the brook, the two of them had played together, equals almost. Then the scene vanished, replaced by the distorted face of a young woman who hissed and then spat twice, once into each of Alice's eyes.

The numbness enveloped her body, and soon it would capture her mind. With her head firmly on the nag's neck, arms slumped at her sides, Alice could just make out the cries: "Baby killer! She even murdered her own sister!" "The devil is her familiar!"

She saw herself with Richard at the Green Pool, her young body firm and vibrant, matching his. The water was icy, but his mouth was so warm.

"Sit up!" yelled the soldier riding beside her, and her heavy body was lifted and held by rough arms. It did no good, though, for as the nag started the climb up to the top of Gallows Hill, she fell forward once more. "Revive her!" came the call. She smiled. It was too late.

Tommy's image came to her, his brilliant eyes and his mouth creased in a mischievous smile as he chased crickets in the meadow behind the farmhouse in Ivycombe. As she watched his young body run across the grass, he turned and waved to her, then ran back and picked her up in his strong arms. Pride and joy filled her as her son held her aloft before the applauding crowds gathered to see her in her moment of triumph.

⁂

The sergeant-at-arms had to lift Alice Molland's body up to place the rope around her neck, for she was no longer breathing. Mr. Hann, the clergyman, stepped up to her and asked her to repent, but only a pair of vacant eyes stared back at him.

Hung between Carol Twist, the deserter, and John Bowden, the thief of forty shillings, she had already escaped her torment by the people of Devon in the only way that she could. But as the crowd stared at her body, swinging in the chill morning rain, they noticed her left hand was still moving. It carried the shape of a slightly raised oak leaf, which shone brightly through the gray July drizzle.

A great cheer went up from a number of wise women and healers who had come from all over the county and were gathered beneath the gallows.

"Hail to Alice Molland, the greatest healer that Devon has ever seen!" they called out. "Hail to Alice Molland!"

Historical Note to THE MAKING OF A WITCH

On March 20, 1685, Alice Molland, my ancestor, was sentenced to death at the Exeter Assizes Court in Devon, England. She was the last person to be legally executed for witchcraft in England. Between 1500 and 1700, at least 250,000 people, and perhaps many more, were labeled "witch" and condemned to death in Western Europe. Presumably because they were mostly women, they were deemed unimportant by the writers of history textbooks in the England of the 1970s, where I grew up, and never rated a mention.

I first came across Alice Molland's name in *Religion and the Decline of Magic* by Keith Thomas. As a young woman in her twenties, I was thrilled to see my last name printed in a book for the first time. My father, a vicar in the Church of England, did not share my excitement; he grabbed the book, closed it, and told me never to speak of this woman again.

Many years later, I received a grant from the National Endowment for the Humanities and spent several summers researching, or trying to research, the life of Alice Molland, but I was only able to unearth one link to her: her death sentence.

When I visited the National Archives, located in leafy Kew, in London, UK, I was able to hold the seventeenth-century record book containing Alice Molland's sentencing to death for "witchcraft on the bodies of Joane Snowe, Wilmott Snowe, and Agnes Furze."

However, the script of the manuscript was indecipherable to me, being a mixture of seventeenth-century script and some unusual graphics. The clerk in the office pointed to a sign above her head as she handed me the dusty volume: "Librarians are not translators." It took me a further several months to find an expert in seventeenth-century English script: Audrey Erskine, a historian at Exeter Cathedral, who was able to translate Alice Molland's death sentence.

Since that is my lone piece of evidence, I have built the story of Alice Molland upon my studies of seventeenth-century England, particularly South West England, and have anchored my novel in the historical context in which Alice lived. I believe I have captured this accurately, but I have taken one liberty with a historical date. Alice Molland was hanged in March 1685 and not July 1670, as I have written in my story. This change became necessary for the pacing of my story and its narrative arc.

The Witchcraft Act of 1735 made it a crime for a person to claim that any human being had magical powers or was guilty of practicing witchcraft in the Kingdom of Great Britain.

I have drawn from numerous resources in the research for my novel. Here are just a few of them:

Religion and the Decline of Magic by Keith Thomas

The Witch-Hunt in Early Modern Europe by Brian P. Levack

Malleus Maleficarum by Heinrich Kramer and James Sprenger

The Weaker Vessel: Women's Lot in Seventeenth Century England by Antonia Fraser

Working Life of Women in the Seventeenth Century by Alice Clark
Two Thousand Years in Exeter by W.G. Hoskins
Devon and Its People by W.G. Hoskins
Witchcraft in Exeter 1558–1660 by Mark Stoyle
Diary of a Witch by Sybil Leek
The Complete Art of Witchcraft: Penetrating the Secrets of White Magic by Sybil Leek
Culpeper's Complete Herbal by Nicholas Culpeper

ACKNOWLEDGMENTS

I am grateful to Brooke Warner and She Writes Press for giving me the opportunity to publish this book, which has been my obsession for many years.

My journey began when I received a grant from the National Endowment for the Humanities to study the witch hunts of seventeenth-century England. The truths I uncovered gave me the germ of a vision for my novel.

Yet where would I be without the intelligence and insights of my amazing editors, Christine DeSmet and Ellen Sussman?

Numerous friends and colleagues have helped me realize my dream: Mary Schultz, Natasha Nummedal, Courtney Rediger, and Jennifer Walworth, my beta readers. Also, Levannah Morgan, Martha Jackson, Ellen Nordberg, Laurie Scheer, Kathy Emery, Sylvia Braselmann, Janet Simms, Matt and Caroline Simms, Jean Fitzpatrick, and Colin Lomas.

Lastly, I would like to thank my family: Will Molland-Simms and Kline Swonger, Jane and Peter Huxham, Elizabeth Courtauld, and my wonderful nieces Sarah Courtauld and Catharine Hart, who have let me hold forth about Alice Molland for hours. And above all, Joe, the brightest, best, most beautiful person in my life.

ABOUT THE AUTHOR

Photo credit: Ali Windberry

Judy Molland began her career as a high school teacher of French, English, and Spanish, and soon added freelance writer to her job description. Her articles and blog posts have appeared in numerous publications including *Parents*, *New York NewsDay*, and *Care2.com*. She has published two non-fiction books: *Straight Talk About Schools Today* and *Get Out! 150 Easy Ways for Kids and Grown-Ups to Get Into Nature and Build a Greener Future*. *The Making of a Witch* is her first work of fiction. She grew up in England before moving to California. She now lives in Missoula, Montana.

Looking for your next great read?

We can help!

Visit www.shewritespress.com/next-read or scan the QR code below for a list of our recommended titles.